"Don't tell me you're so afraid of the empty nest that you're going to try to win your ex back," my mother exclaimed.

"Get serious, Mother."

"Never mind. I don't want to know." Bernice stood. "Take a look at what's in the shopping bag. And don't be stubborn about it." She kissed my forehead, then clicked her way to the foyer. "Good luck with... whatever," she yelled before the door slammed.

I kept glancing over my shoulder at the bag. Curiosity finally won out and I went to investigate.

Another little black dress. I drew it out and held it in front of me. Not bad. Maybe I'd wear it tonight. If it fit. I looked at the tag and was surprised to see that it was actually my size. Maybe Bernice had finally gotten it into her he~~ad~~ ~~~~ver going to be a size eight. I grinned. ~~~~ possible?

Nikki Rivers

Nikki Rivers knew she wanted to be a writer when she was twelve years old. Unfortunately, due to many forks in the road of life, she didn't start writing seriously until several decades later. She considers herself an observer in life and often warns family and friends that anything they say or do could end up on the pages of a novel. She lives in Milwaukee, Wisconsin, with her husband and best friend, Ron, and her feisty cairn terrier, Sir Hairy Scruffles. Her daughter, Jennifer, friend, critic, shopping accomplice and constant source of grist for the mill, lives just down the street.

Nikki loves to hear from her readers. E-mail her at nikkiriverswrites@yahoo.com.

Window

Dressing

NIKKI RIVERS

From the Author

Dear Reader,

Don't you just love a road trip? Music blasting, wind in your hair, brand-new pair of sunglasses perched on your nose? I've been taking road trips with my best girlfriend, Deb Kratz, ever since we've been old enough to drive. The destinations have changed over the years—and so have we. But we always have a blast.

Window Dressing starts with just such a road trip between Lauren Campbell and her best buddy, Moira Rice. Lauren, divorced for ten years, thinks she knows exactly where she's going—taking her son, Gordy, to start his freshman year, after which she will do all the things she'd always planned. But, as we all know, the roads we take in life don't always get us to the destinations we've planned on. Too often there are detours.

In some ways, I'm like Lauren. I had my trip planned, too, but found myself on a different highway in midlife. As Lauren does, I discovered that an alternative route can turn out to have an even better view. It's not easy leaving some of that window dressing behind. After all, it's not nice to litter on the highway of life—but everyone does. And along the way, we also pick up things—other ideas, other people, other careers. Other ways of living.

Window Dressing celebrates the choices we make in our lives—and the friendships and loves we find along the way.

I hope you will always stay open to the journey.

Nikki Rivers

P.S. I would just like to add that neither Deb nor I ever flashed any truckers on those road trips. Really.

This book is dedicated to friends and road trips and the millions of chips and snack cakes eaten along the way.

I'd also like to thank my editor, Kathryn Lye, for her continued support and encouragement over many years and many journeys. Special thanks to Ron, my husband extraordinaire, who leaves me little treats to find among the manuscript pages on my desk and keeps me fed when I'm on deadline and my daughter, Jennifer, who helps me keep my sanity in this insane process we call writing. Both of them, by the way, are excellent road trip companions.

CHAPTER 1

"Welcome to weirdness," Moira Rice said as she rode shotgun in my aging Chevy.

"Put on your glasses, Moira. That sign said Welcome To Indiana."

Moira shrugged her shoulders. She was the only woman I knew who could make a shrug look sexy. It didn't hurt that she was wearing a turquoise off-the-shoulder sweater and that her long, wavy chestnut hair was pinned loosely on the top of her head.

"Same thing," she said. "I mean, Lauren, just look—" she jutted her chin toward a steak and waffle house we were passing, "—they don't even have normal fast food down here. And every other car on the road is a pickup truck. And, have you noticed, they all have gun racks? And every driver is wearing a cap extolling the virtues of farm equipment or beer. Even the women. Like I said, welcome to weirdness."

I craned my neck so that I could see the backseat in the rear view mirror. "I'm sure Indiana has no more weirdness than any other state and I'd prefer you didn't make comments like that in front of Gordy," I said primly.

Moira arched her brow and gave me a sideways look. "Gordy isn't hearing anything but whatever passes for music these days via that wire attached to his ear."

It was true. My eighteen-year-old son, Gordy, his head

leaning back on the headrest, his eyes peacefully closed, had been hooked up to his iPod since we'd taken I-94 out of Milwaukee just after dawn. He'd only unplugged long enough to order when we'd pulled into a drive-through south of Chicago.

"I just want him to be happy with his choices, that's all," I said defensively.

Gordy was going to be living in Bloomington, Indiana, for the next four years while he majored in finance at Indiana University. Like the slightly obsessive mother I am, I wanted him to be enraptured with his surroundings. As much as I was going to miss him, I wanted him to be happy enough to justify my agreeing to let him go away to school.

Moira checked out the backseat. "Looks happy enough to me," she said. "You know," she added with a frown, "the kid is starting to look like the shirt more and more every day."

Moira had been calling my ex-husband, Roger Campbell, *the shirt* ever since she'd discovered that he had his business shirts custom made. I glanced in the rearview mirror again. Gordy did look like his father—which wasn't necessarily a bad thing. Like his father, my son was a brown-eyed blonde—handsome with an athletic body. But I knew that he also got some of his beauty, style and grace from his grandmother. My mother. Who I am nothing like.

"How can he not be nervous?" was my question. The fact was, Gordy seemed as cool as the Abercrombie and Fitch clothes and the hundred and fifty dollar sunglasses he was wearing—all gifts from the shirt.

"Honey, how can you not be relieved?" was Moira's comeback.

Moira was that rare thing in Whitefish Cove—the suburb of Milwaukee where we were neighbors—a mother who'd managed to completely let go of her children. Kenny and Gina had gone east to school and stayed to work on Wall Street and the Garment District, respectively. They made one trip home every year and Moira and her husband Stan made one trip to NYC every year and everyone seemed satisfied. But here I was having heart palpitations at the thought that I wouldn't see my son until he came home for Thanksgiving break. I was already planning the first meal in my head.

His favorite meat loaf. Garlic mashed potatoes. Glazed...

The blare of a semi's horn and the hoots of its driver snatched me from my recipe revelry.

"Nice rack!" the trucker yelled before blasting on his horn again.

"Are you crazy?" I demanded.

"Just trying to liven this funeral procession up a little," Moira said as she stuffed her sizable boobs back into her sweater.

I frantically checked to see if Gordy had witnessed Moira's flashing but his mouth was hanging slightly open as he softly snored, oblivious to the recent show. Of course, chances are, he'd already seen something of what Moira had to offer. She was fond of sunbathing topless in the back yard and exercising semi-nude in the living room with the drapes open. Whitefish Cove's Junior Leaguers didn't quite know what to make of her. But I liked her. I thought she was funny and audacious—different from anyone I'd ever known. My ex had never shared my appreciation of Moira's quirkiness so I didn't start to really get to know her until after my divorce. Now, after a few years of dancing around each other, we were starting to become best girlfriends and I was loving it.

I did, however, expect her to stay completely clothed on interstate highways.

"It's a wonder you don't get kicked out of Whitefish Cove," I snapped as I stepped off the gas and pulled in behind the semi, hoping the driver would see the maneuver as a sign that the show was over.

"That's the beauty of being married to a brilliant CPA, girlfriend. Half the men in Whitefish Cove have Stan on retainer. Several, who shall remain nameless, of course—"

"Of course," I hastened to agree.

"—would be peeling potatoes in some country club prison if it weren't for Stan."

Although I didn't know any details, nor did I want to, I knew she wasn't kidding. Stan might have been the neighborhood savior as far as the men were concerned, but to the women, Moira was the neighborhood thorn. She loved to shock the uptight wives and flirt with the bewildered husbands. More confident in her sexuality than any woman I'd ever met, she made no apology for carrying around twenty extra pounds while I seemed to be constantly apologizing for my extra fifteen. Although on Moira the pounds were mostly in the right place while I tended to be somewhat lacking in the rack area. Under similar circumstances, I was pretty sure that truckers would not be honking in my honor.

"Are we there, yet?" Gordy moaned sleepily from the backseat.

"Such enthusiasm for higher education," Moira drawled.

"Nah," my son, the college-bound, said, "I just gotta take a whiz."

I flicked on the van's blinker and took the next exit.

A huge bag of potato chips and three diet sodas later, we were there.

Indiana University looked like it had stepped out of central casting. It was that perfect. Big, ancient limestone buildings, gorgeous landscaping and students who didn't know the meaning of the word acne.

"Stepford U," muttered Moira.

"Behave yourself," I hissed as I pulled the van onto the U-shaped drive in front of the residence hall Gordy had been assigned to and claimed a parking space just vacated by a Mercedes. A few dozen kids were lugging trunks and duffels and what looked like several thousand dollars worth of electronics out of upscale SUVs. Gordy spotted his roommate—a boy named Dooley from Michigan that he'd been getting to know via email for the past month—and was out of the car and shaking hands before I even had a chance to turn off the engine.

"Isn't that cute," Moira said. "Acting like little men."

I gave Moira a stern look. "Am I going to have to make you sit in the car?"

"You and what fraternity?" she asked over her shoulder as she got out.

I opened my door and stepped into cloying humidity. "Holy hell," I gasped.

"You've got that right. What floor did you say Gordy is on?" Moira asked as she fanned herself with the empty potato chip bag. "Maybe I'd rather wait in the car, after all."

I slammed my door. "Nothing doing. You're hauling. In this heat it'll be no time at all before you'll be too dehydrated to open your mouth."

Close to the truth. Several trips to the second floor later, we were gasping for breath and begging for bottled water from some kids who'd had the foresight to bring a cooler full of drinks.

Moira and I sat under a tree to catch our breath while we re-hydrated and watched Gordy mingling and laughing and acting like this was a homecoming instead of a goodbye.

"I don't think I was ever that confident," I said.

"You did a good job, girlfriend," Moira stated.

"Can it be as easy as it looks for him?" I wondered.

Moira sighed. "In my experience, hon, it's never, ever as easy as it looks."

By the time we'd finished unloading, Gordy had gone full sail into his brave new world.

"Call if you need anything," I said for the hundredth time as I lingered outside the car trying to hold back my tears.

Gordy rolled his eyes. "Mom, if you cry, I swear I'll—"

Moira, waiting in the car, started to honk the horn.

"I'm just a little misty," I promised. Moira honked again and I said, "Just take care of yourself, okay?"

"Deal," he said, then added, "You, too," and looked at me long enough for me to know he meant it. Finally, he grinned. "See ya, Ma," he said, then turned and ran from me without a backward glance.

Which was a good thing.

So how come it made me so sad?

I sniffed back tears and went around to the driver's side of the car.

"Well, that was subtle," I said when I got in.

"Someone had to save the kid from humiliation."

I sniffed again, turned the radio to a classical station, which I knew Moira would hate, and started the long drive home.

But I can never stay mad at Moira for long and by the time we pulled off the interstate north of Indianapolis in search of more road snacks, I'd changed the station to oldies rock.

The convenience store/gas station that beckoned us from the night had seen better days. The florescent lighting inside was so cheap it hummed like a tree full of cicadas and I could feel my shoes stick ever so slightly to the badly mopped floor. Apparently, a sweet tooth's needs override fear of germs because the smeared and cracked self-service bakery case drew us like a couple of flies.

"Are you sure you don't mind driving right through?" I asked Moira as we peered at a couple of questionable looking donuts hiding behind the fingerprints.

"'Course not," Moira said. "It'll be an adventure—speeding across state lines in the middle of the night. Besides, we're both kid-free now. We can sleep as late as we want to tomorrow."

I had no intention of speeding and I wasn't at all cheerful about my new freedom to sleep late. I decided to change the subject. "Is it the bad lighting in here or do those donuts look a little green to you?"

"I consider myself somewhat adventurous," Moira said, "but in this case I think we should stick to packaged snacks with readable expiration dates on them."

I agreed and we went in search of the junk-food aisle.

"Cupcake?" Moira asked, once we'd buckled in again.

I grabbed the chocolate cupcake with the white squiggle of frosting bisecting the top and ate it the way I'd been eating them since I was ten—by tearing off the frosting with my teeth. It easily came off in one piece.

"Now that's talent," Moira said before downing half a bottle of soda in one chug. Her burp could have rivaled anything Gordy ever emitted.

"That was truly disgusting," I said as I pulled out of the gas station and into local traffic.

She burped again. "Don't tell me you're not acquainted with the car rule."

I glanced at her then back at the road. "The car rule?"

"Yeah, if it happens in a car, it doesn't count."

I hooted. "I bet some guy told you that back in 1978."

Moira stuck her nose up in the air. "That may well be, but even so it is one of the few known laws of the universe," she insisted. "Why do you think so many people pick their noses at stoplights?"

I pulled up to a stop light and we both looked to the right then started screaming with laughter. A guy with long greasy hair in the pickup next to us actually did have one of his digits shoved halfway up his bulbous nose.

"Seriously, Mo," I said after the light had changed and we'd pulled away from digit man and turned onto the ramp that would take us back to the interstate, "what if Gordy isn't as cool as he pretends to be about going to school? What if he's really been acting as phony as that knock-off Fendi on the floor at your feet?"

Moira gasped and grabbed her purse. "How did you know?" she demanded as she scrutinized it. "Is it that obvious?" she implored, the threat of handbag humiliation burning in her eyes.

I sighed impatiently. One of the many things Moira and I don't share is a love of all things fashion. "No, it's not that obvious. You told me it was a fake—that you'd bought it when you and Stan went to Mexico last spring."

Moira frowned. "Oh, right," she said.

"Forget your damn purse, will you? We were talking about Gordy, remember?" I asked her testily, certain that the happiness of my son was more important than whether women more in the know than I would spy that Moira's bag was a fake.

"Hey," Moira said, obviously satisfied that the bag would pass inspection as she tucked it back down by her feet, "you're not allowed to get serious on a road trip. Plenty of time for that once we're back on Seagull Lane. Here," she said as she tossed a cellophane bag at me, "have some pork rinds and listen to me sing backup to this song. You'll swear it's Cher."

As long as it didn't count, I ripped open the bag of pork rinds with my teeth and dug in. The thing was, Moira really did sound like Cher.

Thousands of calories and several dozen oldies later, I was maneuvering the car through the softly curved streets of a dark and sleeping Whitefish Cove.

As usual, Moira had to comment on the street names. Sea Spray Drive. Fog Horn Road. And her all time favorite Perch Place.

"Absurd," Moira pronounced, "considering you couldn't see Lake Michigan if you climbed to the roof of the largest Cape Cod in the Cove with a pair of binoculars."

"But you can sometimes feel it on your skin or taste it on your tongue," I said, parroting my usual argument in favor of all things maritime.

"Leave it to you to glamorize humidity and lake-effect snow," Moira said as she stuffed wrappers and half-eaten junk food into a bag so we could dispose of it discreetly and avoid possible ridicule by late-night joggers or carb counting insomniacs.

The Cove was reportedly first settled by fishermen which made the street names somewhat less absurd. To me, at least. Moira, however, was sure that the khaki wearing denizens liked to think of themselves as New Englanders, which made their collective fantasy of being related to the founding fathers doable.

It was true that the Cove had a lot of white picket and waving flags and many of the houses were more than one hundred years old. Which was why I'd been so thrilled when Roger had announced that we were buying our "starter house" in Whitefish Cove. It had looked so stable. So family oriented. Two things, at twenty-two, that I'd craved more than anything.

I pulled into the meager driveway of my two story wood frame cottage. The original clapboard siding was painted white and the window boxes under the first story windows, bursting with red geraniums, were painted the same blue as the front door. I loved the place now as much as I had when we moved in, but I was in no hurry to go inside now that Gordy wouldn't be there. When I cut the engine, the last of my energy seemed to go with it. I just sat there, arms clinging to the steering wheel.

"You're going to have to get out and go inside sometime, honey," Moira said. "Look at it this way, you'll never have to wait for the bathroom again."

Not very comforting, but true. My house was probably the only one left in the Cove with only one bathroom. It was one of the reasons Roger had wanted to dump it. Right around the same time he'd decided to dump me. In the years we'd lived there, I had bonded with the house like it was an old friend. I knew every creak. Every draft. But to Roger, the house had been nothing but an investment and, as with me, the time eventually came to trade it in on something that had a higher market value. He'd traded the house for a high-rise condo overlooking Lake Michigan. He'd traded me for a twenty-one-year old flight attendant named Suzie with a z.

Finally, Moira got out of the car and came around to the driver's side and opened my door. To save her the trouble, I dragged myself out.

"Geeze, girlfriend, you really are in bad shape." She put her arm around my shoulders. "Come on over and I'll scramble us some eggs and shake us up some martinis. A couple of those and you'll forget you have a kid."

"Tempting, but I think I'll just go inside and wallow a little." I didn't want to forget. At that moment, with the summer coming to an end and my nest newly empty, everything just seemed too precious. What I really wanted to do was put on my oldest, softest pair of cotton pajamas and climb into bed with a couple of photo albums. I truly did intend to wallow.

By late September, with the leaves starting to turn on the maple tree outside my living room window, I began to think there had to be a limit to how much a woman should be allowed to wallow. Not that I hadn't been out of the house since Gordy had deserted it. And I'm not just talking about the twice-weekly trips to the post office to send fresh baked cookies and care packages to Bloomington.

Whitefish Cove wasn't exactly a bedroom community, miles from real civilization where the cul-de-sac ruled and there wasn't a decent restaurant you didn't have to wrestle traffic on the freeway to get to. We were really a village that was only fifteen miles from the trendy east side of Milwaukee and just a few miles more to downtown. But I'd done the "meeting old girl-friends for lunch" thing to death. Moira, who'd recently started to collect art, had dragged me to every new gallery show in town. I'd gone to enough regional theater performances to fill the bottom of my purse with programs and parking stubs. I hadn't turned down one single invitation since I'd left Gordy in Bloomington. I'd even issued a few, determined not to become a forty-one year old recluse. But I was quickly becoming sick of hearing about how lucky I was to be divorced with my only child two states away.

"Why, you can do just about anything you want to do," a friend from my college days exclaimed over her basil, tomato and fresh mozzarella salad. I'd taken the initiative of inviting her and a former roommate to lunch at the latest trendy sensation—an overpriced café in a building that had once been a garage for city buses. The huge door at the front was left open at the owner's discretion, which was one of the big draws. *The excitement! The suspense!* It was rumored that he'd opened it during a March snowstorm last year and there was a big buzz going on about whether he'd leave it open for the first snowstorm this year. Personally, I couldn't get past the fact that I was eating a fourteen-dollar sandwich in a place where someone once drained motor oil from a city bus.

"Like what?" I asked after I'd swallowed a bite of my baby spinach and radish sprouts on asiago foccacia.

"Well—anything. You're footloose and fancy free," pointed out the former roommate who was trying to overcome bulimia, so she was eating nothing at all.

"Well, I have been considering finding a new kind of volunteer work—"

My former roommate laughed. "That's Lauren. Always the good girl."

These kinds of conversations did not make me feel better about my situation. Neither did spending the money on overpriced sandwiches since Gordy's support had started going into a trust on the day he started college and the maintenance Roger had to pay me was in nineteen-ninety-six dollars. So I went back to wallowing and baking until Gordy called one afternoon. I was absurdly pleased to hear his voice when I picked up the phone.

"Ma," he said before I could tell him how happy I was that he called, "you gotta stop sending all the cookies. One of my roommates saw a roach last night."

"You're not eating my cookies?" I asked with a modicum of mommy devastation.

"Ma—come on. Who could keep up? We get a package like every three days."

Perhaps I'd gone a little overboard, I thought as I eyed the two batches of oatmeal cookies cooling on the kitchen counter. "Okay," I vowed, "no more cookies. So, how are things going?"

"Things are cool, Ma. Gotta go, though. Class. See ya."

"But—"

But he was gone.

I packed the cookies up and took them next door to Moira's.

"Listen, hon, I know you've got time on your hands," she said as she chewed on her fifth cookie, "but you can't bring stuff like this over here. I have to be able to get into my new red dress for that cocktail party next month. CPAs and their wives. Big Yawn. I plan on being the most exciting aspect of the event and these cookies aren't helping."

That was the night I started watching the shopping channels on TV. Looking forward to finding out what the deal of the day was at midnight was about all the excitement I was getting. One night I found myself reaching for the phone while the on-air personality rhapsodized about a kitchen tool that would replace just about every other implement in the house—and all for $19.95. I snatched my hand back and vowed right then and there that there were going to be some changes made.

With butterflies in my stomach, the next day I called the University of Wisconsin, Milwaukee campus, ordered a catalogue of courses, and made an appointment to speak with a counselor in the department of continuing education.

Two days later, my heart did one of those funny little stalls when I opened the mailbox to find the catalogue had arrived. Oddly, I was not comforted that the postal rules hadn't changed since I was a twelve. Good things, like free makeup samples, took forever to arrive. Things that you'd just as soon not see, like report cards—and catalogues that were going to force you to start thinking about where your life was going—showed up in no time at all.

I took the catalogue to the breakfast nook, poured myself a cup of coffee, and started to page through it. After a half-hour I was wishing I'd made decaf. I felt lost and nervous as a high school freshman trying to find her locker.

I'd always intended to finish college someday. I'd even taken a college course here and there over the years. I'd sit in lectures thinking about the Halloween costume I could be sewing or the party I could be planning or the soccer game I was missing or the committee I could be chairing. Pretty soon I'd drop out, vowing to go back again when Gordy got older. Well, now Gordy was older and it was going to be different. It had to be. When Gordy graduated from college, maintenance from Roger would stop and I'd have to buy him out of the house if I wanted to stay on Seagull Lane. Which I did. I intended for my grandchildren to someday visit me in my little cottage.

Before I'd dropped out of college to marry Roger, I'd planned to major in elementary education. The prospect of being a teacher no longer interested me, I knew that much. But I had no idea what else I wanted to do.

Hoping to brainstorm, I called Moira but Stan said she'd gone shopping so I switched on the tube, found an old Bette Davis movie and lost myself in how Paul Henreid looked when he held two cigarettes in his mouth, lit them, and handed one to Bette. It wasn't a bad way to spend an evening. Afterwards, I made myself a peanut butter and jelly sandwich on, horrors of horrors, soft white bread. Since I no longer had to set a good example for my son, cheap white bread had become my new guilty pleasure. I dug in the refrigerator and came out with a can of chocolate syrup. I poured some into a big glass of milk and stirred. Then I tucked the UW catalogue under my arm, picked up the sandwich and milk and took everything up to bed with me. Maybe if I slept with the catalogue under my pillow, I'd dream about what I wanted to be when I grew up.

The phone woke me up the next morning. I sat up and grabbed it on the first ring. The college catalogue, still open in the vicinity of my lap, slid to the floor with a thump.

"Hello?" I croaked as I squinted against the sun filtering through the semisheer curtains in my bedroom window.

"Mrs. Campbell? This is Sondra Hawk from Priority Properties. I'd like to set up an appointment to check out the house. Today if possible. What time would be convenient?"

"Check out the house?" I asked dumbly as I pushed hair out of my face and looked at the alarm clock on the bedside table. Ten a.m. I never slept this late. Ever. I swear. The shame of it made my body go hot all over. I sat up straighter in bed and tried for a more cheerful, wakeful tone. "You want to check out the house?"

"Yes," Sondra said then gave a little laugh. "You know, get acquainted with its idiosyncrasies."

"Why would you want to do that?" I asked as I got out of bed. That way if Sondra, whose voice sounded like she was one of those alarmingly well put together women who knew how to accessorize, asked me if I'd still been in bed I could honestly answer no.

But, of course, she didn't ask.

"We here at Priority Properties," she explained, "pride ourselves in getting to know a house before we list it. The first step—"

I frowned. "Wait a minute—did you say *list?*"

"Yes—list."

"Excuse me, but you seem to be under the false impression that I'm selling my house."

Sondra didn't miss a beat. "I have the signed agreement right here in front of me."

I shook my head. "No—that's not possible."

There was a slight pause before she said, "Mrs. Campbell, your husband signed the agreement."

"Nonsense," I insisted, knowing this must be a mistake. "I don't even have a husband. I have an ex-husband," I conceded. "But he no longer lives here. *I* live here."

"But it's his name on the deed, Mrs. Campbell. It's his house. And he's putting it up for sale."

I told Sondra I'd get back to her and hung up the phone. I started to punch in the number for Weidermeir, Junket and Sloan Associates Engineering but thought better of it. This was something I had to do in person. I showered in record time, pulled on a white T-shirt and an ankle-length, army-green drawstring skirt that was only slightly wrinkled and ran a brush through my wet hair. My dark blond hair is chin length, parted in the middle and tends to be stick straight if I don't blow dry it. But this was no time to worry about volume. My adrenaline was shooting into high gear. I needed to confront Roger while the anger was still pumping through my veins. I shoved my feet into some brown leather clogs, grabbed my purse, and headed for the garage.

Southeastern Wisconsin likes to keep you guessing about the weather. October had arrived and the leaves on the trees were gold and crimson but the day was as steamy as an August heat wave. I was practically to Roger's office before the air conditioner in my aging car had any effect on the sweat factor under my T-shirt. I arrived downtown looking as haggard and bewildered as I felt.

The attendant at the underground parking facility wouldn't let me in. No spaces reserved for ex-wives, apparently. I managed to snag a parking spot on the street five blocks away. Which meant, of course, that I was noticeably damp by the time I reached Roger's building. The ride up in the elevator made me feel queasy and I wished I'd eaten something before leaving home.

The receptionist didn't have a clue who I was and looked dubious when I told her my name. She was as crisp and unwrinkled in her tightly tailored taupe suit as I was sweaty and disheveled. I noticed her giving me the once over while she buzzed Roger's office, making me wish I'd spent some time with a blow dryer and an iron, after all.

"He's with clients," the receptionist said as she hung up the phone. "If you'd care to wait—" She waved her hand toward the sumptuous waiting area. But I wasn't interested in being awed by the Mies van der Rohe knock-off chairs or in paging through this month's copy of *Structural Engineering*.

"I really don't care to wait, thank you. I'll just go on back."

She was on her feet and out from behind her desk before I could open the door to the inner sanctum.

"Of course," she said smoothly, like she was used to managing uncooperative people. "Please come with me."

I followed her down the plushly carpeted hallway to a small room that wasn't a conference room, nor was it an office. Perhaps it was the place they led all irate ex-wives to. The Ex Waiting Room. How modern. How sophisticated. How condescending.

"Can I get you anything? Coffee?"

Coffee? I was boiling inside and out. "No, thanks," I muttered.

"As you wish," she said, then left.

"As you wish," I singsonged to myself as I flounced around the room. Her poise was pissing me off almost as much as that immaculate taupe suit she was wearing. I noticed the furniture in the Ex Waiting Room didn't even bother to be knock-offs of anything. No doubt I'd have gotten my coffee in a plastic cup.

So not only was I getting my house sold from under me, I was now labeled second class at Weidermeir, Junket and Sloan.

Which, of course, was what I was. But having my nose rubbed in it didn't make me happy. Not that I would ever want Roger back. In fact, every time I saw him I believed just a little bit more in divorce.

I was pacing and mentally counting up Roger's deficits in the husband department when the door opened and he walked in.

He was still handsome and I suppose you could say he looked intimidating standing there in a suit that probably cost more than the contents of my entire closet and a shirt that was custom made. On the other hand, I knew he got gas from cucumbers and that he had the hair on his back professionally waxed. These things saved me from being intimidated by cashmere or thread counts.

"What is this about, Lauren?" he asked impatiently.

I crossed my arms. "What do you think it's about, Roger?"

He sighed again. "I take it Sondra called you. She wasn't supposed to do that. Not until I'd had a chance to warn you."

"Warn me? About what?"

"Lauren," he said with that blandly condescending way I'd come to hate when we were still married, "try to focus. I meant warn you about Sondra listing the house, of course. With winter coming, now is the best time to put it on the market. Plus, with interest rates—"

I only partly listened while Roger quoted a raft of statistics.

"Roger," I finally interrupted, "why does the house have to be put up for sale at all?"

He sighed and looked up at the ceiling before turning back to me. "Lauren, that was the agreement," he said slowly, like he was explaining something to a child. "I pay you maintenance, child support and pick up the tab for the house until Gordon goes to college. At which time, the house reverts back to me, the maintenance ends and the child support goes into a trust to pay for Gordon's education and other expenses."

I stared at him for a moment. Could this be right? I shook my head. "The agreement was until he *finished* college, Roger. Which means I've got four more years until—"

He gave a derisive chuckle. "Delusional, as usual," he said. "You've always lived in your own little dream world, Lauren."

I gasped. "Me? Are you kidding?" I demanded. "Dream world? I've been a single mother for ten years, Roger. I was the one who stayed, remember? I'm the responsible one, while you—"

"Now wait just a minute! If you were really responsible, we wouldn't even be having this conversation. You'd have a career in place and you'd be able to buy the house yourself if you wanted to stay there so badly."

"My career," I said tightly, "was raising our son."

"Fine. But now that's over."

"Over?" Okay, maybe I knew that. And maybe I knew that this day was eventually coming. But it made no sense to me that *eventually* had suddenly become *now*.

"That house is Gordy's home, too," I pointed out. "What do you expect him to do during the holidays? Summers?"

Roger shrugged. "He'll do what most children of divorced parents do. He'll spend part of the time at my condo and part of the time at your apartment."

The word apartment still had the power to make me cringe inside—and not only because, without a job, I couldn't possibly afford one. The reason I'd fought to stay on at Seagull Lane, fought to bring my son up in exactly the manner he would have been raised had his parents not been divorced, was because he wasn't going to have my childhood. Not if I could help it.

Roger looked at his watch. "Look, I've got to get back to my meeting. This has taken up too much of my time already. I'm sorry the Realtor's call shook you up, but I think if you check with your lawyer, you'll see that I'm well within my rights. So don't try to make me out to be the bad guy, Lauren. I've been patient with you long enough."

After Roger left, I slumped into a chair, fished my cell phone out of my purse and called my lawyer's office. She was with a client so I asked for her voice mail and left her a message detailing precisely what I needed to know. Namely, was I about to become homeless?

On my way out, I managed to give the receptionist a bright smile and wish her a good day but I was glad once I was back on the street and I didn't have to hide how scared I was.

I walked without purpose, trying to remember the details of the divorce agreement. Could I have actually gotten wrong something as important as this—a roof over our heads? Bread on the table? Was it possible that my life was about to change even more than I thought it would? Was I going to go from an empty nest to no nest at all?

I started to feel sick. I wasn't sure if it was lack of food or the humidity or the fear, but when I passed a restaurant, I decided to go in. I didn't even notice the name of the place. The air conditioner was pumping out cool air and there was food to be had. That was enough for me.

The waitress showed me to a booth and I ordered iced tea. When she left, I opened the menu and immediately honed in on the dessert section. Chocolate Suicide. Yeah, I could use a little suicide, especially if it was sweet. But then I remembered the receptionist's tight, taupe skirt. When the waitress came back, I ordered the salad of field greens with grilled chicken.

When it came, it was huge and it occurred to me that maybe I should eat half and take the rest home for dinner. I mean, maybe I was going to have to start doing that kind of stuff. Maybe I was going to have to start doling out my food so a loaf of bread would last me a week and a jar of peanut butter would last me a month. I'd have to start putting milk in my coffee instead of more expensive flavored non-dairy creamers. Unless, of course, I ended up living under a viaduct in a discarded washing machine carton where I'd only have refrigeration from October to May.

I nibbled while I thought of the humilities I might have to suffer, but as soon as the food hit my stomach I started to feel stronger.

I was right about this and Roger was wrong. I had four more years to get my act together. Not that I was admitting that I'd been irresponsible. You can't be irresponsible and serve as PTA president, block watch captain and room mother. You can't be irresponsible if you tucked your child in every night and made him breakfast every morning.

I stabbed a hunk of something green and ruffly and shoved it into my mouth. I was getting angry again. After all, marriage was a contract. A bargain between two people. Both Roger and I had been up-front before we'd gotten married about what we wanted and expected. I had kept my end of the bargain. Roger was the irresponsible one who hadn't. It was hard to believe that in the beginning we'd both wanted the same thing.

I met Roger the summer before my junior year of college. I was working at a day-care center and I'd taken a group of seven and eight year olds on a field trip to the Milwaukee Art Museum, perched on the edge of Lake Michigan. We'd brought bag lunches and eaten them on the lawn near some huge, metal sculptures. Afterwards, I'd passed out little disposable cameras, given the kids a quick lesson and told them to get snap happy. It was such a joy to watch them decide what they wanted to shoot. I was grinning ear to ear when Roger came up to me and told me that he'd never seen anything as beautiful as how I was with those children. I was speechless. I mean, here was this terrific-looking man dressed in a gorgeous suit, looking at me like I was the best thing he'd ever seen. He handed me his business card and asked me to please give him a call so he could ask me out to dinner. I watched him walk away then looked down at the card.

An engineer. And at a firm I'd heard of. A firm everyone had heard of. You bet your life I called.

He wanted a traditional wife, he'd told me on our first date. Someone who would stay at home and raise his children. Someone who would care about his career, which was just starting to take off, as much as he did. It sounded like heaven to me. Raised by a single mother, I was a latchkey child before the term was even coined. Being a stay-at-home mother was exactly what I dreamed about being someday. I loved kids. I was only twenty-two, but my biological clock had been ticking ever since I'd started babysitting at fifteen.

After six dates, Roger declared himself enchanted and proposed. How could I refuse? He was offering me everything I ever wanted. This handsome, ambitious man wanted to take care of me and our offspring for the rest of our lives? Blame it on fiercely independent mother backlash, but I was more than happy to let him.

I became pregnant with Gordy when we were married less than a year. We bought the house in the Cove. Bought the minivan and the infant car seat. Life, as far as I was concerned, was beautiful.

Until Roger made partner. The youngest ever in the firm. He started to travel more on business. He started to buy more expensive suits. He started to complain about how I dressed. But the real fighting began when he enrolled us in a wine-tasting club. I just couldn't get behind the idea of spitting out deliciously expensive wine once it was in my mouth.

By the time Gordy was six, Roger was no longer enchanted. Two years later, we were divorced.

Just as I was signaling the waitress for more iced tea, my cell phone rang. I dug in my purse for it and flipped it open. It was my lawyer.

"So, I'm right, aren't I?" I asked in a rush of certainty that I really wasn't feeling in my belly anymore. "I still have four more years."

There was a moment of silence, then, "Lauren, maybe you should make an appointment and come in so we can discuss this."

I closed my eyes. "No, give it to me now."

She sighed as the waitress refilled my glass.

"All right," she said. "No. You don't have four more years."

My mouth went dry. I looked at the retreating waitress in a panic. I didn't have enough spit to call her back, so I took a gulp of iced tea then yelled, "Excuse me? Miss?"

She turned around and I said two words. "Chocolate Suicide."

CHAPTER 2

Buzzed from the caffeine in two orders of Chocolate Suicide, I ran up the stone steps of Moira's Tudor and jabbed the doorbell.

"Door's open," Moira yelled.

I found her in the living room, wearing only a pair of French-cut panties, rolling around on a Pilates ball.

"Jesus, Moira, what if I'd been the UPS guy or something?"

Moira jumped off the ball, her breasts bouncing with enthusiasm. "Then I guess I would still be getting some exercise," she said with a smart-ass grin.

Moira was always alluding to other men and rumors were rife among the neighbors on Seagull Lane. I'd taken a "don't ask, don't tell" attitude and had no idea if the rumors were true.

"Geeze, honey," she said as she took in my appearance, "you look like hell. And what's that all over your shirt?"

I looked down. "I've just done two rounds with Chocolate Suicide."

"Well, it obviously didn't kill you, but, sweetie, you sure look wounded."

For one harrowing moment I thought she was going to hug me. I don't consider myself to be all that narrow minded, but that didn't mean I wanted to feel Moira's bare breasts against my T-shirt. Thankfully, she grabbed a kimono off the sofa and slipped into it. But not before I had enough information to put another Seagull Lane rumor to rest. Not an ounce of silicone on that body. I'd never seen them in action this long before. They were real, all right.

Heavens, was this any time to focus on another woman's breasts? My world was crumbling. What did I care about silicone? "Something terrible has happened—" I began.

"Well, I'm here to listen and help but you seem awfully rattled. Before you start spilling your guts, you need a martini." She peered at me again from under her false eyelashes. "Or maybe three."

I was in no shape to argue. I followed her into the kitchen and watched her make a shaker of martinis.

"Here," she said, handing me one. "Drink up."

I'm usually a white wine kind of gal, but the first sip went down easily. Delicious and cold enough to ice skate over the surface. I took another sip. And another.

"Good," Moira praised. "The color is starting to come back into your cheeks. Now let's go get comfortable so you can tell mama everything."

I followed her into the living room and sank onto one of the two white sofas that flanked the fireplace. While the women of Whitefish Cove often worked for years at taking layers of paint off their woodworks and crown moldings, Moira had done just the opposite. Everything was painted a creamy white—even the stone fireplace. Sacrilege to most of the ladies of the Cove, but I thought it was really quite striking. The color in the room came from a red shag rug on the floor and the artwork on the walls— which were mostly bold slashes of color on canvas—the kind of stuff you look at and think you could do yourself just as well. But what did I know about art?

"So," Moira said once I'd let the down-filled cushions of the sofa enfold me, "spill it."

I chugged the rest of my martini, put the empty glass on the coffee table, and spilled. The look on Moira's face grew more horrified with each word.

"Honey," she said when I'd finished, "you must have had a man for a lawyer."

I shook my head. "Nope. A woman."

"Traitor bitch," Moira mumbled.

"Not really. I insisted on doing it this way." I braced myself, figuring Moira would look at me and say *stupid bitch*. But she didn't. Instead, she asked me why.

"Okay," she said, "you're not dumb. So what were you thinking?"

"I was thinking that I wanted my life to go on just as I'd planned it," I said. "I wanted to be a 'stay at home mother,' I wanted to be a block watch captain, room mother, chairman of the annual Christmas cookie exchange. I wanted to drive a minivan to soccer games and sew Halloween costumes. I wanted everything that Roger had promised me when I'd married him, damn it. And I didn't see why Gordy should have to suffer having his life uprooted just because his parents had fallen out of love. Besides, I'd always planned to go back to school and eventually support myself. I mean, I had no intention of living off a man who didn't love me for the rest of my life."

"I'm not sure I share your ethics on that one," Moira murmured as she refilled our glasses from the shaker she'd brought with her from the kitchen.

"The most important thing to me was to know that Gordy would be taken care of until after college." I shook my head in disbelief. "I guess that's how I screwed up. I thought I was going to be taken care of for four more years, too." I leaned forward again and buried my face in my hands. "Don't you see? I thought I had four more years to figure out what to do with the rest of my life."

Moira set her glass down on the table, then gathered me to her ample, unfettered bosom. "You poor thing," she murmured as she rocked me in a way that my own mother certainly never had. I closed my eyes and settled in. Of course, Bernice wouldn't have been nearly as comfortable to be held against, either. My mother had good bones and never put anything into her mouth that could lead to hiding them. When she was upset, she lost herself in sit-ups or yoga, not double helpings of dessert.

My eyes popped open. *OMG! My mother! How was I ever going to face my mother with this?*

Comforting as they were, Moira's arms weren't going to cut it. I pushed away from her and grabbed my glass off the coffee table, downing the second martini, which wasn't nearly as cold or delicious as the first, in one huge gulp. I burped then wailed, "How the hell am I going to tell Bernice?"

"I think we need more booze," Moira said.

She'd met my mother.

Moira was back in the kitchen, shaking up the last of a bottle of Stoli, when Stan came home. I sat up straighter and tried to look less like a tearful lush, then I remembered that Stanley Rice, who at six foot three and about one hundred forty pounds looked like Ichabod Crane in Ralph Lauren, wasn't known for a keen sense of observation when it came to anything other than business and his model railroads in the basement. He barely glanced at me.

"Hello, Lauren," he murmured absently while he sorted through the stack of mail he'd brought in with him.

"Hi, Stanley," I said, trying not to slur my words. Not that he'd notice that, either.

Moira came into the living room with the shaker and another glass. She poured Stan a martini. "Here you go, snookums. Something to fortify you."

Stan looked blankly at the glass Moira had thrust into his hand. He took a sip and a small smile played around the corners of his thin mouth. "Ah," he breathed.

"That's a good boy," Moira said. "Now you go downstairs and play with your trains until dinner is ready."

Stan shuffled off like an obedient mental patient. I still hadn't figured out how someone as vibrant as Moira had ended up married to the barely breathing Stanley Rice.

"I should go," I said as I tried to stand up.

"Don't be silly." Moira refilled our glasses. "You're staying for dinner."

I looked around the room. "What dinner?"

She raised a perfectly arched brow. "You have heard of delivery, haven't you?"

She fished a cell phone out of her kimono pocket and ordered a pizza.

With a tummy full of pepperoni pizza to help soak up the vodka, I wove my way back home under darkness, hoping that the ladies on Seagull Lane were all too busy either scrapbooking or exfoliating to see the shameful condition I was in.

At nine o'clock the next morning, I shot up from a dead sleep into a sitting position. *Someone is in the house*, was my first thought, followed closely by *Something must have crawled inside my mouth and died last night*. My third thought was spent wishing

I could unscrew my head and set it aside for the day because the pounding going on inside of it was driving me crazy.

And then I heard the noises from downstairs again.

I threw back the covers on my four-poster bed, then crept to the top of the stairs.

A woman was standing at the foot of them, shaking the newel post.

"Excuse me," I said. "What are you doing in my house?"

The woman looked up at me. "Oh, hello, there. I guess you didn't hear the bell."

"I guess I didn't," I muttered.

She held up a set of keys. "So I just let myself in. I'm Sondra Hawk. We spoke on the phone."

I'd been right. She did know how to accessorize.

Shiny black boots, shiny black purse, shiny black belt, shiny black hair cut as severely as the black and white houndstooth check suit she was wearing. The jewelry all looked like real gold. And there was just enough of it to announce that Sondra Hawk was both successful and tasteful.

Suddenly, I was keenly aware of what I must look like. Not to mention smell like. According to my T-shirt, I'd had chocolate, and something red. Most likely something Italian because I was pretty sure it was garlic fermenting in my mouth.

Damn it. Sondra the Hawk was probably wondering how someone like Roger Campbell could have ever been married to someone like me. A thought, unwelcome as a swarm of wasps at an ice cream social, entered my mind. I wondered if they'd had sex, yet—Ms. Coordinated of 2006 and Roger "I have all my shirts custom made" Campbell. If they hadn't, I figured they'd eventually get around to it. And on sheets with a minimum 600 thread count. I thought longingly of the yellow sprigged sheets currently on my bed wishing I were still snuggled between them even though I was pretty sure that no one had ever bothered to count their threads.

But there was no running away from the woman with the leather notebook that matched her bag. Anyway, was I woman or wimp? I decided to hold my head high, despite the map of indulgence on my T-shirt. I started down the stairs. "May I ask what you're doing here, Ms. Hawk?"

"I'm here to inspect and get to know the property, Mrs. Campbell. We at Priority Properties pride—"

"Yes, I know. You pride yourself in getting to know a house before you list it."

She gave me a frosty smile. "So if you don't mind, I'll just make myself at home and take a look around."

"And if you don't mind, I'll accompany you."

"Certainly," she said. "Of course, some people find it too emotional an experience—"

She let her voice trail off as she shook the newel post again then jotted something down in her notebook.

"No entrance hall," she murmured as she jotted some more.

There had once been a tiny entrance hall and an enclosed staircase. The one big change Roger and I had made in the early years was to tear down the wall so that the narrow staircase was now open to the living room. Which meant that there was really no entrance hall, but I'd always thought it was worth it because it had opened up the living room so much.

"Small, isn't it?" Sondra commented as she moved to the center of the room and inspected the ceiling. "This should really be replastered," she said. "And I would strongly suggest changing your window treatments."

I'd made the simple tieback muslin curtains that hung in the front windows myself. I'd always thought them charming. Sondra's tone had reduced them to rags. I didn't want to know what she thought of the rest of my decorating. She was probably inwardly sneering at my blue-and-white check camelback sofa and my chintz wingback chair, the cushion worn down to fit my tush like a baseball in a glove.

"You're lucky wide-plank floors are back in style, but this one needs refinishing—or you could just carpet over it. It would probably make the room warmer."

The dining room didn't fare much better than the living room, but it was the kitchen that really took a beating.

"You'd be wise to have a new floor put in and the built-in booth in the breakfast nook should be torn out to open the room up."

She wanted me to get rid of the booth where Gordy had eaten Froot Loops and fish sticks? Where he'd helped me decorate Christmas cookies and did his homework while I cooked dinner? I was debating whether to cry or to kick her out on her tight rear end when something she said caught my attention.

"Excuse me—what was that you just said?" I asked.

"I was just saying that you'll have to get right on this list of improvements. It'll be a miracle if we're ready to show by the end of October. Once we hit November, things slow down until well after the holidays."

"You mean the house could just be sitting here, empty, all through the holidays?"

She gave me another frosty smile. "Well, we don't like to think so. I mean, our sales staff is excellent. But, this house hasn't got much more than location going for it. I suggest we get it on the market as soon as possible. But, even with the best of properties," she added in a tone that made it clear that this was not one of them, "people just don't like to relocate during the holidays." She sighed. "Now let's take a look at the upstairs."

I followed her up but I hardly heard anything else she said as she inspected the larger bedroom in the front and the two smaller ones in the back and I only vaguely heard her outrage when she discovered the one small bathroom with the claw-footed tub. I was too busy forming a plan.

Once she was gone, leaving a list of problems behind, I called Roger's office. His secretary tried to put me off but I told her to tell him it was regarding the sale of the house. She put me on hold but it wasn't long before Roger picked up.

I didn't waste any words. "Roger, I think we need to talk. Could you drop by after work today?"

"If you spoke to your lawyer, Lauren, you know I'm well within my rights—"

"Roger," I said pleasantly, "please. I know the house is going on the market. Sondra was here this morning and we went through the entire house together," I said, making it sound like we'd bonded while discussing cracks in the ceiling. "She made a list of liabilities that I think we need to discuss."

"Liabilities?"

I smiled. I'd gotten his attention.

"What kind of liabilities?"

"Well, the list is quite detailed and I thought we should probably go over it together."

"Just fax me a copy, okay?"

"Roger, since I'm going to be living here while these repairs are being done, I'm the one who will have to handle the plasterers and painters and the carpenters. So I think—"

"Plasterers? Carpenters?" he grumbled before giving the kind of sigh that would have made me nervous if we were still married.

"Yes, maybe we better discuss it." I could hear him flipping pages on his day planner. "I'll be there around six-thirty."

"Perfect," I said. When I hung up the phone I headed for the shower. I needed to get rid of the stench of yesterday's pity party, then start making a grocery list.

I'd decided to splurge on ingredients, so I drove to the Market in the Cove in the heart of the village. When I pulled into the parking lot my heart did a little flip. God, I used to love this place. When Roger and I were still married I relished shopping here on Friday mornings, planning special dinners for the weekend. Once Roger split I'd started going to the bigger, less expensive chains. But they were just grocery shopping. The Market in the Cove, with its low green awnings and its clusters of pumpkins and corn stalks flanking the entrance, was an *experience*.

Buckets of fresh cut flowers greeted me as soon as I was through the door. Warm gold and vibrant orange zinnias. Jaunty brown-eyed Susans and roses of yellow and pink and red. There was a bucket of pale, creamy giant mums. I decided I had to have some of those. I grabbed a shopping cart and chose half a dozen. After the flower girl, in an adorable cobbler's apron, wrapped them for me, I moved on to the butcher's counter. The butcher wasn't the same one as in the old days, but he was just as friendly when he held out the length of white butcher paper where an expertly trimmed loin of pork reclined for my approval before he wrapped it.

The fresh vegetable section was even more beautiful than the flower department. Every tomato appeared to be the same size and fully ripe. The asparagus was thin and tender enough to make one doubt the calendar and there were varieties of mushrooms I'd never even heard of. I chose a selection of vegetables to marinate and pan grill and was sorting through the fresh rosemary when I heard a familiar voice behind me.

"Lauren! I haven't seen you shopping here in ages!"

I grimaced. Amy Westcott. The biggest gossip in the Cove. I made myself smile before I turned around.

"Amy! What a surprise!"

Amy lived across the street from me in a huge Colonial that was decorated within an inch of its life. She had parlayed a fondness for painting vines, flowers and birds on assorted surfaces into a business. Amy's Ambience, her little gift shop in the village, was stocked with the overflow from her house as well as hand-dipped candles, homemade soaps and a selection of useless, overpriced gifts. Moira and I had often speculated on how she managed to keep her shop open since there never seemed to be any customers.

"Is it true what I've heard?" she asked with that overly concerned air that people affect when they're hoping that whatever horrible thing they've heard really is true.

My stomach clenched. Had Amy somehow heard that I was soon to be homeless? "I don't know," I answered pleasantly. "That depends on what you've heard."

"That you're selling your little house!" she exclaimed, her fresh-scrubbed face looking the picture of innocence. Amy never wore makeup. She didn't have to. This was a woman who'd sailed through high school without a zit or a blackhead to slow her down. And she was sailing into middle age with barely a crow's foot to her name. "I mean, I saw Sondra Hawk over there this morning, so I just thought—"

"Oh, that," I said as I turned my attention back to the rosemary. "I was just having the house—um—appraised."

"Appraised?"

I didn't have to look at her to know that she was skeptical.

"Yes. I'm thinking of having another bathroom put in," I said, a little astounded that I'd grabbed this idea out of thin air.

"But, didn't Gordy just leave for college? I would think the last thing you'd need is another bathroom at this point."

I looked at her in her white button down and sixteen inch strand of pearls and wanted to tell her that it was none of her business but it's like I was programmed to be nice. So instead I gave her a bright smile and said, "Well, you never know what the future will hold, do you?"

I could see that this response had whetted her appetite for more information. I decided to counterattack. "So how is Chuck doing? The stock market is so unpredictable these days." Chuck was a stockbroker who liked to brag that his clients were the only ones who hadn't lost money in the '90s.

"Oh—well—Chuck is fine. And, as always, he just has a knack for picking the right stocks," she said with a brief laugh, then opened her mouth to pounce again.

I beat her to it.

"And the girls? How are Annabelle, Belinda and Camille doing?"

"Oh, the ABCs are doing terrifically," she gushed. "I'm sure you heard about our Belinda coming in first at her twirling contest and—"

I nodded, smiled, oohed and aahed in all the right places as Amy talked batons and gymnastics and swim meets. The ABCs, as Amy and Chuck liked to refer to their girls of eight, ten and twelve, were, as Moira liked to put it, "nauseatingly talented." Not to mention Amy's favorite subject. She could go on for hours. And that's exactly what it felt like she was doing.

I looked at my watch. I didn't have any more time to be nice.

"Oh, gosh, look at the time!" I interrupted. "Gotta rush. Nice to see you." I tossed a bundle of rosemary onto my other groceries and took off, rattling my cart down the aisle and leaving her standing there in her Eddie Bauer khakis with a dumbfounded look on her face.

Shameful, maybe, but I fully admit that I enjoyed every minute of preparing that meal, even though I was going to be feeding it to Roger.

The plan was to fill the house with the scents of home cooking so he wouldn't be able to resist accepting my invitation to stay for dinner. Then I'd whet his appetite with baby spinach and fresh pears tossed with his favorite vinaigrette and a sprinkling of blue cheese and walnuts and wow him with my honey mustard pork loin and my pan grilled vegetable medley. I'd lull him with freshly baked yeast rolls then move in for the kill with warm apple crisp.

First I'd have him eating off our wedding china, then I'd have him eating out of my hand.

One thing in life I was sure about. I was a damned good cook. It was one of the reasons Roger had married me.

It was just past noon and I was kneading the dough for the rolls when I heard the front door open and close, followed by the tap-tapping of high heels on my liability floors. I thought at first that it might be the Hawk again, back to insult the backyard or something. No such luck.

"Hello, Mother," I said when I looked up to find her standing in the kitchen doorway. "What brings you out to the Cove?"

But I didn't really need to ask. She had a shopping bag from the upscale boutique she managed dangling from her arm. The only time my mother made a visit was when she'd plucked something tasteful from a clearance rack that she was certain would be perfect for me. Luckily, with her discount, she got the stuff for next to nothing so I didn't really feel guilty that I never wore any of it. I was totally honest with her about this, but Bernice, who'd done some modeling in the fifties and sixties and still dressed, groomed and moved like she was camera-ready at all times, just could not seem to give up trying to dress me. It'd been a battle between us since I was about ten and decided I'd rather be comfortable than look "pretty."

My mother, even at sixty-two, was still what I thought of as a Hitchcockian beauty. Tall and blond and sophisticated with a very chilly edge. She was wearing a pencil-thin camel skirt and a cream cashmere twinset. Her skillfully colored champagne hair was drawn back in a perfect French twist. Her earrings were small swirls of gold surrounding pearls. I looked down at my flour-dusted denim coveralls and sneakered feet.

Like I said, my mother and I are nothing alike.

"I brought lunch," she said as she held up a little shopping bag from the café near her boutique, "but it looks like I needn't have bothered."

"Actually," I said, "I could use some lunch. This is for dinner."

"Are you having a party?" she asked skeptically.

"No," I answered as I went back to kneading the dough.

"Surely you don't bake this kind of thing for yourself?" Her voice held the kind of horror mothers usually reserved for something worse than the possible consumption of carbohydrates.

"No, Mother, I don't."

She reached into the refrigerator and brought out a pitcher of iced tea.

"Is that your honey mustard pork loin marinating in there?" she asked.

"It is."

She poured herself a glass of tea, then sat down in the breakfast nook and started to lay out what she'd brought for lunch. Salads sans dressing. My mother carried her own fat-free concoction in a handsome little bottle she kept in her huge, tote-size purse.

"Well, it can't be that you're seeing someone," she said.

Although she was right, her tone still pissed me off. "Why can't it?" I asked with the petulance that only she can bring out in me. "Just because I haven't dated anyone since that excruciating blind date back in nineteen ninety-eight—" I sprinkled more flour on the ball of dough "—doesn't mean that I couldn't date if I wanted to."

"Well, *are* you seeing someone?" my mother asked, her voice icily amused.

"As it happens, no," I answered curtly.

"Then what's with all this mess?"

To Bernice, a mess in the kitchen was anything that eventually led to washing dishes. My mother's idea of preparing dinner is to stop at the deli or pick up the phone. I probably teethed on biscotti and I was pretty sure my first solid food had been something with olives and feta cheese.

"Actually," I said, despite my reservations, "I'm expecting Roger for dinner."

"Oh, my God," Bernice exclaimed, a forkful of arugula halfway to her mouth, her beautifully made-up green eyes wide, "don't tell me you're so afraid of the empty nest that you're going to try to win that asshole back."

I stared at her, wondering if her latest Botox treatments had somehow affected her mind but she didn't seem to be drooling or anything.

"Get serious, Mother. I would prefer," I said, picking up the dough and giving it a good bashing, "to never be in the same room with him again if I could help it. It's the nest I'm after—empty or not."

Okay, I'd said it. And I knew it would bring on the questions. And I knew what her reactions to my answers would be. My mother was not going to be pleased to find out that I was willing to flatter and feed my ex-husband just to keep from getting my ass tossed into the street. But what the hell, might as well get it over with.

I took a deep breath. "Mother, there's something I have to tell you," I began, preparing to spill my guts while my mother sipped her tea.

"This has too much sugar in it," she said before I managed to get one word out. "I don't see why you don't leave it unsweetened and offer your guests the option of artificial sweetener."

I rolled my eyes like a teenager. "Well, Mother, it's not like I have crowds coming through here every day asking for iced tea."

She eyed my hips. "Then do it for yourself," she said.

Maybe I'm too sensitive, but I'm not fond of pouring my heart out to someone while they're insulting me. The fact that it was my own mother just added to the fun.

I slapped the dough against the breadboard, sending up a little puff of flour. And then I told her my story.

And what did she say?

"Of course, it would never occur to you to just go out and get a job."

I had to force myself to stop kneading the dough. It was long past time to shape it. Face it, the last five minutes had been overkill, but I'd needed to keep my hands busy while I told my mother what a mess I'd made of my life. "Of course, I'm going to get a job," I said as I opened a cupboard door and searched for a baking sheet. "But I need time to find one, Mother."

"Right. You've only had ten years," she answered.

That my mother disapproves of my choices in life is no secret to anyone who has ever seen us together. But, just in case I might have forgotten, she was kind enough to take this opportunity to remind me.

"I honestly have never understood why you didn't finish college. You weren't raised to be dependent on anyone, Lauren. Certainly not a man. I've been taking care of myself since I turned sixteen. I've—"

I found the pan I needed and slammed it onto the counter top. "Just because you programmed yourself to be the woman you wanted to become when you were twelve years old and first discovered that you had cheekbones doesn't mean—"

She didn't let me finish. "Oh, you think that isn't exactly what you've done?" she asked.

I gasped. "That's nothing like what I've done!"

She shrugged. "Keep your little delusions, Lauren, if it makes you feel noble. At least I have the consolation of knowing you aren't trying to win back that jerk you married." She stood. "That said, I hope you intend to do some grooming before Roger gets here. It wouldn't hurt to have him feel sorry that he screwed up for a change." She picked up her enormous purse. "Take a look at what's in the shopping bag," she said. "And don't be stubborn about it." She came over and kissed my forehead—easy since she was about five foot eleven, even without the mules, and I was five foot six—murmured disapprovingly over my hair for a few moments, then clicked her way back to the front door. "Good luck with Roger," she yelled before the door slammed.

"That woman drives me nuts," I muttered to the dough as

I started to shape it into dinner rolls. Face it, we drove each other nuts.

I'd always suspected that my mother had "career girl" stamped on her birth certificate. It wasn't that she didn't like men—there had been no shortage of men over the years to take her to dinner, the theater, New York—she just didn't want to be married to one. She certainly hadn't wanted all the things that came with marriage in the fifties and early sixties. I was obviously an accident. She'd stayed married to my father just long enough to give birth to me. Gorgeous and irresponsible, Daddy had set out for the Florida Keys before I'd learned to talk, but I still heard from him every Christmas and on my birthday. And I still kept a picture of him, wearing swim trunks and a tan George Hamilton would envy, on my bedroom dresser.

I finished shaping the rolls, covered them with a gingham linen towel and went to the sink to wash my hands. I kept glancing over my shoulder at the shopping bag Bernice had left in the breakfast nook. Curiosity finally got the better of me and I wiped my hands on a towel and went to investigate.

Another little black dress. I drew it out of the bag and held it in front of me. Not bad. Maybe I'd wear it tonight. If it fit. I looked at the tag and was surprised to see that it was actually my size. Maybe Bernice had finally gotten it into her head that I was never going to be a size eight. I grinned. If that was the case, then anything was possible.

CHAPTER 3

For a few minutes I almost forgot.

As I started down the stairs, wearing the dress my mother had delivered earlier, the scents from the kitchen took me back to evenings when the sound of music had come from Gordy's room upstairs and the house had felt cozy and safe. That's how I'd felt in this life I had built for Gordy and me. Home safe—like a kid who'd been playing kick the can and had rushed out madly from the shadows of dusk to hit goal. But I'd forgotten something about how the game was played. The win was always only temporary. You never knew what was going to happen in the next round.

I was bending over the open oven door, basting what I'd hoped was going to help me win the next round, when I heard the front door open and Moira's voice loudly purr, "Yum-mee— something smells good enough to eat. And look at that table," she said as she came through the dining room. "And look at you, girlfriend!"

I shut the oven door while Moira stood in the kitchen doorway and studied the dress I was wearing.

"Donna Karan?" she asked.

"Right," I answered.

"Bernice was here," Moira said.

"Right again."

She grimaced. "How did it go?"

"It was typical Bernice. First she cut me down at the ankles and then she wished me good luck."

"Good luck? Don't tell me you're expecting a man for dinner!" Moira put her hand to her chest and slumped dramatically against the wall. "Oh my god, you're dating and you didn't tell me!"

"I am expecting a man for dinner. But it's not a date. It's strictly business."

Suspicion brought her upright again. "Business with whom?" she asked.

"Roger," I answered as I walked past her to check on the table one last time.

Moira scurried after me, her arms outstretched. In the fringed peacock-blue cashmere shawl she was wearing over a matching V-neck sweater, she looked like a horrified exotic bird. "Cloth napkins and a Donna Karan dress! I had no idea you were this desperate." She swept me into her arms. "Sweetie, don't you know Stan and I would never let you starve? You don't have to resort to this!"

It took me a moment to disentangle myself from her shawl.

"Resort to what?" I demanded once I'd spit fringe out of my mouth.

"To trying to woo the shirt back into your life," Moira stated like the answer was obvious.

"Damn it, does the entire world see me as *that* pathetic? Bad enough that my mother jumped to the same conclusion. I expected more from you, Moira. Give me a little credit, will you?"

Moira flapped a hand at me. "Simmer down, hon. I mean, it's a gigantic *whew* that I was wrong, but why the big production if there's gonna be no seduction?"

"Well, I didn't exactly say there wasn't going to be any se-duction," I said demurely as I fluffed the giant mums in the short amber color vase in the middle of the dining room table. "But not," I added before Moira could erupt again, "sexual seduction. I'm using food to have my way with the man, true," I admitted, "but only so I can convince him to let me stay in the house for a few more months."

Moira digested this information for a few seconds. "Hmm, shrewd," she said, nodding sagely. "Very shrewd."

"I'm glad you approve."

She pulled a pout. "Well, I am a little hurt that I wasn't consulted since you know how I love mischief, but it's a solid idea, sister. Roger was always a sucker for your cooking. That dress isn't going to hurt, either."

I looked down at myself. For once, my mother had gotten it right. The dress fit like it was tailored for me. Made of something black and soft, it had a wide V neckline and hugged my body to the waist where the skirt flared gently to just above my ankles. It made the most of my flat midriff and decent waistline while it hid my slightly generous hips and backside. I looked good and I knew it.

"Thank you," I said.

Moira followed me back into the kitchen and plucked a crumb of topping from the apple crisp cooling on the counter. "I could easily be bribed into something for a dish of this stuff."

"Come over for leftovers later. You can dry the dishes."

"I'll dry the dishes as long as you dish the dish. I want to hear every little crumb of what goes on between you and the shirt," she said.

I assured her that I would spill like a toddler trying to pour a glass of grape juice, then steered her toward the door. The last thing I needed was Moira hanging around when Roger arrived. But as she was leaving, I suddenly wanted to grab onto her fringe and make her stay. "I wish you could hide under the table and feed me lines if Roger gets difficult."

She pulled me into a quick hug. "Hey, you can pull this off. Just let your inner diva meet your inner bitch queen." She did a little shimmy, fringe flying and breasts bouncing. "Mix 'em up a little. After all, God wouldn't have given us multiple personalities if he hadn't wanted us to use them."

Moira could always make me laugh.

And Roger could always drive me crazy.

"If this is some sort of attempt to win me back, Lauren," he said as he surveyed the table twenty minutes later, "I can tell you that you're only embarrassing yourself. I'm with Tiffany now. You remember—the twenty-eight-year-old aerobics instructor?"

I resisted the urge to lunge at his neck. For just a moment it flashed through my mind that no jury with at least one female member would convict me. After all, it was the third time that day that I'd been accused of trying to lure Roger Campbell back into my life. Surely I was expected to have limits.

I managed to keep from curling my fingers into weapons and tried for a reasonable tone. "I don't know what your fantasies are, Roger. But I assure you, winning you back isn't one of mine. I was just trying to make our discussion more pleasant. I mean, you gotta eat, right?" I said, with a shrug. "But if you'd rather *not* join me, that's not a problem. I'll go turn the oven off and then we can go into the living room and talk."

He followed me into the kitchen. I'd been pretty sure he would.

"What's in the oven?" he asked, then, "No, don't tell me. Your honey mustard pork loin."

"Well, that's just amazing, Roger," I said with what I thought was just the right amount of awe. "After all these years your senses still recognize it."

He opened the refrigerator door without asking, a territorial infraction that ordinarily would have driven me nuts. This time it was just part of the plan.

"You're marinating vegetables," he said as he breathed in deeply.

For all his faults, Roger knew a decent balsamic vinegar when he sniffed one. When he shut the refrigerator and saw the apple crisp on the counter, I knew I had him.

He looked at his watch. "I have to be out of here by eight," he said. "Tiffany's car is in the garage again and I have to pick her up after her last class."

"No problem. Go fix yourself a drink while I start grilling those veggies."

To keep him out of my hair while I cooked, I'd set up drinks on the coffee table in the living room, complete with a silver ice bucket and tongs. This was the kind of thing Roger had wanted me to do when we were married but usually by the time he got home from work the coffee table was full of puzzles pieces or finger paints or homework assignments.

Once we were seated in the dining room with our salads, I could see that he appreciated the vinaigrette. But I decided to wait until he had some protein and carbs in him to make my pitch. I did, however, point out the list Sondra had given me, folded like a napkin next to his water goblet. He shoveled in salad while he started to read. But the longer he perused the list, the less eating he did until finally he threw down his fork where it clattered against the salad plate. The noise didn't even make me flinch. Pleasure spread through me like the warmth of good wine. I no longer felt responsible for Roger's anger.

"There's nothing wrong with that kitchen," he fumed while

I enjoyed my salad. "It's—well, it's quaint. And as for the living room ceiling, who doesn't expect an old house to—"

"Roger, that's exactly what I told Sondra," I said. "People expect some—um—quaintness when they buy a house this old."

"Right," Roger agreed as I got up to clear away the salad plates and bring in the entrée.

"Did you explain to her that the floors are original to the house?" he asked as I served him slices of perfectly roasted pork loin from a platter we'd gotten for our wedding.

I nodded. "Yes, I did, Roger. But she still suggested wall to wall carpeting."

Roger was offended at the notion, but not so much that he wasn't able to cut into his meat and seize a hunk between his teeth.

"Mmm—you always could cook," he said as he chewed.

I sat down across from him and handed him the basket of rolls. He slathered butter on a warm roll and took a bite.

"You know, I was thinking—" I began. Then I went into my spiel about how Sondra the Hawk said the house probably wouldn't sell until after the holidays if we didn't get it on the market soon.

"So, it occurred to me that since the house will be empty anyway, maybe I could have just a tiny little extension before I have to get out."

"Lauren—" he began warningly.

I plowed on. "It would really help you out, too, Roger. I could be here to supervise the work on the house, which would free you from having to deal with workmen. Besides, just think what it would mean to Gordy to have one last Christmas in his childhood home."

He raised his brows and I wondered if he had started having them shaped. I could tell that he was definitely using some sort of skin products on his face. Probably frantic to keep up with the twenty-eight-year-old aerobics instructor, Tiffany.

"Are you sure you aren't talking about yourself?" he asked while he cut into his third helping of the other white meat.

"Well, *of course*, I'd love it *too*, Roger. I mean, I know that soon Gordy may not even want to come home for the holidays—"

He raised his knife in triumph. "Didn't I warn you not to make Gordon your whole life?"

I knew right away I was going to go for humble agreement, even though it made the grilled asparagus in my mouth hard to swallow.

"You were right, Roger," I said, shaking my head like I was really too bewildered to fathom why I hadn't listened to him in the first place. I was beginning to wish that Moira *were* under the table. I was giving the performance of my life and I had no audience.

"But putting all that aside," I went on, "the main thing is, it would be a shame if the house just sat here empty all winter when your son could be having the stability of coming home—I mean *really* coming home—for the holidays."

He gave in before he even tasted the apple crisp.

"But you're on your own financially this time, Lauren," he said. "I'll give you a month to find a job and then the maintenance stops for good. I'll agree to have the work done on the kitchen, but there's nothing wrong with the rest of the house. If Preferred Properties doesn't want to handle it, there are plenty of other companies out there who would jump at the listing. Meanwhile, it'll be your responsibility to find someone to do the work. And stay away from those national companies. They charge a fortune. Better to find some local man. Just make sure he has references."

"Of course," I said, proud of hiding my panic at the idea of finding a job in a month.

"So," he asked as I served him another helping of apple crisp, "how is our son doing?"

I filled him in on what I knew about Gordy's new life, then pointed out that it was time for him to leave. "You've got to pick up Tiffany, remember?"

At the door he lingered, giving me that little smile of his that I used to find sexy and now just seemed arrogant.

"Come on," he said, leaning in a little closer and cocking his head like he thought he was Robert Redford, "tell the truth. Even if you weren't trying to get me back, you were kind of hoping this whole sexy Martha Stewart scene would at least get you a roll in the sack for old times' sake, weren't you?"

"No," I said sweetly. "Were you?"

I saw by the look on his face that my mother had, indeed, been right about the dress.

An hour later the dishes were done and Moira and I were sitting in the breakfast nook, eating the rest of the apple crisp right from the baking dish while perusing the employment section of last Sunday's newspaper. It was a warm enough evening to have the back door open. The faint neighborhood sounds drifted in and I felt safe again. But I had to keep reminding myself it was only temporary.

"Here's one," Moira said. "Dog grooming assistant. Says they're willing to train anyone who can demonstrate a love for dogs."

"I wonder what that means?" I asked suspiciously.

"It probably means you have to not mind getting your leg humped by a German Shepherd with performance anxiety."

I laughed.

"Or getting pissed on by a poodle. Or lapped by a—"

Sometimes it didn't do to encourage Moira. "Stop it," I said nearly choking on my apple crisp. I tossed a pen at her. "Circle it."

The circle looked pretty lonely on that big page, even though it was the miscellaneous employment section—the last hope of the unskilled.

I sighed. "Face it, I'm not qualified for much."

"I still think this one about dancing at the Leopard Lounge is your best bet."

"I'm not seeing me wearing an animal print thong and wrapping myself around a pole anytime soon. Not with my thighs."

"It'd be the best thing for your thighs, sweetie. It's become very chi-chi to use stripping moves as a workout, you know."

Hoping Moira wasn't going to tell me that she'd had a stripper pole installed in her bedroom, I picked up the page where we'd circled an ad for a day care aide. The pay was paltry and I could no longer see myself wiping noses and helping with snow boots.

"Wait!" Moira yelled as she circled an item in red ink. "I think I just found the solution to your employment problems!"

I grabbed the section of the paper out of Moira's hand. "A temp agency?" I asked dubiously when I saw what she'd circled.

"Why not? Look," she said, poking the newsprint with her finger, "it says they have a variety of jobs for inexperienced people and that they offer free refresher courses in computer and clerical skills."

"I don't have anything to refresh," I muttered.

"You've done a lot of volunteer work. That shows you've got people and organizational skills. The rest," she said with a flap of her hand like it was the easiest thing in the world, "you can fake."

* * *

Temporary Solutions had a suite of offices downtown in a glassy building that had a shiny marble lobby and a wall of elevators. I was glad I'd borrowed one of Moira's more conservative suits for the occasion. When I caught my reflection in the mirrored wall of the elevator I was convinced I looked like employee material.

Unfortunately, the first thing they did at Temporary Solutions was test my skills. As far as I could see, there was absolutely no way to fake it. Excel? QuickBooks? PowerPoint? Lotus Notes? The only lotus I knew was a yoga position—about as unobtainable by me as a position at Temporary Solutions was beginning to look.

"You never have worked in an office, have you?" Christy Sands asked.

Christy, who had the harsh hair of a woman who'd been bleaching it for most of the twenty-something years of her life and the slightly red tan of a tanning bed addict, was what Temporary Solutions called my *personal career counselor*. She was supposed to help me find the job with a *perfect fit*. What good would it do to lie?

"No," I admitted. "I've never worked in an office. But I'm a fast learner and I really, really—"

"Please," she said. "I've heard it all before. There's nothing worse than a premenopausal woman begging for a job because her husband just dumped her for a younger woman."

I gasped. We'd barely met and my existence had already been reduced to a one-line cliché. It was degrading. And, in my case, not exactly the truth. I considered setting her straight but the truth wasn't going to make me look any better, was it? I was still a premenopausal woman looking for a job because her husband dumped her. I'd just managed to avoid it for ten years.

Having waited so long to take the plunge, I decided I wasn't going to be deterred by someone who looked like she could be a future candidate for Roger's harem. ("You remember Christy—my twenty-six-year-old-career-counselor girlfriend?")

"It says right here," I said, thrusting the ad I'd clipped from the newspaper in her face, "that you have jobs that require no—"

"Whoa—take a chill pill," Christy said. "We do have a few jobs that you actually don't need qualifications for." She eyed me up and down. "I might have something," she said as she turned to her computer and started to type. "What size dress do you wear?" she asked as she scrolled through a screen.

I thought I better not lie. Christy was wearing a turquoise Chanel knock-off bouclé suit with a skirt that was about ten inches long. She already knew I wasn't a size nine. "Fourteen," I said.

Hmm, the world didn't stop spinning. In fact, Christy didn't even blink.

"You don't mind working with the public, do you?" she asked.

I assured her that I didn't. "In fact, I've had a lot of experience with—"

"Yeah, I know. The PTA fund raiser, the Girl Scout cookie sale, the soccer candy-bar sale," she recited wearily.

Okay, so maybe I was a tad bit of a cliché.

"Just show up at eight tomorrow morning. I'll see if I can work something out. Meanwhile, if I were you, I'd come into the office as often as you can. Here's a list of times when tutors are available in our computer room. Here's a list of classes we offer for a nominal fee. Now just fill out these forms and—"

I was nearly giddy as she loaded me down with forms and folders. Cliché or not, I was in! I'd been hired!

By ten the next morning, I was standing in the dairy section of Market in the Cove, dressed in a milk maid's costume, complete with fake blond braids hanging out of my bonnet and white Mary

Janes on my feet. Somehow, when I'd thought of the humiliations I might have to suffer as unskilled labor, this one had never occurred to me. When Christy said there were no qualifications necessary, she hadn't been kidding. I was, however, getting twelve bucks an hour to hand out samples of a new brand of yogurt.

Moira would have been proud because I wasn't alone. One of my personalities kept reminding me that this was honest work and nothing to be ashamed of while another was praying that I wasn't going to run into anyone I knew. Still another personality was considering lobbing a few four letter words at a group of teenagers giving me a walk-by heckling when I spied Amy Westcott and Bonnie Williams standing in front of the deli counter. I quickly ducked behind a display of imported cheeses.

Bonnie Williams lived across the street from me in the Victorian next to Amy's Colonial. They were very chummy but Moira and I still liked Bonnie—and not just because she had more weight to lose than either of us did. Despite the fact that she was naive enough to swallow almost anything Amy told her and that she was overly fond of scrapbooking, Bonnie was really a sweet woman who was prone to sharing her homemade strawberry preserves and bread and butter pickles. It didn't hurt that her husband owned the hardware store in Whitefish Cove's quaint little downtown, either. He was a font of information for a woman living sans male in a house as old as mine was.

I could have handled Bonnie witnessing me prancing around among the curds and whey, but Amy? If I knew Amy, she would squeal and gush about how adorable I looked and then speculate endlessly up and down Seagull Lane about what had driven me to make such a fool of myself for a buck.

I peeked out from behind the display. Amy was being waited on in the deli. Bonnie would be next. I decided that maybe people in the flower department deserved some free yogurt, too. I headed that way and found a vigorous Boston fern that offered camouflage but still allowed me to see the checkout lanes. As soon as my neighbors got into line, I could hustle back to *dairy* where I belonged.

"Is this yogurt organic?" asked a thin young woman in black whose arms were loaded with little pots of herbs and sprouts.

I looked down at my basket of yogurt. "Um—well, I'm not sure—"

"Well, I just thought because you're in front of the potted organics that the yogurt was somehow connected."

"Oh—no." I picked up a little plastic tub from my basket. "It has active yogurt cultures," I said, "but—" The young woman seemed to be looking over my shoulder.

"I think that woman in the checkout line is waving to you," she said.

I squatted out of sight so fast that I practically lost my fake braids, but not before I'd seen that the woman waving was Bonnie. Hopefully, Amy was too busy checking that her gourmet goodies were being bagged appropriately to have noticed me lurking about like a demented trick-or-treater.

"Are you all right?"

I looked up to find the seeker of organics staring down at me. "I'm fine," I said even though I wasn't. I was pretty sure my knees had locked on my way to a squat. I decided to use it to my advantage and managed to waddle back to the dairy aisle without anyone in the checkout lines catching sight of me. There, I was able to grab onto the rim of a refrigerated case containing six kinds of goat cheese and hoist myself upright.

"Care to try our new yogurt?" I asked the flabbergasted woman I'd popped up in front of.

She not only declined, but turned tail and ran over to the

bakery department like they were giving away their five-dollar brownies, leaving me to wonder if it was possible that I was under-qualified for a job that required no qualifications.

"Christy said I moved less product than any other milkmaid before me," I later whined to Moira as I sat in her kitchen eating cold shrimp and perfectly ripened mango. Moira always had these types of exotics in her refrigerator. "I mean, I couldn't even give the stuff away."

"Well, it stands to reason that if you're going to hide from half the customers and scare the other half off, you're not exactly going to be queen of the milkmaids, are you?"

Weren't girlfriends supposed to be sympathetic? "Well," I said defensively, "I probably won't have to hide much tomorrow. I'm appearing at that little supermarket on the east side. I'm not likely to run into anyone I know."

Moira looked thoroughly disgusted with me.

"What the hell," she demanded, "do you care what the neighbors think of the kind of job you've got? Especially someone like Amy Westcott?"

She was right, of course. And I'd never been a job snob. "It's not the job I don't want people to know about," I told Moira. "It's the *reason* for the job. It's the fear that people like Amy are going to find out how stupid I was about my divorce. I mean, Roger left me for a younger woman and I didn't even get the house! I didn't even ask for a settlement! I just wanted to keep pretending that everything was just as I'd been promised it would be. I was living like a married woman whose husband just never came home. I feel so damned stupid."

"There are worse things than feeling stupid," Moira said.

"Like what?"

"Like having your feet hurt. Yours are swelling even as we speak. You better go home, hon, and soak them or you're not going to get your Mary Janes on in the morning."

I smiled weakly. "Now that's a warning I never thought I'd hear at the age of forty-one." I picked up the scuffed white shoes and ambled to the door.

Moira followed. "Just keep reminding yourself that it's not going to last forever. Nothing ever does." She grabbed me into a big hug. "And you're not stupid. You're human. A good human. One of the best. But you're not mistake proof—none of the species is."

When I walked home that night, I paused under the maple tree in front of my house and took a deep breath, letting the crispness of the night fill my lungs. There was a sudden wind and orange-and-crimson leaves fluttered down all around me and skittered across the sidewalk. Soon the tree would be bare and my hands would be blistered from raking. Autumn would be over and winter would come blowing in.

Moira was right. Nothing lasted forever. Even blisters, I thought with a small smile. They only felt like they were going to.

Buoyed by Moira's pep talk last night, I tied on my pinafore the next morning, vowing to move product. I arrived at East Side Groceries in a good mood and in full costume. For three hours I was charming and chatty and sweet enough to turn those braids into the real thing. And then my mother spotted me.

Her hand had been hovering above a carton of fat-free cottage cheese when she got a look on her face like Tippi Hedren in the movie *The Birds*. And I don't think it was because she suddenly remembered what fat-free cottage cheese tasted like.

In my freshly polished Mary Janes, I skipped over to her just to see the mortified look on her face. "Care to try our new yogurt, ma'am?" I asked in my best milkmaid voice.

"You know," she said, her mouth tight, "I was glad when you didn't immediately run to another man after Roger. I wanted you to have time just for you. To discover yourself. But look at you. You've wasted the last ten years of your life."

"What do you expect, you old bat, when you make the kid dress like that?"

Both my mother and I swung around toward the raspy voice to find a tall, scruffy-looking man, leaning on a cane, and eyeing my mother beneath a critically lowered brow.

Bernice was momentarily speechless. I was pretty sure that no one had ever called her an old bat before.

"A joke," he said, staring at her and then looking at me with the bluest eyes I'd ever seen. "Doesn't have much of a sense of humor, does she?" he asked.

"Afraid not," I answered while I noticed that the scruffiness wasn't so much scruffy as it was a rather attractive five o'clock shadow.

"Excuse me," Bernice said, "but I'd rather not be talked about like I wasn't here."

"Then perhaps you should leave," the man suggested. "In fact, that probably would be for the best. Leave, woman," he intoned like he was playing to the back of the house, "and let your unfortunate daughter get on with earning an honest day's wages."

"I'll thank you to mind your own business," Bernice said in her best ice-maiden-of-the-'50s fashion.

The man leaned closer to her. "I think the manager is on his way over to see what the commotion is about. If I were you Mama, I'd get my skinny ass out of here. If you get sis here fired, she's gonna have to move back in with you and that would sort of cramp your style, wouldn't it, doll face?"

Regal as a queen, my mother turned away from him. "Expect a phone call tonight," she said to me before she headed for the seafood department.

"You're my hero," I said to the man with the mouth. "Have some yogurt."

"I'll take the yogurt, Heidi, but I reject the mantle of hero. Those suits they have to wear are always so confining," he said with a look of distaste and a little shiver. Then he tossed the free carton of yogurt into his cart, hung his cane on the handle and limped out of the dairy department.

"Mother," I said into the phone later that night, "I swear to you that I have no idea who he was."

I was in the wingback chair in the living room, my feet in a basin of sudsy hot water, waiting for a cup of tea to steep and listening to my mother tell me for the fifth time how appalled she'd been to find me handing out samples at the supermarket.

"To think that you would settle for being a vendor—a hawker in a ridiculous costume. I have important clients who live in that area, you know."

My mother didn't have customers. She had clients. *I found the perfect dress for a client during my last buying trip to New York,* she'd say. The same women had been keeping her in business for years. And they brought in their friends and their daughters and their daughter's friends. The boutique, in a converted townhouse east of the river on a little street off Wisconsin Avenue in Milwaukee, was so exclusive you could barely find the sign. The kind of women who dressed like my mother just seemed to know how to find it. I was sure that if my mother didn't manage the place, I'd have absolutely no idea where it was.

I wiggled my toes in the satiny water, took a sip of chamomile tea, and let my mother elaborate on all the ways I was a disappointment to her. When I could get in a word, I said, "Mother, I have to start somewhere. Besides, it's only temporary." I added a good-night and hung up.

The phone immediately rang. I picked it up.

"The least you could do is let me wish you a good-night," Bernice said. "And I know you have to start somewhere and I'm proud of the fact that you've at least *started*. But for heaven's sake when you're walking around with that basket of yogurt, stand up straight. That slouch just makes you look even more ridiculous. Goodnight, dear."

CHAPTER 4

"I'm Your Handy Man," the deep voice on the other end of the line said.

Oh, my, I thought. The name of the company was the reason I'd decided to call it but I hadn't expected someone with a deeper voice than James Taylor's to answer the phone.

"Hello?" the deep voiced asked.

"Oh—uh, I need an estimate."

"For?"

"Some work in my kitchen. A breakfast nook has to come out—"

"I always liked breakfast nooks," said the voice.

"Oh, me, too. But the house is going up for sale and the Realtor said they weren't popular anymore, so—"

"Well, that's just sad."

Who was this guy? A deep voice and an appreciation for breakfast nooks. Quite a combination.

"I think so, too," I told him. "But it's kind of not my decision."

"Oh. Then what is yours to decide?"

I was left sort of speechless. His voice was so—well, deep—and a little unnerving for it's lack of inflection. Cave man stuff with a kinder, gentler edge.

"Well, it's for me to decide who to hire to do the work."

"Then I suggest you hire me."

There was a smile in his voice this time that I found hard to resist. "Maybe you should come over so I can have a look—um, I mean so *you* can have a look at the work I need and then you can um…" What *was* the word? For the life of me, I couldn't remember it.

"Give you an estimate?"

"Right," I said, rolling my eyes at the woodwork.

"Sounds cool. Tomorrow morning? Nine o'clock?"

"Can you make it earlier? I've got to be at work at 9:30." I was scheduled to hawk cereal in a superhero costume at a grocery store on the south side.

"Eight, then. I like my coffee strong and black. I'll bring the bagels."

He not only brought bagels, but he brought a carton of cream cheese spread—and a set of shoulders that filled out a softly worn flannel shirt better than any man I'd actually ever seen in person.

He held out the bag. "Your voice told me honey and cream cheese," he said with a quirk of the corner of his mouth. "Am I right?"

"Actually, you are right. But, come on, how could my voice tell you that?"

"Okay, it wasn't just your voice. It was a combination of your voice and your fondness for breakfast nooks."

"Ah," I said. It made perfect sense to me. After all, I had decided he was one of the good guys because of his voice and his fondness for breakfast nooks. His dark, almond shaped eyes held my gaze for a beat too long. I cleared my throat. "Uh—why don't you come into the kitchen and meet the doomed booth."

He treated me to a sudden, lethal grin. "Lead the way," he said.

"Toasted?" I asked, once we were in the kitchen. It seemed like a good idea to keep my hands occupied.

"Is there any other way?"

I split a bagel and popped it into the toaster then poured him a cup of coffee and handed it to him.

He took a sip. "Hmm. Nothing like the first cup of the day."

Watching him appreciate my coffee was such a pleasure I could barely take my eyes off him. He ran a hand through his hair—dark, parted in the middle and long enough to brush the back of his collar—and it dutifully fell back into place.

"You're going to join me, aren't you?" he asked.

I thought about my hand joining his in that silky, straight hair but I had a feeling he meant the coffee.

"Of course," I said and turned away from him to fill a mug. I turned back to find him studying the breakfast nook. "So," I said, after I'd taken my first sip of coffee, "what do you think?"

"I think it's a shame to get rid of her—"

"I know, it breaks my heart." I ran my fingertips over the scarred wood. "This is where my son did his homework while I cooked supper. Where he frosted his first Christmas cookie. Where—" I stopped, suddenly embarrassed by my emotional display, as well as the deepening grin on his face.

"You sound like a hell of a mom," he said. "My mom was like that. I miss her."

"She doesn't live nearby?"

"Actually, she died a few years ago."

"Oh, I'm so sorry," I said, just as his bagel popped up.

"That's okay. It was cancer. By the time she went, it was a relief just to know she wouldn't be in pain anymore."

I felt immediately more comfortable with him. I reminded him of his mother. That was safe. That was a role I knew how to play.

"Sit down. I'll get you some butter," I said as I put his bagel on a plate. He slid into Gordy's side of the booth, which just made things more comfortable still.

After my bagel popped up, I slid in across from him. My mother would not approve of this familiarity, nor would she approve of the sweats I was wearing. I could almost hear the lecture she'd give me on preserving decorum and boundaries. It was like she was in my head and I couldn't get her out.

"I'll rip her out for free if I can have her."

"Excuse me?" I said, wondering how he'd get Bernice out of my head and, more puzzling still, why he'd want to keep her.

"This booth. I'll take it out for free if I can have her."

"Oh—the booth." Of course he was talking about the booth. "For free? Really?" Roger would be overjoyed at this perk, although I would have preferred that Quint was ripping my mother out of my head for free. Oh, hell, who was I kidding? I'd pay.

He shrugged. "What can I say. I have a thing for breakfast nooks."

I saluted him with my coffee cup. "I'll be glad to see her go to a good home. Now, what about the floor? How much do you think that will cost?"

"Well, that depends on what you have in mind…"

Over toasted bagels slathered with cream cheese swirled with honey, we discussed ceramic tile versus vinyl flooring with a smattering of laminated wood tossed in. I had no idea what I wanted—after all, it's not like I was going to be walking on the new floor. Or sweeping it. Or scrubbing it. I looked at the old linoleum that shined only because I was willing to wax it once a month. Finally, a new kitchen floor and it wouldn't even be mine.

"I could take you shopping," Quint said.

I looked up at him, wondering how he knew I was bummed. How he knew that shopping would cheer me up.

"I could even get you a discount in a couple of places."

Oh, of course. He was talking about flooring.

"Does that service usually come with the contract?" I asked with a careless laugh to hide my embarrassment.

He shrugged, his mouth quirking again. "That's one of the cool things about being your own boss. I can do pretty much anything I want."

"I bet you can," Moira shamelessly purred from the back door.

"Hello," Quint said, flashing his brief, kilowatt smile.

"Quint, this is my friend and neighbor, Moira Rice. Moira, Quint Mathews."

Quint rose as Moira sashayed into the kitchen, looking spectacular and mussed in a long silk robe the color of champagne.

"I had no idea you had company," she lied demurely. I knew it was a lie because she was already wearing false eyelashes and frosted lipstick. She'd obviously seen Quint arrive.

"Quint is here to give me an estimate on some work."

"Work?"

"I'm Your Handy Man," Quint said in that same deep voice that had gotten to me on the phone. Moira's mouth dropped open. I'd rarely seen her speechless.

"It's the name of his company," I told her.

"Oh," Moira said recovering enough to flip her hair back. "How clever."

"Thanks," Quint said, treating us to another smile. "Well, I'd better get a few measurements."

"Good idea," I said before turning to Moira. "Something I can do for you?"

She held up a cup. "I find that I am in need of sugar this morning."

I took the cup from her and muttered, "Funny, you seem cloyingly sweet to me."

Moira ignored my witty remark. And who could blame her? Quint had taken out his tape measure and was crawling around the kitchen floor, giving us a very impressive view of his very impressive backside. I could tell Moira was starting to sweat so I hustled over to the sugar canister, filled her cup, and herded her toward the door.

"Hire him," she whispered just before I shut the door in her face. When I turned back to the room, Quint was under the breakfast nook, examining something with a flashlight.

"I think I can take it out without damaging the wall much, but if you let me have it, I'm going to have to give you a discount on my bill. This baby," he gave a couple of knuckle raps to the underside, "is solid maple."

Forget his almond shaped eyes and his solid buns, his honesty was the real seduction. I made up my mind right there and then that I was hiring I'm Your Handy Man, no matter what the estimate was.

After he left, I scurried upstairs to get ready for work. I'd graduated from milkmaid to superhero but I wasn't sure the transition was a step up. The cape wasn't all that flattering but it was a relief to trade in the Mary Janes for superhero boots. Knee high black rubber, they weren't exactly trendy but at least they didn't pinch. And, even though the skirt was short, I got to wear tights, meaning I didn't have to shave my legs everyday, so, I guess there were advantages.

Usually, I didn't put the cape on until I got to whatever grocery store I was working at that day but I was running late, thanks to my little breakfast with Quint Mathews. I tied it around my neck as I headed downstairs, then grabbed a tote bag where it hung from the newel post and opened the front door.

Quint Mathews was standing on the other side of it, his hand poised for knocking.

"I forgot my—" he began then stopped when he took in the costume. "You know," he said in that deep, serious voice, "I sensed there was something exciting about you, but a superhero—"

"Very funny. Actually, I'm in marketing."

"Oh?" he looked me up and down.

"I pass out samples of Hero cereal at the supermarket," I said, hoping my thighs didn't look lumpy in the tights.

"That's my favorite cereal," he said in a tone that sounded like he'd just discovered something profound. "I've been eating it since I was a kid."

I managed to avoid telling him that the cereal hadn't even been around when I was a kid. "Um, if you don't mind, I'm sort of in a hurry," I said, checking my watch.

"Oh, of course, sorry—"

He took off for the kitchen. While I waited I pondered whether it would have been any less humiliating if Quint had seen me in my milkmaid costume, then decided that since I was forty-one and reminded him of his dead mother, it didn't really matter anyway.

"Got it," he said as he came out of the kitchen holding up his tape measure. He passed me, crossed the porch and clattered down the stairs, heading for his truck. He opened the driver's door, then paused. "Have a great day saving the world for cereal," he called. "I'll be in touch."

At four o'clock I ducked into the bathroom at the supermarket that was my last stop of the day and turned in my cape for the dress I'd stuffed into a huge tote my mother had given me years ago. The designer was apparently a big deal and Bernice had been appalled when I'd used it as a diaper bag. I wasn't sure she'd approve of it as luggage for my cape, either, but I was headed downtown to the Temporary Solutions offices and I had no intention of swooping through the window in full costume. I'd signed up for a computer workshop at six and I planned to use the extra time to eat a dinner of low-fat microwave popcorn and badger Christy about finding me a job where I didn't have to leave my dignity at the door.

I cut through the city on residential streets, avoiding the early rush hour traffic on the freeway. It was getting near the end of October and the trees were nearly bare, squirrel nests swaying gently in the chill air. There were jack-o-lanterns in windows and ghosts made of bed sheets swinging from porches. In the old days, I'd be home sewing Gordy's Halloween costume while something simmered on the stove. Not much had simmered on the stove since Gordy left for college. I was becoming well acquainted with the microwave. But I missed cooking. At a stoplight I allowed myself to fantasize about Quint staying for dinner once he started work on the kitchen. That boy could probably use some mothering and I was just the woman to do it.

I was still absurdly pleased when my pass got me into the underground parking garage of the building that housed Temporary Solutions. It meant that I belonged somewhere. I found the idea of that comforting.

I found a parking spot and took the elevator up to the fifth floor.

"Oh my god," Christy cried when I walked into the office. "Is that a Donna Karan?"

"It is," I admitted. It was the only thing I owned that I was sure would still look good after spending the day stuffed into a tote bag.

"Well, you look fabulous," Christy said.

"Speaking of fabulous, I don't suppose you've found me a fabulous job yet," I said, mentally patting myself on the back for the inventive segue. "One where I could maybe wear this dress instead of braids or a cape?"

"You people are all the same," she said, shaking her head sadly. "You come in here begging for anything at all and before you know it you're off your knees and nagging me for something better."

"It's called evolution, Christy."

"You've already evolved. You're a superhero. Besides, you're just getting good at this. The guy at Innovative Marketing said you moved more product yesterday than anyone else in the state."

I couldn't help but feel a flash of pride. The numbers meant that I was finally getting better at approaching people who were trying their best to focus on something far away when they pushed their carts past me. Still, I was getting tired of playing characters. I wanted a chance to play myself. When the credits rolled at the end of the day, I wanted them to read: Lauren Campbell as herself.

Whoever that was.

"As flattering as it is to be the best cereal superhero in the state, I'd like to move on as soon as possible."

Christy sighed. "Innovative Marketing will not be pleased. You've already stayed at the job longer than anyone else we've sent them. They were hopeful."

"So am I," I said, as I headed for the break room so I could microwave my popcorn dinner.

While I munched my dinner it occurred to me that what I'd told Christy was really true. I was hopeful. It made no sense. I mean, here I was, eating popcorn for dinner after having worked all day in a ridiculous costume, waiting for a free computer workshop because that's all I could afford at the moment. This might not sound like progress to many women my age, but I realized that that's exactly how I saw it. I was making progress. I still felt like crying at the thought of losing my house. But, lately, I'd been too damn busy to actually shed tears. I was never one to cry in public. Which turned out to be a really good thing, because two hours later Gwen, the woman who taught the computer workshop, declared in front of three other displaced homemakers that I was the worst student she'd ever had. Things weren't looking good for that fabulous job I was hoping for.

When I got home that night there were two messages on the answering machine. One was from Moira wanting to know if I'd hired Quint the hunk. No surprise there. The other message was a surprise. It was from Gordy. Surprising because I'm pretty sure this is the first time he'd called me since he'd gone to Bloomington. But even more surprising because I realized that I'd barely thought of him for days now.

I knew that Bonnie and Amy across the street would be horrified at that admission, but to me it was another sign of progress. I'd gone from overloading the poor kid with homemade cookies to not even worrying.

I frowned. But maybe I should be worrying. Why would Gordy call? I played back the message, trying to gauge his voice, searching for any sign of distress. It was hard to tell. Thanks to his doting mother, Gordy had seldom been in distress.

I picked up the phone and called his dorm room. No answer. I left a message and went for the refrigerator. All that popcorn had made me thirsty. But by the time I opened the door, I'd forgotten what I wanted. Worry was back on me like a harness. Maybe I should try his cell phone. But there was no answer there, either, so I left another message.

I paced. I tried to read a magazine. I picked up the phone to make sure there was a dial tone, then checked my cell to make sure it was charged. I paced some more. Finally, I punched in Moira's number.

"Can you meet me on the back porch?" I asked. "I'll bring the beer."

"I'll bring the pretzels," Moira said.

"Could you make it peanuts?" I asked, figuring I could use the protein after nothing but popcorn for dinner.

"Peanuts it is."

Another thing to love about Moira is that she doesn't waste time asking a lot of questions before she comes to the rescue.

Of course, as soon as we were together, I told her about Gordy's call.

"He's probably out somewhere having the time of his life," Moira said as we sat on the steps of my back porch, my cell phone and cordless between us and a couple of Miller High Lifes to keep us company.

"Is that supposed to make me feel better?" I said, popping a small handful of peanuts into my mouth.

"Okay, then he's too busy studying to return your calls. That better?"

"It would have been better if only you'd said that first but I'm already thinking of him having the time of his life."

Moira took a swig of beer. "How about this—instead of obsessing about your son, who is probably just fine, let's obsess about Quint Mathews. You *are* going to hire him, aren't you?"

"Not if you're going to parade in front of him in lingerie every morning, I'm not."

"I was subtle."

"Please—the word isn't even in your vocabulary."

"All right. I'll learn subtle. After all, I wouldn't want to deprive you of what is probably the handiest man in the Cove. But you'll have to share."

"You and Stan are planning to have some work done?" I asked with exaggerated innocence.

"Very funny. Don't tell me you didn't notice the finer points of his male charms because I happen to know that you do breathe in and out like the rest of us."

"Of course I noticed how good-looking he is. But he's also about fifteen years younger than me—"

"Maybe ten."

"And," I added emphatically, "he told me that I remind him of his late mother."

Moira visibly slumped. "Now you're just trying to depress me."

I laughed and zipped up my hoodie. The night was almost cold—a preview of the nights to come—but it felt good. The branches of trees rustled and I could smell wood smoke from someone's fireplace. There was a hush in the neighborhood that came with the closed windows of colder weather and the earlier onset of darkness. Whitefish Cove was already tucking in for the night.

"I see you decorated your windows for Halloween again this year," Moira said.

"Why wouldn't I?"

Moira shrugged. "With Gordy gone and you working—"

"You think it's silly," I accused.

"Jesus, Lauren, I was just trying to change the subject, not make a judgement. Maybe you're the one who thinks it's silly."

"No," I said defensively. "Of course not. I wouldn't do it if I thought it was silly. Although—"

"Although what?" Moira prompted when I let the word just hang there.

"Oh, it's just that working for a living takes a lot of time and I will admit that while I was decorating the windows I kept thinking of other things I could be doing instead." I took a swallow of beer and leaned back against the stair behind me. "Honestly, Moira, I don't know how working mothers with young kids do it. How can they not drop a ball once in a while? Gordy is eighteen and I'm sitting here feeling guilty that I wasn't around to answer the phone when he called."

"If every mother worried as much as you do, Madame Curie never would have invented penicillin."

I frowned. "Did Madame Curie have kids? Besides, she didn't invent penicillin. She had something to do with radio-activity, I think."

Moira sighed. "Okay, fine. But my point is that I bet you'd even worry about your ceramic pumpkins if they didn't get to come out of the attic every October."

Okay, so it was true. I did think that the paper bats and the grinning ceramic pumpkins deserved their time in the sun before being packed away in the attic for another year. And then the Thanksgiving turkeys and pilgrims would come out. And after that, the snowmen and Santas. It wasn't in me to deprive decorations.

Moira peered at me in the darkness. "Oh, my god—I'm right, aren't I? Yeah, you're definitely full time mama material."

And that, I thought, was exactly why I was in the mess I was in. It wasn't that I hadn't chosen a career. I had. I'd chosen wife and mother. I thought back to what my mother had said to me that day in the kitchen. The day I was cooking for Roger. Had she been right? Had I programmed my life as much as she had programmed hers?

"I'm nothing like my mother," I said.

Moira shook her head. "I don't know where that non sequitur came from but it's stating the obvious."

"Thank you."

"You're welcome. Now why don't you try calling Gordy again before we get hemorrhoids sitting on this cold concrete."

"Isn't that an old wives' tale?"

"I'm not willing to test the theory. Are you?"

I laughed, then took a huge gulp of the fresh, cold air, prolonging the moment when I tried Gordy's number again. Because I knew there would be no answer this time, either.

And I was right.

It was silly, I told myself at three a.m. After all, I hadn't known where Gordy was on practically every night since I'd left him at IU. Not for sure, anyway. I'd done a lot of assuming—assuming he was in class, assuming he was studying, assuming he was sleeping. So why worry now? Why not just assume that—for instance—he didn't check his messages when he got back to his dorm room, because he was too tired from studying at the library.

Yeah, I liked that assumption. I decided to go with it. But my sleep was fitful, full of the kind of dreams where you lose something and can't find it.

Two nights later, I still hadn't been able to get in touch with Gordy. So when I heard the phone ringing as I unlocked the front door after work, still wearing my cape, I dove for it like it was a live grenade and I was a real superhero.

"Hello!"

"You sound winded," Roger said.

"I just came in from work," I said.

"You found a job already?" he asked dubiously. "In what field?"

"Um—marketing," I said vaguely. Up to now, I'd avoided

having this conversation. It hadn't been hard. Roger and I often went weeks without talking. I knew that now that we were having this conversation, he was going to want details. I had no intention of telling him that my job involved wearing a super-hero cape so I quickly changed the subject.

"I found a contractor for the kitchen," I said.

"Where did you find this guy?" Roger asked after I told him about Quint Mathews.

"Um—I got his name from Amy Westcott," I lied. After all, I wasn't about to admit to Roger than I'd hired Quint because of the cleverness of his company name and the deepness of his voice. "She said that Chuck just loved him."

Roger thought that Amy was Martha Stewart and Sharon Stone rolled into one and he and Chuck played golf together on occasion—a ritual that often bonded the strangest of bedfel-lows. I didn't like to lie, even to Roger, but I'd endured enough praise about Amy during our marriage to feel like I had a "get away with a lie free" card or two coming.

"Fine," Roger said. "Hire him. But I don't want him putting in anything too expensive on that kitchen floor. No ceramic. None of that laminated wood."

"Yes, Roger," I said.

"And while we're on the subject of money, I understood that the quarterly payment from Gordy's trust fund was supposed to cover all his school expenses for this term. I was surprised when he called last night and hit me up for a hundred."

"Gordy called you last night?" My annoyance was tempered somewhat by the fact that at least I now knew my son was still alive.

"He said he spoke to you first and that you told him to call me for the money."

I opened my mouth, then closed it again. I knew I was

breaking all the rules, but I couldn't bring myself to rat my son out to his own father, not without more details. "Well, Roger, you know that odd expenses sometimes come up."

"Nothing odd about a hundred dollar book for lit class. But it is a little odd that the teacher didn't request he have it when the semester started."

"Right. I thought that, too." Oh, boy, was I going to burn in mommy hell. I'd never played these kinds of games with Roger, and I didn't want to start now. But I also wasn't up to admitting that I didn't have any idea what Roger was talking about, not when I was still trying to deal with the fact that Gordy had called his father but hadn't seen fit to return my calls. Once again, I changed the subject.

"You know, Roger, maybe we should consider a ceramic tile floor. The Realtor said the house had little but location going for it, so maybe it needs a really good kitchen floor."

"You may have a point. Okay, let's go with ceramic. But something plain and not too—"

"Expensive," I finished for him. "Don't worry. Quint says he can get us a discount."

"Sondra suggested we get something neutral."

So he was still in touch with Sondra the Hawk. Perhaps Tiffany's days were numbered.

"It'll be as bland as egg custard," I assured him.

CHAPTER 5

"**I** just love these red tiles," I said, running my hand over their cool, slightly rough surface.

"I guess a superhero would consider red a bland color," Quint murmured.

"Behave or I won't give you the case of Hero cereal that's stowed in the trunk of my car."

"No shit?" he exclaimed. "Wow. A case."

We'd been browsing the aisles of Home Depot for the past hour and I kept going back to the red tiles.

"Your ex won't be happy," Quint said. "Neither will the Realtor."

"Roger just might be happy since the price is half off."

"That's because nobody else wants them."

"You don't like them?"

"Sure I do. They're cool. I can see them with your walls sponge painted yellow. Sort of a Tuscany thing."

I stared at him. "You could be a decorator."

He laughed. "Nah. Chicks would think I'm gay."

"Trust me," I said. "Never gonna happen."

His dark, almond shaped eyes sparkled. "Promise?" he asked.

Good thing, I thought, that I remind him of his mother. "Promise," I said.

"Okay, then let's get these red tiles and then I'll help you pick out the right shade of yellow paint."

While Quint put the order in for the tiles, I happily browsed among the paint chips. I was in a good mood, and not just because it was Saturday and I was out shopping with a guy who was actually enjoying the situation. I'd put aside my hurt that Gordy had called his father instead of me to bask in the fact that I'd worried for nothing. Gordy was fine. He'd called because an unexpected expense had come up, that's all. When he hadn't been able to reach me, he'd called his father. Simple as that. I'd worried for nothing.

I started to get into checking out all the different shades of yellow paint available. I was holding two chips in my hand, comparing them, when Quint came back.

"That one, I think," he said, tapping the one on the left.

"I thought so, too."

"You're the easiest woman I ever shopped with," Quint said. "You make a decision and that's that."

"Don't forget, I can afford to make mistakes."

"How so?"

"I'm not going to be living with my choices."

The thought subdued me and I was mostly quiet while Quint figured out how much paint we'd need. We loaded it into his truck, then drove around back to the loading dock to pick up the cartons of tiles. At the house, I offered him a beer after he'd unloaded the tiles and paint into the garage.

"How about a sandwich to go with that?" I asked him when I handed him a Miller High Life.

"How did you know I was starving?"

"Probably because I'm starving myself," I answered.

I grilled a couple of Muenster cheese and tomato sandwiches on whole wheat and handed him a plate.

We sat across from each other, swigging beer and eating in silence.

"This is some great sandwich," Quint finally said.

I gave a weak smile and took another swig of beer.

He put his sandwich down. "Something's been bothering you since we picked out the paint. What is it?"

I shrugged. I wasn't about to pour out my heart to the poor guy, even if he had asked.

"You don't want to sell this house, do you?"

I blinked, hoping to avoid disgracing myself with tears. "It's the only real home I've ever known."

"You know something," he said. "I think you could probably make a home just about anywhere you went."

His dark eyes held mine steadily. I was deeply grateful for his words—and deeply self-conscious about it.

"Eat your sandwich before it gets cold," I said.

He grinned and obeyed.

Late on the afternoon of Halloween, I came home from work to find the booth in the breakfast nook gone. I stared at the empty spot. It felt like a piece of my heart had been ripped out. Okay, a small piece, but painful nonetheless. That booth held so many memories—the warm, fuzzy kind I'd missed when I was a kid. But even more painful, it meant my days in this house were numbered.

It was a melancholy night. I'd even considered the unpardonable sin in Whitefish Cove of turning off all the lights and pretending I wasn't home. But in the end, I filled the ceramic pumpkin I'd been using for years with treats and dutifully answered the doorbell all evening, exclaiming over all the pretty costumes and feigning fright at all the scary ones.

Memories filled my mind, filled the house, and once or twice, filled my eyes with tears. I was missing Gordy like crazy.

When the phone rang around ten that night, I snagged up the cordless like it was a lifeline. "Hello?"

"Ma?"

"Gordy! Hi! Happy Halloween!" I said in a rush, my heart singing at the sound of his voice.

"You, too," he said.

"Gordy, I've been trying to call you. I left messages—"

"Ma, come on, I didn't call to get a lecture."

"I wasn't lecturing," I said, feeling a little hurt. When had I ever lectured? Now was probably not the time to discuss the small lie he'd told his father. "Your Dad told me you were okay," I said instead. "I just wished you'd returned my calls, that's all."

"Yeah, okay. Sorry. It's just that I've been—you know—busy. There's a lot going on."

"Yeah, Moira told me you were probably having the time of your life."

"Right." He sounded weary suddenly. "The time of my life."

I frowned and told myself to tread softly. "Classes okay?"

"Sure. Everything's solid, Ma. It's just that—" there was a pause, and then, "I was kind of remembering all those costumes you made and how we used to go pick our own pumpkins, so—"

I waited.

"—so I just thought I'd call to say happy Halloween."

"Gordy—"

"Gotta go, Ma, some dudes are waitin' for me," he said and hung up before I could say anything else.

I put the phone down and slumped into the wingback and waited for the relief I figured I should be feeling at finally talking to Gordy. It didn't come.

* * *

"You know, you really suck at this," Christy said as she leaned over my shoulder while I tried to figure out how to build a spreadsheet. It was late Friday afternoon and I'd stopped in at Temporary Solutions to get a little computer time in.

I moaned. "I know I suck. It's because I'm right brained."

"Whatever. The point is, I don't think your future has a keyboard in it."

"If you tell me that I'm destined to play characters in supermarkets the rest of my life, I'm going to—"

"Well, Innovative Marketing *is* looking for someone to play a giant candy cane for the Christmas season—"

I opened my mouth to scream.

"Will you chill and let me finish, please? I do have another opening you might be interested in. It's seasonal, though—"

I groaned. "What is it? Shoveling snow?"

"Working in the display department at Grant's Department Store."

I pushed back the desk chair and jumped to my feet. "I'll take it!" I yelled. I *loved* Grant's.

"Don't get too excited. You'll be decorating Christmas trees in the Holiday Department."

"Are you kidding? I love decorating Christmas trees! And what's more," I declared in triumph, "I actually have experience at it."

"The hours are all over the map—including a lot of late evenings," she added almost as if she was trying to dissuade me.

"Perfect," I said, refusing to be dissuaded. After all, it's not like I had anything to do with my evenings. But even if I did, it wouldn't really matter. Shopping at Grant's during the Christmas holidays was the only time my mother and I had ever really bonded when I was a child. The only time we were ever in sync. The only time we hummed the same melody.

"If you're sure—"

"Oh, I'm sure," I interrupted emphatically.

"—you can start Monday, then. When you finish up here, stop by my desk and I'll give you the info."

After she left I stared at the computer screen. I couldn't make any sense of what I was trying to do. And now I was too excited at the prospect of handling all those expensive glass ornaments, all that glittery garland, all those treetop angels. What did I need spreadsheets for? I deleted my dismal attempt, packed up my stuff, and headed for Christy's desk.

Info on the car seat beside me, I was waiting my turn to exit the parking garage when it hit me that there was no one waiting at home for me to tell my news to. Moira? It was Friday night. Moira and Stan always went out for dinner on Friday nights. I could call Gordy, but our last conversation hadn't exactly gone all that well. I was doing my best not to dwell on that weariness I heard in his voice and, call me a coward, I was far from ready to face it again.

I pulled out into a break in traffic onto a one way street and realized that it was heading in the direction of my mother's boutique. Hmm…why not?

On the other hand, *why?*

Well, for one thing, I reasoned as I dodged a city bus that had decided to change lanes like I wasn't there, the job at Grant's was definitely a step up from hawking products in silly suits for Innovative Marketing. I mean, Bernice wouldn't be embarrassed to say, for instance, "My daughter, Lauren, works in the display department at Grant's." Besides, we had memories there. Probably the best memories of my childhood—and her motherhood. Every year we'd spend a day at Grant's, choosing my Christmas outfit, buying gifts, eating tiny, fancy sandwiches and little cakes in the ornate tea room—now sadly closed and only used for special events. I'd be on my best behavior because I knew Santa was coming and Bernice, who still knew people who worked there from her modeling days, would be her most charming. I got to bask in the reflected adulation she'd receive from all her old friends and admirers. Maybe telling Bernice about the job at Grant's would bring back some of those same, sweet memories for her.

And, for another thing, I was, let's face it, a little lonely. Who knows? Maybe she was, too. She was probably getting ready to close up shop, getting ready to face another solitary dinner. She might just be thrilled to see me walk through the door.

My mother was not thrilled to see me walk through the door.

"When was the last time you had your hair trimmed?" she asked.

"Well, I've been sort of busy—"

"Right." She went back to rearranging a cashmere sweater set thrown across a slipper chair. That was the kind of place it was. They didn't have anything so prosaic as a mannequin. The high-end merchandise was displayed on various antiques, art deco pieces and Lucite poles that appeared to be levitating. "Well," she said as she gave the cashmere one last smoothing with her elegant hand, "with that job you've got I suppose it doesn't really matter."

"That's why I'm here. I'm starting a new job on Monday."

She'd moved on to a coat tree to adjust the leather handbags hanging from it and didn't bother to look up. "What is it?"

"I'll be working in the display department at Grant's Department Store."

She finally looked at me. "Really?" she asked in a tone that was all too doubtful.

I bobbed my head up and down like an excited child. "Really."

She smiled, an act that melted the ice and made her even more beautiful. "Why, Lauren, that's wonderful." The click of her heels was muffled by the Persian carpet that covered a good portion of the gleaming wood floor as she came up to me, put her hands on my arms and kissed my forehead.

I was happier than a twelve-year-old bringing home a perfect report card. "I thought maybe we could go out to dinner and celebrate. My treat."

"Nonsense. It will be my treat." She looked down at the shapeless denim jumper I was wearing with a turtleneck sweater. "You can't go dressed like that. I'll find you something."

I sighed. "Mother, I'm sure what I'm wearing is fine—"

"Trust me, it's not," she said as she went over to the clearance rack and pushed garments to and fro.

"Black again?" I said as she pulled out a rather severely cut suit. "Couldn't we do something with a little color. And maybe something a little—softer?"

"Yes. I suppose this suit would accentuate your hips." She pulled out a pale pink cardigan and a charcoal gray skirt and handed them to me. "These should work." I looked at the price tags and gasped. Both pieces had already been marked down twice but their combined total was still more than what I'd paid for my sofa.

She looked at me disdainfully. "Haven't I always told you to never look shocked at the price tag?"

"But—but—" I sputtered.

"Close your mouth, dear. It's a gift from me. Not many of my clients are a size fourteen. It would probably just sit here all winter, anyway."

Bernice giveth and Bernice taketh away. Oh well, it was a gorgeous outfit. I slipped into the dressing room and tried it on. Damn, I looked good. Amazing what a five-hundred-dollar sweater can do.

When Bernice finished closing up, we emerged from the boutique and I stood at the top of the long, graceful stairway, waiting for her to lockup. The boutique occupied a cream city-brick Italianate building that used to be a private residence in the area of Milwaukee known as Yankee Hill. It is elegant, on a street of other elegant houses turned into apartment buildings and lawyer and architect offices. Its pewter sign, the only one it possesses, is small and tasteful and low enough to be nearly buried in the bright yellow mums planted on the tree lawn.

We descended the curved staircase to walk under the old-fashioned black iron street lamps to the corner. Across the street, a long arched green awning marking the entrance, sat the residential hotel where my mother lived, complete with doorman, maid service and a wonderful restaurant that delivered food to the residents on linen covered carts. We crossed the street and walked under a smaller green awning to enter the restaurant.

My mother was well known here. The hostess was friendly yet deferential. She seated us at one of the best tables in front of a tall, arched window so that we could look out onto the glossy autumn evening. Our handsome waiter's name was Scott. He was obviously a favorite of my mother's.

"Let's order a bottle of wine to toast your new job," Bernice said.

The candlelight flickered across her face and played in the highlights of her hair as my mother discussed the wine list with Scott then ordered a bottle in perfect French. I suppose in a way it was just as hard for me to accept that this beautiful, poised creature was my mother as it must be for her to accept that I was her daughter.

"What's happening with the house?" she asked when Scott left to get the wine.

"The breakfast nook is gone—"

"No great loss," Bernice commented dryly.

"Quint is tearing up the old flooring on Monday," I went on, deciding not to spoil the evening by defending a breakfast nook that I no longer even possessed.

Bernice raised a brow. "Quint?"

"The man I hired to do the work in the kitchen."

"What's he like?"

I was surprised at the question. "He's nice—in his twenties. Easy to be around."

My mother waved away my description with her hand. "I mean, what does he *look* like?"

I described him.

"That makes him perfect," Bernice said when I'd finished.

"Perfect for what?" I asked warily.

She leaned farther over the table. "Lauren, a younger man is exactly what a woman your age needs."

My jaw dropped. "Are you crazy? I'm practically old enough to be his mother! It would be ludicrous. I'd feel foolish. I'd—"

"For heaven's sake, Lauren, I'm not suggesting you marry the man and procreate. A fling—that's all."

"I'm not the fling type," I said. And I wasn't. If I had a fling with a younger man I'd have to start thinking about things like underwear and lingerie and, heaven forbid, push-up bras. I just wasn't up to it. "Besides," I added, "I remind him of his mother."

Bernice settled back in her chair, clearly disappointed. "How charming."

She studied me and I waited for another one of her jabs. Something about using the wrong skin cream or that it's never too early for micro-dermabrasion. Instead she said, "That shade of pink is just lovely on you, dear."

Scott came with the wine and while he poured a smidgen for her to taste, I reflected on how my mother could always catch me off guard with a sudden burst of motherly tenderness. I guess it had always been that way. Why had I never come to expect the good with the bad? Why was it the bad that always stood out in my memory?

When my mother had approved the wine, Scott filled my glass and I took a sip. It was a crisp white, cool and a little fruity.

"Now," Bernice asked as we opened our menus, "tell me all about that handsome grandson of mine."

I told her about Gordy's failure to return my phone calls. "And then he called me out of the blue on Halloween night, but he didn't sound right."

"What do you mean?"

"He sounded—I don't know—weary. He just didn't sound happy."

"Nonsense. Of course he's happy. My grandson doesn't have a neurotic bone in his body."

She meant, of course, that he wasn't anything like me. Which is why I'd decided it wouldn't do any good to discuss Gordy's lie with her. She'd brush it off as a misunderstanding. Or suggest that Roger was the one lying. The acceptance she had always denied me she easily lavished on my son.

"This is your time to let go, Lauren. The boy will be just fine."

Scott came back for our order. "We'll have the wild mushroom soup and the broiled salmon," she told him.

"Speaking of letting go, Mother," I said once we were alone again, "I do know how to order my own dinner off a menu."

"Do you? My guess is you were considering the meat loaf." She saw by the look on my face that she was right. She shuddered. "Whoever decided to make meat loaf into fine dining should be hung by their undoubtedly unfashionable necktie."

I'd been taking a sip of wine. It snorted out of my nose when I started to laugh.

"Oh, perfect," she said, as she sat up straighter and tilted her chin at its haughtiest level. My mother's way of dealing with possible public embarrassment was to go into what I called her Princess Grace act. No one would dare laugh at royalty.

I plucked my napkin off my lap and dabbed at my face. "Sorry."

"I'll try not to say anything funny while you're eating your soup," she said in her iciest tone. But I could see that her eyes were sparkling with just a little merriment.

It ended up being a good dinner. The soup was delicious, the salmon was excellent and my mother was animated, telling stories of her days in New York City and of the summer she spent in Paris on a shoot for *Vogue*.

"Isn't it delightful," she said, "that we're both going to be working in the same field?"

It was true I would be in a field—of artificial trees. I decided this wasn't the time to tell Bernice the whole truth about my new job.

"And how lovely that you'll be working at Grant's. Remember all those Christmas shopping trips? We had such fun. Remember the year we bought you that adorable red dress with the striped sash? You should let me treat you to a few more outfits, darling. You'll need a new wardrobe for work."

"Mother, I'm only a temp in the display department. I'll be working a lot of nights, after the store is closed. Hardly anyone will see me."

"Always dress for the job you want, not the job you have,"

Bernice pronounced like an oracle sitting on a mountain of designer duds.

I couldn't help it. I burst out laughing. Luckily, nothing came out of my nose this time. "How did someone like you ever end up with a daughter like me?" I asked.

She looked like she was about to say something but Scott arrived to try to sweet talk us into dessert and my mother never did answer.

CHAPTER 6

What a pleasure it was to not have to wake to an alarm clock on Monday morning. Natural, gradual awakening was so much less jarring to the soul. Maybe I'd only been a member of the work force for a short time, but as a mom who believed in breakfast I'd been ruled by the alarm clock for years.

I opened my eyes and stretched languidly. I could smell coffee brewing, which made no sense to me at all. Maybe I wasn't really awake after all. Just dreaming of coffee.

I sniffed deeply. Definitely coffee.

I threw back the covers, grabbed my robe, and followed the scent down the stairs and into the kitchen. Quint was on his knees, ripping out the quarter round in preparation for pulling out the old linoleum. It wasn't really a shock to see him there. I'd given him a key so he could come and go while I was at work. I hadn't spoken to him since Friday so he didn't know that my job and work hours had changed.

He hadn't heard me come in so I leaned in the doorway and watched him for a minute or two. He was wearing a black T-shirt and I could see the muscles in his arms and back gather and bunch while he worked. These were real muscles. Work muscles. Somehow more attractive than anything a man could get in a gym.

My face grew a little warm as I remembered what my mother

had said at dinner Friday. Just what I needed, she'd said. A fling with a younger man.

The quarter round ripped away with a crack and he sat back on his haunches and wiped sweat from his brow, then picked up a small crow bar and started to work on another section.

Behind me, I faintly heard the front door open and close but still I stood there, entranced by the man who was ripping out flooring that was older than he was.

"Pardon me while I swoon," Moira murmured as she stepped up behind me.

Quint looked over his shoulder and gave us a grin. "Good morning," he said. "I didn't know anyone else was here." He got to his feet and gave me that quizzical tilt of his head that really was quite adorable. "You're not sick, are you?"

"No, I—"

"She got a new job. Grant's Department Store. Works nights," Moira said as she pushed past me and headed for the coffeepot.

"No kidding? I'm sorry. I hope I didn't wake you?"

I pushed the hair out of my face. "Actually, I think it was the coffee that woke me. And for that you don't have to apologize. It's been a long time since anyone else made the morning coffee around here."

Moira poured two mugs and handed one to me. "Will you be joining us?" she asked Quint with a flutter of her false eyelashes. At least today she was fully dressed. And I do mean fully. Tailored black pants, high-heeled black boots, and a silk shirt the color of chocolate. Her glossy chestnut hair was loose, waving artfully to her shoulders. I looked down at myself. My fleece robe was hanging open to reveal plaid flannel drawstring pants and a faded T-shirt. I wrapped the robe around me and tied the belt but I still felt at a disadvantage.

"Tempting offer," Quint said, "but I want to finish tearing out that quarter round before I take a break."

After my very un-mommy-like musings, I was relieved to not have to sit across the dining room table from him with the morning sun glowing on my guilt-ridden face.

"So," Moira asked once we were seated, "was the ice queen properly impressed with the new job?"

"Actually, I think she was. But you know my mother, for every good word there are about three bad ones. We did reminisce about Grant's, though." I told Moira about the Christmas shopping trips and how it was one of the few times we felt like mother and daughter. "It was kind of like we went through those front doors and some kind of magic occurred. For the next five hours we were perfect together."

I sipped coffee while Moira asked, "So when did that perfection stop?"

I had to think for a moment. "Probably the year I decided I didn't want to wear tights and velvet anymore. I think I must have been about ten. We had a huge fight in the dressing room because I wanted a pair of pants from the Army Surplus store and some earth shoes."

Moira shrugged. "Every daughter rebels at that age. Besides, earth shoes are a pretty tame form of revolution."

"Not to my mother. After all, she'd been on the cover of *Seventeen* when she'd been in high school. She acted like her little girl had been abducted by aliens. After that, nothing I ever did was right."

"My mother was too busy protesting the war and Nixon to give a shit about anything I wore."

"In Bernice's eyes, failure to accessorize was right up there with the Watergate break-in."

Quint came into the dining room, steaming mug of coffee in one hand and a plate of hot buttered toast in the other. "Your mother sounds like a trip."

Damn. I'd forgotten he was in the kitchen. I wondered how much he'd heard—and how pathetic I'd sounded.

"Toast?" he asked as he put the plate before us then took a seat.

"You know," Moira lamented, "the guy I hired to paint my living room never fed me hot buttered toast."

"Well, that's just a shame," Quint said.

"You're telling me," muttered Moira. "What are you doing after this job?"

"Why? Are you in need of a handyman?"

Moira's grin was slow and totally carnal. "If you answer that," I told her, "I'm banishing you from the house for the next thirty days."

"Honestly, Lauren, you can be such a prude."

"Someone needs to keep you out of jail."

Quint laughed. "I'm not even going to ask the history of that statement."

"Good," I said.

We munched and sipped for a few companionable minutes and then Quint said, "I couldn't help but overhear your earlier conversation."

I groaned inwardly. Well, that answered that question.

"I remember Dr. Phil saying one day that it takes a parent saying like a thousand nice things to a kid to wipe out one bad thing."

Moira and I looked at each other over the rims of our mugs. We both knew what the other was thinking. I mean, how many hunky twenty-something guys quoted Dr. Phil?

"So, what you're saying," I said as I put my mug down, "is that I'm basically doomed to feel mediocre in my mother's company?"

"Well, no," Quint answered. "At least not in my opinion. I

mean," his face grew sheepish, "I don't know what Dr. Phil had to say about it—I didn't get to hear the rest of the show over the buzz of the floor sander—but, it seems to me that at some point you have a choice. I mean, you could choose to believe only the good things. Or choose to just figure your mother is wrong—" he shrugged "—or weird or something. I mean you're an adult, right?"

Was I?

"Well, I always *thought* I was an adult. I always thought I was supermature and responsible." I grimaced and thrust my hand into my hair, trying to think how to put what I was feeling. "I guess lately, though, I've had to rethink my choices—and my perceptions."

"Then," said my sage of a handyman, "you could rethink your mother, too." He shrugged. "Maybe it's just her way. Take my dad—"

We were a rapt audience, Moira and I, while Quint told us about how his father had all but abandoned him and his mother when he was eleven years old and how he'd been angry for years. "I got into fights at school constantly. But every time I acted out I could see more clearly how it hurt my mom." He shook his head. "Man, she didn't deserve that. So I kind of decided I better accept who my old man was and get on with the business of becoming the kind of man I wanted to be. I mean, it was a cinch. *He* was never going to become the man I wanted *him* to be."

We all reached for another piece of toast and munched quietly. But it wasn't my mother I was thinking about. It was my father. Why had I never been angry at him the way Quint had once been angry at his father? Why didn't his absence and indifference bother me as much as just about everything my mother said or did?

Two phone calls a year didn't exactly make for discovering

someone's irritating foibles. Quite possibly the only reason my father wasn't critical of me was because he didn't know me. And I didn't know him. He was just an overly tan guy in a silver picture frame.

At least my mother was in my life. She'd been there on my wedding day—even though she'd disapproved of the groom. She'd been there for Gordy's birth—even though she thought we should have waited longer to have a child. She'd been there when we'd bought this house—even though she thought we should get a condo instead.

I squirmed in my dining room chair. Was I guilty of perpetuating a double standard when it came to my parents? The word *delusion* came into my thoughts, unbidden. *Keep your little delusions*, my mother had said. *Delusional, as usual*, Roger had said.

Quint pushed his chair back and stood up. "So, anyway, I guess what I'm saying is you might as well cut your mother a little slack. She's the only one you've got."

Moira and I watched him as he walked back to the kitchen.

Moira sighed. "He shops, he watches Dr. Phil, he discusses his feelings, he does stuff around the house and he makes toast."

I laughed. "What more could a woman want?"

"Oh, a woman could want more—but I bet he's good at that, too."

"You look outstanding," Quint said to me when I came down the stairs dressed for work later that afternoon.

"Thank you," I said as I pulled on a navy peacoat. My mother had messengered over the tailored gray pants and the blue cardigan I was wearing. I felt a little overdressed considering I was going to be working behind the scenes. Left to my own devices, I would have worn jeans and a pullover.

I noticed that Quint had his leather jacket on. "Are you leaving, too?"

"Yeah, I thought I'd quit a little early today."

"But that floor will be finished by Thanksgiving, right?"

He laughed. "Don't you trust me?"

"Well," I said as I opened the front door, "it's just that, you sort of come and go and when you're here you make toast—I mean, it's all very nice and I enjoy your company, but—"

"You do?" he asked as he followed me out onto the porch.

I blinked at the brightness of the sun. "I do what?"

"Enjoy my company?"

I was a little taken aback. "Well, yes, of course, but—"

He grinned. "Good. Because I enjoy your company, too."

"But the floor *will* be ready by—"

"Thanksgiving," he finished for me. Then he took my hand and placed it over his heart—or over where his heart would be beneath the soft, worn feel of his leather jacket. "Cross my heart," he said, looking down at me with that intent, still gaze of his.

I swear, my temperature went up ten degrees despite the fact that we were standing on the front porch.

"Hi, Lauren!" someone called.

I tore my gaze from Quint's face. Hell. It was Amy.

I twisted my hand out of Quint's. "Hi, Amy!" I called out, waving like a maniac with my newly liberated hand. She apparently took my gusto for an invitation and crossed the street.

"This is Quint Mathews," I said. "He's putting in a new kitchen floor for me."

"Oh? I thought it was a new bathroom you were considering," she said.

Actually, I was considering pushing her off the porch.

"Um—well—I thought the kitchen needed sprucing up first.

Quint was just promising me that it will be finished by Thanksgiving," I added, knowing I was giving too much information—something that could only make me look guilty. Although, guilty of what, I wasn't sure. I just knew that Amy was an expert at twisting things she'd seen and heard.

A horn honked. "Woops, there's my ride to book group," Amy said. "Good luck with that floor."

"Did you know you're blushing?" Quint asked me softly after she'd left.

"I have to get to work," I mumbled, as I turned away and started down the stairs.

"Hey," Quint said when I was halfway to the car.

I stopped and turned around. He was grinning at me.

"Good luck on your first day," he said.

I grinned back. "Thanks," I said.

The grin stayed on my face all the way downtown. Usually, I wouldn't be expected at work until eight at night when the store closed, but on this first day I had to report to the display department at Grant's at four o'clock so that the director could acquaint me with the department. What excited me most about this was that it meant I got to walk through the front doors of Grant's for the first time as an employee. I deliberately parked in a lot down the street just so I could join the late afternoon throng of downtown workers on the sidewalks of Wisconsin Avenue.

Grant's was one of only two remaining privately owned department stores in Milwaukee. It was by far the more elegant of the two. The five-story building, just east of the bridge that crossed the Milwaukee River, was made of white terra cotta tiles. It had twin classic colonnades on either side of the main entrance and a brass plaque above that read Grant's Department Store.

Eagerly, I opened one of the double front doors and stepped into warmth and color and the murmur of shoppers. I walked through the glittery jewelry department, smelled the leather as I passed purses and shoes and wove through the dreamy fragrance of the cosmetics department to the elevator. I rode down to the basement, then took a sheet of paper out of my purse.

I knew the sales floors at Grant's like I knew my own name, but I had no idea where the displays were planned. The directions Christy had given me to the display department led me through a labyrinth of narrow hallways painted a disappointing institutional yellow. Occasionally I passed an open doorway and caught glimpses of huge, ancient looking boilers, gauges and electrical-looking thingies. It was all a little dismaying after the shiny brightness of the sales floors. But when I finally came to the huge swinging doors and pushed them open, it was like entering Oz.

There were mannequins and papier-mâché animals. There were huge urns, Roman columns of every height, and baskets and baskets of silk flowers, feathers, and wild, twisted twiggy things. There were bolts of wide ribbons hanging from the ceiling and fake wreaths and topiaries. There was even a full-size Santa's sleigh with some reindeer in need of a coat of paint. I didn't see any people but I heard voices.

"Hello?" I said.

A young man in a sweater-vest and short, spiky hair poked his head around one of the reindeer.

"Yes?"

I held up my paper work from Temporary Solutions. "I'm reporting for work."

He came out from behind the reindeer, took my papers and glanced down at them.

"Oh, you're the temp," he said. Then, "Dora!" he yelled, "the temp's here!"

A woman poked her head out from behind a huge topiary to take a look.

"The last one they sent us was wearing dungarees," she said as she emerged from behind the greenery. "At least you look like you consider this to be a real job."

I silently thanked my mother for the clothes—and myself for taking her advice and wearing them. Dora herself was wearing a version of pretty much the same outfit. She was short, but formidable looking as she came toward me, her stride long and forceful for someone of her stature. She was probably around the same age as my mother, but she'd allowed her closely cropped hair to go gray and she clearly wasn't a slave to Botox. But, every line on her face just seemed to add to her attractiveness.

"I'm Dora Reynolds, the director of this menagerie." She held out her hand and I shook it. "The loud mouth there is Stuart. He's my assistant. If you don't take orders from me, you'll be taking orders from him. The girls at the drafting boards," she threw an arm toward the right side of the room where drafting tables and desks where crammed together, "are Lola and Sienna. They're apprentices, sent to us from the Institute of Art and Design. Right now they're putting the finishing touches on the design for this year's Christmas windows."

They looked up from their sketches long enough to say hello.

"We have a few worker bees who come and go as we need them and another temp who—" Dora frowned at her watch "—appears to be late. We do things the old fashioned way here at Grant's," she went on. "Everything for the windows and displays is done in-house, if at all possible. We don't have the budget of a Macy's or a Bloomingdales, but we strive always to be creative and fresh—no matter how cheap the front office is. Now—you do understand that you'll be mainly setting up and decorating the artificial trees on the third floor?"

"Yes, ma'am," I answered.

"Heavens," said Stuart, "don't start calling her ma'am or she'll start believing that poor imitation of Bette Davis she does."

Dora smiled wickedly. "Stuart might be helping you trim those trees."

"Hey, I've done my time in Winter Wonderland, sister."

Dora laughed and I decided to relax. "I'm looking forward to working in Winter Wonderland," I said.

"Teacher's pet," Stuart mumbled.

"No, really. I love Christmas. Some of my happiest childhood memories are of Grant's at Christmas."

"That's very touching, my dear," Dora said. "I've worked here for over forty years and I must say that the Christmas holidays were always my favorite, too. Now, you'll be working mostly nights for the time being, but if you're interested in learning more about the department, I encourage you to come in a little early and observe and explore."

"She means run errands and sharpen pencils," Stuart said.

"Quiet, dear," Dora said sweetly, "or I'll demote you to playing one of Santa's elves."

"The threats never end," Stuart said as he stalked off.

"As you can see, you have to be something of a good sport to work here."

"I raised a son to eighteen pretty much all by myself, so I know how to be a good sport."

"Excellent. Now, if you'll follow me to my office, I'll show you the sketches we've been working on for the third floor trees. Any input you have, will, of course, be appreciated—"

* * *

"It's all so fabulous," I told Moira and Quint a few afternoons later over coffee. "The head of the department is like something from a forties movie—you know one of those clever career types. Hard as nails but totally fair."

"Bette Davis," Quint said.

Moira and I stared at him, although you'd think we'd be long past being surprised by anything that came out of his mouth.

"Right," I said.

Since it was lunch time—I now slept later—Quint had made a plate of grilled cheese sandwiches.

"I can't make them as good as you can," he said.

"Are you kidding? These are great." I took another bite then licked melted butter and cheese from my fingers.

"All I can say is I'm quite sure that I've never had a man— any man—grill me a cheese sandwich before," Moira said. "I'm not even sure Stan knows how to turn on the stove."

"My mom taught me to cook basic stuff. She always said that a man should know how to take care of himself so that he never marries a woman for the wrong reasons."

"Smart woman," Moira said, while I tried to remember if I'd ever taught Gordy to make a grilled cheese sandwich. I was pretty sure I'd always been there to make one for him. I was also pretty sure that this was the first time I'd felt a little apprehensive about it. Just a small current of uneasiness spreading from my neck to my shoulders. Sort of like the same feeling I'd had when Gordy had sounded so weary on the phone.

Of course Gordy was weary, I kept telling myself. He was on his own—doing his own laundry for the first time. Being responsible for his own meals. Deciding on his own when to go to bed, when to study, when to do—um—other things. The point was that soon I'd have him home again to cook for and to take care of. And then, at last, something familiar would be back in this life that was becoming barely recognizable to me.

Moira pushed her chair back. "Well, sweeties, I've got to get to the day spa. Stanley and I are going to a function tonight and I figure if I have to be bored I might as well look beautiful. I'm getting the works," she said as she gathered up her purse and jacket. "Body polishing, seaweed wrap, pedicure—"

Quint laughed. "I'm not even going to ask what a seaweed wrap is."

"Wise man. Catch ya later," Moira said as she blew us kisses then headed for the door.

"So you're sure the floor will be finished by Thanksgiving?" I asked Quint after Moira left.

He threw up his hands. "Again with the floor! Yes! I'm sure."

"It's just that now you've started painting the walls, and—"

"It's best to get the mess out of the way before I put in the new floor."

"But I know you can't walk on a newly tiled floor right away, so I just—"

He tilted his head at me quizzically. "Didn't I cross my heart?"

Oh, boy, I didn't want to think back to that morning. So I thought of pumpkin pie, instead. "It's just that—"

"It's just that you're thinking of all those goodies you're going to make for Gordy. Am I right?"

I sighed. "Guilty as charged. Is that so wrong?"

He stood up. "No," he said. "It's what makes you so sweet." He bent down and kissed my cheek, then picked up his mug and went back to the kitchen.

* * *

I'd decided to take Dora's advice about arriving early every day so I could observe. Yes, I ended up fetching coffee and sharpening pencils. I also followed Stuart around, taking notes while he brainstormed and now he had me on the phone calling secondhand and antique stores looking for props. Namely, a pair of those tinsel trees that had come out in the fifties. Stuart decided he just had to have them for one of the window displays. Dora and he argued budget while I made the phone calls.

"I found one!" I called out in triumph after my first successful call.

"One? I said I wanted two," Stuart pouted. "I can't possibly do it without a pair. I thought I made that clear."

"But, I thought we might as well buy this one then if we find another one—"

"And if we don't?" he asked petulantly.

I chewed on my lip. "You could sort of rework your design so—"

Stuart was glaring at me so I decided not to finish that particular sentence. "Should I cancel the order?" I asked meekly.

"Let it stand," Dora said. "And come away from that phone. You're doing Stuart's job for him. And Stuart, stop pouting. I'm sure we'll find another tree. I need Lauren to start sorting and numbering these boxes of ornaments so we can have them shipped upstairs."

She showed me how to check off the stock numbers and gave me the diagrams of how each tree was to be decorated so I could mark the cartons accordingly.

I was rechecking the cartons a few hours later when Dora asked me how it was going.

"We seem to be missing some doves," I murmured as I re-checked the last carton. "All the other ornaments for the Peace Fantasy tree are here. Just no doves."

"Bother. The Peace Fantasy tree is the one shoppers see first, as they're coming up the escalator. We need those doves. I'll have a chat with the buyer. Maybe she knows something. Meanwhile," she said to Stuart, "call stock and tell them we need to borrow a few of their burliest."

"I'm on it, Chief."

"I thought you would be," Dora said dryly. "Just don't use it as a dating opportunity. I want these cartons ferried to the third floor ASAP."

"Chief, please, I'm on the clock."

Dora laughed, then turned back to me. "As soon as the store closes, I want you up on the third floor. Tonight we start assembling the trees."

Assembling the trees! It sounded like such fun. But let me tell you, two hours of straightening branches had my back aching and my skin itching.

"What are these things made of?" I asked Kelly, the other temp working with me.

"Whatever it is, it can't be good for the environment," she answered.

"The environment? I'll be lucky if I have any skin left on my forearms by the time the night is over."

"How many more do we have to go?"

"Six."

Kelly groaned. "And I thought this was going to be an easy way to make money for Christmas."

"It'll be more fun once they're all up and we get to start trimming them."

"Tell you what—let's stick it out here tonight until we've finished them all."

I was game. Might as well get the worst of it over. Dora checked on us a couple of hours later and approved the plan.

"I'll be here until dawn, anyway. Just come down to the department when you're finished and I'll let you out of the building."

While we worked, Kelly told me the story of her life—all twenty-four years of it. She'd been raised in Minnesota and had followed a guy in a band to Milwaukee.

"He turned out to be a real loser, but I liked Milwaukee, so I stayed. It's a pretty good party town." She looked like a club kid—black hair, trendy clothes, weird colors of eye shadow.

She was currently working as a receptionist in a tanning salon. "The hours are pretty flexible and the people who run the place are pretty cool, but the pay is lousy. That's why I ended up at Temporary Solutions."

We worked on in silence for a little while until someone turned on the sound system and Christmas music started to fill the empty store.

"Well, that settles it," said Kelly. "They're trying to drive us crazy."

"Don't be silly," I protested. "They're trying to get us in the mood."

"It's not even Thanksgiving yet."

I didn't care. I liked it. And, truthfully, I couldn't wait until tomorrow night when we could start trimming.

"Imagine," I said out loud, "getting paid to trim Christmas trees."

"You're worse than the music. It's like working with Snow White."

I frowned. "I don't think she had anything to do with Christmas."

"Whatever."

Was it me, or did I seem to be associating with a lot of people lately who used that word?

I hummed along to the music for a while until Kelly sighed for about the fifth time, after which I shut up and we worked in silence for another hour.

"One more to go," I said.

"I'm starving. If I don't get something to eat soon, they're going to find my emaciated body draped around this damn thing like a goulish garland."

"Now that you mention it, I'm pretty hungry myself."

"Want to do breakfast when we're through here?"

"Oh—I don't think—" I started to automatically decline the invitation. But why should I? There was no one waiting up for me at home. I was free to go to breakfast in the wee hours of the morning with a coworker if I felt like it. And, damn it, I felt like it.

"I'd love to," I said.

"Cool. I know a place that does the best hash…"

I followed Kelly's car through the empty streets of downtown to the east side and found a parking spot right next to hers in the crowded parking lot of the all-night diner. Sound, heat and heavenly scents rushed at us when we opened the door.

We were shown to a booth and given menus. I already knew I wanted the hash and eggs so I scanned the people sitting at the counter. I was wondering what their stories were, what had brought them out at this hour, when I did a double take and looked again at the man sitting at the last stool.

It was him. The blue-eyed stranger with the cane.

I quickly slouched in my seat and held the menu up to my face. I have no idea why. I was just suddenly awash in embarrassment. Maybe he wouldn't recognize me without my bonnet and braids. Maybe he wouldn't remember that I'd called him my hero for telling my mother off and then rewarded him with free yogurt. But I wasn't taking any chances.

I peeked over the top of my menu just as he slid off his stool and started to limp his way to the cash register. He was just as interesting looking as I'd remembered. His eyes were just as blue, his scowl was just as sexy.

"You know that guy?" Kelly asked.

"Huh? Um—no. Why do you ask?"

"'Cause you're looking at him like you wish he was on the menu."

I straightened in my seat. "That's ridiculous," I said.

"Good. I mean, you're a little old, but believe me, you could do better."

The sun was starting to come up when I crawled into bed, my body exhausted, my arms still itching, but my tummy and my heart full. I smiled into my pillow. I'd just had coffee, eggs and hash at three o'clock in the morning with a young woman that I had absolutely nothing in common with except that we worked together.

And, I'd seen the blue-eyed man again.

Apparently, there really was life outside Seagull Lane.

CHAPTER 7

The Monday before Thanksgiving I stood in the kitchen eating a casserole Quint had made from some leftover chicken I'd had in the fridge and watching him dab cream-colored paint over the newly painted yellow walls with a sponge. He was on the second wall. Two more to go.

"Quint, the walls look beautiful and this casserole is yummy, but the floor really needs to be done. It's less than a week till Thanksgiving."

"It will be done. But—"

"But, what?" I wanted everything perfect for Gordy's home-coming. I'd even found a table and chairs at a second hand store for the kitchen so that Gordy could still sit and study while I cooked. Or maybe break up the bread for stuffing like he used to. While I sautéed at the stove, he'd tell me all about college and the new friends he'd made. Quint's deep voice brought me tumbling back from my mommy daydream.

"You know," he said, "you could offer extra incentive to get the job done by inviting me for Thanksgiving dinner."

I was surprised. And something more. That feeling you get when you're a kid and you're about to do something just a little bit out of character. A little bit dangerous. Although what could possibly be dangerous about inviting my handyman over for some mashed potatoes and gravy was eluding me at the moment.

"Okay," I said, "you've got a deal. You get the floor finished in time for me to start cooking Wednesday night and you're invited for Thanksgiving dinner."

"Awesome," Quint said, treating me to his most endearing grin.

"I suggest that if you intend to eat turkey you better get back to work."

"Yes, ma'am," he said, giving me a little salute.

I left him to his sponging and headed for work. As I drove I started to wonder how Gordy was going to take having Quint with us on Thanksgiving. For years it had just been Gordy and my mother—I turned as red as the light I had to stop for when I remembered what my mother had said about Quint being perfect for an affair. Oh, lord—she wouldn't play matchmaker, would she? No. That wasn't Bernice's style. Maybe Bernice would go after him herself. Embarrassing, but still the better alternative.

"What am I worrying about?" I muttered to myself as traffic started to move. Gordy and Quint were sure to hit it off. They'd probably be bonding over a football game in the living room while Bernice and I bonded in the kitchen. I grinned. Okay, maybe thinking of my mother and me bonding over peeling potatoes was going too far. But the important thing was that everything was going to work out just fine. There was nothing at all to be worried about.

At Grant's, Kelly looked even more morose than usual as we touched up Santa's sleigh with red paint while we waited for the store to close so we could head back up to Winter Wonderland.

"Cheer up," I told her. "After tomorrow, every tree will be trimmed."

"That's not it—I'm just bummed that I'm not going home for Thanksgiving."

"Why not?"

"Gotta work Friday, remember? Busiest shopping day of the year."

As lowly temps in the display department, we had to come in on Friday and see to it that Winter Wonderland stayed fresh as newly fallen snow all day. Which meant we'd be replacing and restocking ornaments and cleaning up after the bargain seeking masses. I wasn't happy about having to work, either. It meant much less time with Gordy than I would have liked. But at least we'd be together for the holiday.

"Look, Kelly," I said as I dipped my brush into the paint can, "why don't you come to my house for Thanksgiving?"

Kelly's head jerked up. "Seriously?" she asked with a smile that warmed my heart.

"Sure—I always make too much food, anyway."

"So what am I, chopped liver?" Stuart asked as he joined us. "Invite me and you don't just get Stuart, you get Stuart's heavenly yam casserole."

"The one with the marshmallows on top?" Kelly asked eagerly.

"None other."

"Cool. My mother always makes that."

"It's all the rage again, you know. Very kitschy."

I started to tell him that I'd be making my own maple-glazed yams with toasted Georgia pecans, but they both had such a look of glee on their faces that I couldn't bring myself to do it.

Tradition was important to me. When I was a kid, Bernice and I had celebrated the holiday by going to a different restaurant every year. When I got married, I vowed to go all out with the Thanksgiving at home thing. I'd been serving the same dinner since Gordy had been old enough to chew. This year it seemed more important than ever to hold with tradition since it would be the last Thanksgiving in the house where Gordy had been raised. But how could I deny Stuart, who wasn't much older than Gordy, his own favorite holiday dish?

"I'll bring something, too," Kelly offered.

Okay, I could be magnanimous, but enough was enough. "That's not really necessary," I quickly protested.

"No, I want to. My mother always makes this awesome Jell-O salad. I'll call her and get the recipe."

"Your Jell-O doesn't have marshmallows in it, does it?" Stuart asked suspiciously. "Because that would be overkill."

"Don't worry Stuart, I won't rain on your marshmallow parade," Kelly said. "It's got canned pears and that nondairy whipped topping in it."

"Sounds just yummy," I said, wondering if I could manage to forget to put both dishes out without anyone noticing. That would probably be kinder than what Bernice was going to have to say about marshmallows and canned pears.

While I was trying to figure it all out, Dora, wearing a tartan cloak and a red beret, came through the swinging doors. You could actually feel the frostiness emanating from her.

"It is colder than a witch's tit out there," she said.

"Charming," Stuart drawled.

"What's with the huddle? What are my troops brewing up?" Dora asked as she shed her cape.

"Thanksgiving at Lauren's," Stuart said.

"You're welcome to come," I quickly added. We were already up to three guests. What was one more? "It's sort of an impromptu affair."

"She means," Stuart said sotto voce, "that we pretty much invited ourselves."

"I'm bringing Jell-O," Kelly said.

"And I'm bringing yams with marshmallows," Stuart added proudly.

"What a shame I'm going to miss the Jell-O and the marshmallows," Dora lamented dryly. "But I've already got plans, kids. Now, if any of us are actually going to get Thanksgiving off, we'd better get to work." She pointed at Stuart. "Did we get that FedEx delivery yet?"

Stuart made a face. "Yes, Chief. But I'm afraid it ain't good."

"What does that mean?"

Stuart pushed a carton over with his foot. "See for yourself."

Dora bent and opened the flaps. "Holy Mother of God," she exclaimed, "they've sent us pickles." Using just the tips of her fingers, she pulled one of the blown glass pickles out of the carton and held it at arm's length. "*What* am I supposed to do with these?"

"I think it's an old German custom," I answered helpfully. "It's supposed to bring the family good luck—or something."

She was eyeing me like I was a lunatic. "Dear, the point is, we have two hundred mirrored snowflakes and one hundred mirrored hearts all of which, instead of reflecting white blown glass doves, will be reflecting bright green pickles." Her voice had risen throughout her statement until when she'd reached the word "pickles" it was loud enough to make heads pop up all over the department. Seeing the look on Dora's face, they quickly popped back down again.

"Sorry," I said.

Dora sighed. "No. I'm sorry. I shouldn't take it out on you. We'll think of something," she said, as she patted my arm.

But I could still feel the tension in the air. We were getting down to the wire and I knew that Dora still wasn't happy with one of the window displays. The windows were scheduled to be unveiled on the Friday after Thanksgiving, the official opening of the holiday shopping season at Grant's. Discount and chain stores had, as usual, launched the season weeks earlier. Grant's stayed with tradition—another reason I loved it. They'd always started the season the Friday after Thanksgiving, and they always would. I knew Dora must feel tremendous pressure to get everything finished in time and now, with the missing doves, Winter Wonderland had one very bare tree to add to the chaos.

Kelly and I spent the night setting up Christmas villages and hanging giant stars from the ceiling. When we left at two in the morning, Dora was still trying to fix the problem with the window display and muttering about dwindling budgets.

When I got home, there was a note from Quint on the dining room table.

"I know you're worrying," it said, "but don't. I'll be here at the crack of dawn to start the floor. Don't the walls look great, though?"

Yes, they did. They looked terrific. I'd used my discount at Grant's a few weeks ago on a couple of rustic looking plaques made of terra cotta and a framed print of a vineyard in Tuscany. I'd splurged on wide slatted wood blinds for the windows and Quint had hung everything some time during the day.

I looked down at my feet. The linoleum was gone, leaving a scarred and paint-spattered plank floor. Two days. That's all he had. Because on Wednesday night I intended to be sitting at my used kitchen table with my son, breaking up stale French bread for my stuffing. And I intended for the crumbs to be falling on my new red-ceramic-tiled floor.

I fixed myself a peanut butter and jelly sandwich, poured a glass of milk and took it to the dining room table. Before I sat down, I went over to the desk in the living room and pulled out a pad of paper and some pencils. While I ate, I sketched. I had an idea for the tree of the missing doves and I wanted to get it down on paper.

I didn't get any coffee the next morning because Quint was already at it and the kitchen was off-limits.

"Don't even talk to me," he said. "I'm counting on a drumstick."

I obliged. Besides, I had grocery shopping to do before work. Luckily, the refrigerator was now humming along in the dining room.

I'd decided to once again splurge on The Market in the Cove. When I walked into the place, it felt good to be a customer again instead of an overage milkmaid. But as I started to shop I became painfully aware that the prices were ridiculous. Was all this ambience worth it? Considering I now had to buy turkey and fixings to feed six people, it seemed just plain stupid to pay these prices. I was, after all, still a temp. I abandoned my cart, got the hell out of there and drove to a cheaper chain supermarket.

When I got back to the house, Quint insisted on helping me carry in the groceries. When he saw the bag from the fast food place he said, "Any chance there's something in there for me?"

"Triple cheeseburger, extra large fries and a chocolate shake," I said.

"You must be a mind reader," he said. "That's exactly what I wanted."

"So—have you made any progress?" I asked after we'd carried the last of the bags in and set them down with the rest on the dining room table.

He came up behind me and put his hands over my eyes. Pressing his body against my back, he gently started to walk me over to the kitchen doorway. I could feel the breath coming fast from his chest, feel the slight sweat on his rough palms, feel his muscles against the length of me as he moved. I was keenly aware that I hadn't been this physically close to a man in years.

"Okay," he said, his deep voice very close to my ear, "now."

He took his hands away. "Wow!" I said. At least a third of the floor was covered in those gorgeous, rough-hewn red tiles. The walls had taken on a rustic look and the floor finished it off perfectly.

"Didn't I tell you?" he asked.

I nodded. "Quint, it's going to be just gorgeous."

I couldn't believe it, but what he'd done with the kitchen was making it even harder to think of leaving the house than the breakfast nook had. I suddenly felt far too emotional. Changes were happening fast—some of them good—but I still didn't want to leave the house—couldn't even begin to imagine where I would live after I left or what my life would be like.

"Something wrong?" Quint asked.

I kept my head down, knowing there were tears in my eyes. "Let's go eat our burgers before they get cold."

We sat on the floor in the living room around the coffee table to eat. I started to talk about Thanksgiving, but he reached over and used his fingertips to raise my chin.

"What is it, Lauren?" he asked softly.

How could his fingers be so rough and his heart be so tender? "Oh, the house. Thinking about the future." I shook my head. "Everything. Oh, and there's this." I reached over to the sofa where I'd thrown my tote bag and drew out the sketches I'd made the night before. I told Quint about the missing doves and the pickles and about how I'd put together an idea using some old ornaments I'd found in storage.

"But now I'm a nervous wreck thinking about actually taking the idea to Dora. I mean, I'm a temp. What do I know?"

Quint took the sketch and studied it. "Looks to me like you know a lot. You can draw, too."

I shrugged and surreptitiously wiped the tears from my eyes with my fingertips. "Gordy and I used to draw a lot when he was little. He loved to use watercolors. In fact, he still paints sometimes. I've got a bunch of his canvases in the attic that I'm always meaning to get framed."

"I'd say, looking at this sketch, that he got his talent from his mom. I say go for it. What have you got to lose? If your boss says no, at least she'll know that you have initiative and spunk."

"Spunk? You think I have spunk?"

"Those are red tiles I'm putting in that kitchen, aren't they?"

On the drive downtown, I kept saying it over and over again to myself. *You've got spunk. You've got spunk.* I mean, if a twenty-something hunk tells you you've got spunk, it's probably true, right?

However, my spunk didn't keep the butterflies from my stomach when Dora came in later that afternoon.

"Dora—" I began as I followed in her wake while she swirled out of her cloak.

"If there is another problem, I don't want to hear about it."

I gulped. Okay, now was the time to show that spunk Quint was so sure I had. "Actually, not a problem. A solution."

She turned swiftly. "Really?" she asked—a little dubiously, I thought, but I might just have been a tad sensitive at the moment. "Excellent. Suppose you start by telling me what you have the solution to?"

"The Peace Fantasy tree."

"Don't tell me the doves have landed."

"Well, not exactly. But I did come up with an idea last night that I thought might work." My heart hadn't beat this fast since I waited to find out how I'd done on my SATs. I mean, yeah, big things had happened in my life. Marriage, pregnancy, motherhood. But this was another feeling entirely. This was way out of my comfort zone.

"Well," she asked impatiently, "have you a sketch or something?"

"Oh—um—yes."

"Then come into my office and let's have a look at it."

I followed her into her office, pulled out the pad of paper and put it on her desk. "When Kelly and I were sorting ornaments, we came across a few cartons of pink ones."

"Yes, I remember those. A few years ago one of the buyers decided that pink was the new red for Christmas. They stocked all these gaudy, beaded and sequined things. They couldn't even get rid of them at eighty-percent off. Finally, they sent them down here. But I never have found any use for them."

"Pink has become pretty trendy again, you know. And so has gaudy—the whole boho thing. So I thought that we could incorporate those pink ornaments into the design, using them instead of the doves, and we'd have this luscious pink glow from the ornaments reflected in the mirrored pieces."

"What is this?" she pointed a finger at the top of the tree.

"Oh—I found some wide lace wired ribbon so I thought a bow for the tree-topper—"

"No," she said emphatically. "Been done to death."

My heart tripped a little and was just about to fall to my feet when she added, "But the rest is terrific. You've got to come up with a different top, though. Why don't you take a few hours to scout the storeroom—you could even look around the sales floors. Use your imagination—you apparently have one," she said as she smiled at me. "Now get a move on. You've got to pull this thing together before you can go home tonight."

I might be getting lowly temp wages, but on the other hand it was hard to believe that I was actually getting paid to do what I did that afternoon. I was all over that store, up and down the escalators, in back storage rooms, in racks of stuff that was too old to be put on clearance but too good to be thrown away. I considered a gold sequined hat that looked like a relic from the '50s but decided against messing up the pink-and-silver mirrored exclusivity of the project. I considered a pair of pink Lucite kitten heels that were a size four and might look darling hanging from the top of the tree. But I really fell in love with the most gaudy, most absolutely huge pink crystal broach this side of Elizabeth Taylor. Of course, Liz's wouldn't have been crystals, but still the effect was the same. Overblown but beautiful. I found some faux pink-diamond tennis bracelets hanging around in clearance and confiscated those, too.

I took my bounty back to the display department and sat down at one of the drafting tables and began sketching what I envisioned for the tree-topper.

"Still playing at being teacher's pet, I see," Stuart said as he stopped to look over my shoulder.

"Just an idea I had," I said nonchalantly while my heart was beating in my throat. I was amazed at how much this meant to me. I thought I'd have butternut squash and pumpkin pies on the brain today but the idea for the replacement tree was consuming me. And, I'll admit, I wanted badly for Dora to like what I was doing.

"Not bad, girlfriend," Stuart said. "Those tennis bracelets are an inspiration."

"Thanks," I said gratefully. I'd decided the broach would go on top with the tennis bracelets all hanging off it, cascading down the top of the tree.

Dora had been working in the problem window when I'd gotten back and now she came in on a rush. "Someone find me a rope so I can hang myself."

"What's wrong now, Chief?" Stuart asked.

"One of the damn papier-mâché penguins refuses to stand up. I should have listened when you told me to go with the fiberglass ones but no, I had to have something original, something unique! And wouldn't you know, I gave Lola and Sienna the week off so they could rush home for the holiday like a couple of kiddies out of grade school. If I had either of those so-called artists here at this moment, I'd—oh, damn it all! Why didn't I go with the fiberglass?"

Kelly poked me in the back. "Now might be a good time to lay your plan on her," she whispered.

"You really think so?" I whispered back.

"Trust me, if she doesn't simmer down she's going to pop. Go for it—now."

I slid off my stool. "Um—Dora?"

She whirled around and gave me a look. "Make this good news," she said.

"Well, I think I've solved the problem of the tree-topper for the pink fantasy tree."

She swept over to the drawing board. "Let's see what you've got."

I showed her the jewelry, explained the concept, pointed out the drawing.

"Go with it," she said.

"Really?" I asked like an overeager puppy.

"Listen, genius, since you're full of enthusiastic energy at the moment, come with me. See if you can do something with that penguin."

I couldn't believe it. I was going into one of the display windows with Dora. Never mind that I hadn't a clue of how to make a papier-mâché penguin stand up, it was still a thrill to be invited into a Christmas display window and asked for advice from the woman who'd been overseeing them since I'd been in velvet dresses. Oh, this was way better than passing out yogurt and cereal.

She opened a door concealed behind a heavy drapery and motioned for me to follow her up the three steps to the display floor of the window. The design consisted of a row of penguins, each one carrying a different size gift all wrapped up in Grant's signature Christmas paper. The main penguin, the largest, wouldn't stand up.

"You see," Dora said as she pointed at the bottom of his flippers. "He's got a lump. And it makes him all wobbly and he won't stand for more than minutes at a time."

The bottom of the window was filled with fluffy white stuff that was supposed to look like snow. It was deep enough that the penguins' flippers were mostly hidden.

"This reminds me of the time my son Gordy was supposed to play a—"

"For the love of God, cut to the chase!" Dora bellowed.

Luckily, I had spunk. "Okay, here's what I'd do. I'd slice off the bottom of his flippers and put him at the end of the line. He can be the smaller penguin bringing up the rear. The snow will hide the fact that his flippers have been—um—mutilated."

Dora stared at me. "Oh, my God—it's so simple that it's genius."

This was the second time in less than an hour that I'd been called a genius. I decided I might get to like this accomplishment stuff.

"I'll get the boys in maintenance right on it. Now get back to work on that pink tree!"

In the real world, praise only lasted until the next task had to be done.

It was the last tree to trim and I was in charge of it. I showed Kelly the sketches and we got to work, the sound system keeping us company, as usual, and I was singing my heart out despite how I knew Kelly felt about it.

I was hanging a particularly gaudy pink ornament on the tree when I realized that my voice wasn't alone anymore. I stopped singing and stared at Kelly in amazement. As soon as she noticed me staring at her she stopped singing and burst out laughing.

"Okay," she said. "You've caught me with your fairy dust, Snow White."

"I think you're mixing your fairy tales."

"The point is, you're a bad influence. The next thing you know I'll be ringing the bell for the Salvation Army."

At midnight, I climbed the ladder to arrange the broach and tennis bracelets on the top of the tree.

"Perfect," Kelly said.

When I climbed down the ladder, I stood back to take a look. I sighed. It really was perfect.

When I got home that night, there was another note from Quint: "I kept my promise. You'll be able to walk on the new floor by tomorrow evening. I'll be over around five to move the refrigerator back in. Love, Q."

I reached around the corner of the kitchen door and flicked on the light. The floor was indeed finished. And it was beautiful.

I was excited despite the fact that this would be the only turkey I'd ever roast in this beautiful new kitchen. I tried not to think about that part of it, though. There were a lot of "last times" still to come in the house. But tomorrow, Gordy would be home and we would be together. It felt good knowing that the life I was used to would be back again—even if it was just for a little while.

CHAPTER 8

"I don't know about you," Moira said, "but I miss Quint."

Since I still couldn't walk on the kitchen floor, Moira had brought over a pot of coffee and a box of Danish pastries on Wednesday morning.

"I, for one," she went on, "was hoping he was going to take forever to finish that floor."

"I have six people coming for turkey tomorrow. He had to finish the floor."

"I would have gladly taken all of them with Stan and me to the club for Thanksgiving dinner just to be able to watch I'm Your Handy Man work for a few more days."

"He's coming for dinner tomorrow. Cancel your reservations and come over to ogle and eat."

Moira sighed. "Would that I could, sweetie. But for Stan, the holidays are all about chatting up new clients."

I choked on my coffee. It was hot, so luckily it didn't come out of my nose. "Sorry, but I'm having a hard time picturing Stanley chatting up anyone."

"He can talk business for hours."

"But he's so—um—" I was having trouble coming up with a word other than dull. I finally settled on, "He's so quiet."

"Yeah. I love that about him."

I raised my brows in surprise. "You do?"

Moira laughed. "I bet you've always wondered what brought us together."

"Well, actually—yes. I mean, you're so vibrant, so outgoing, so—well, *out there.*"

"It runs in my family. We never got through a family meal without an argument. Both my parents were activists—and fairly loud about it. Both my brothers were tree-huggers and vegans, which suited my parents just fine. I rebelled by rejecting Birkenstocks, eating burgers and bringing Republicans home for dinner. Which, of course, added to the noise level at the dining room table. When I met Stan, I was ready for some peace and quiet. Seriously—his laconism was like an aphrodisiac to me. I seduced the poor guy with everything I had."

I laughed, imagining that it would have taken a lot just to get Stan to notice that someone was trying to seduce him.

"I knew that with Stan I'd never get a middle of the night call to come bail him out for chaining himself to a nuclear power plant. I always knew where he'd be at night. In the basement with his trains."

We both laughed at that. But as I started sipping my coffee again, I thought about all the reasons women have for marrying. Moira married for peace and quiet and the kind of stability that would still allow her to be a little bit wacky. My mother married because of the mores of the fifties. If you got pregnant, you got married. My guess would be that Amy Westcott got married so she could raise perfect children. Bonnie? Bonnie and Tommy Williams might actually be a love match, as odd as that might seem given their bowling pin physiques and Bonnie's penchant for wearing sweatshirts with appliqued animals on them. They still held hands when they walked down the street.

And then there was me.

Why had I married Roger? Given the way I'd been living for the past ten years, could it be that I got married so I could be taken care of while I played house? Had I craved what I considered a conventional life in the suburbs that much when I'd been twenty-two? I reached for another pastry. What a dismal idea, I thought as I nibbled. If it was true, it made crumbs of any leftover feelings of nobility I still clung to about my choices in life. And worse yet, it meant that maybe I'd never really loved Roger at all. Had it been the image I'd fallen for?

"So when is Gordy due?" Moira asked.

I tried to drown out my thoughts with another sip of coffee before I answered.

"He doesn't have any classes today so I expect him by late afternoon. I just wish I could be here when he gets home. I'm a little nervous about him seeing the kitchen for the first time."

Moira flapped a hand. "Teenage boys don't notice things like that."

"You're probably right. I'm worrying for nothing." I sighed with happiness. "I just can't wait to see him again. Can't wait to cook him breakfast again. To—"

The cordless sitting on the dining room table rang. It was Gordy.

"Honey, I was just talking about you," I told him.

"Look, Ma, I decided not to come home tonight."

"Wh—what?" I managed to croak out.

"I can catch a ride with a guy going to Green Bay first thing tomorrow morning."

"Did your ride today fall through?"

"Nah, I'm just too beat to make it today. I need some REM sleep pretty bad."

There was that weariness in his voice again. "Gordy, are you all right? You're not coming down with something, are you? Maybe you should go to the clinic—"

"Christ, Ma, would you not make a big deal out of this? I just need some sleep. I'll be there in plenty of time to mash the potatoes. I gotta go—I forgot to juice up my phone so I'm about to lose you anyway."

"Well, for heaven's sake, recharge it before you leave so we can be in touch while you're on the road tomorrow. They're talking snow flurries."

"Will do, Ma. Catch ya tomorrow."

"Call me from the road," I rushed to get out, but he'd already hung up.

Moira played the good friend, consoling me, but my disappointment rode shotgun as I drove to work that day.

Luckily, everybody in the department was in a terrific mood. The windows were finished. The mutilated penguin actually looked cute, like the runt of the litter. Kelly and I set up the last of the ceramic Christmas villages in Winter Wonderland and Dora treated everyone to Chinese delivery then sent us all home at nine o'clock as promised, wishing us a happy Thanksgiving and extracting promises from me and Kelly that we'd be there bright and early Friday morning.

I was exhausted, my dissipated energy no longer refueled by the thought of my son coming home that night. I passed a grocery store and on impulse pulled in. I managed to snag the last of the pumpkin and apple pies. It would be the first Thanksgiving I hadn't made my own. But it was also going to be the first Thanksgiving we were having Jell-O and yams with marshmallows so I figured what the hell.

At home, the refrigerator was back in place. The kitchen looked beautiful. But it was empty. I stowed away the pies and headed upstairs to change into my pajamas. Then I went back down to the kitchen to begin breaking up the bread for the stuffing all by myself.

When I woke up Thanksgiving morning it was snowing lightly. I jumped out of bed and hustled over to the window. Flurries? Were they only flurries? Ordinarily snow on Thanksgiving morning would have sent my heart soaring. But this year it was different. This year my baby was out there on the road.

I ran downstairs and turned on the TV, searching for a weather report. Parades. All over the dial. I rushed to the front door. Yes! I was pretty sure the *Milwaukee Journal-Sentinel* put out a holiday edition and there it was, on the front porch like a faithful friend.

Flurries, it said in the little weather box on the front page. In fact, what it really said was *chance* of flurries. I lifted the curtain on the front door and looked out. "Flurries," I said happily to myself. And if there was only supposed to be a chance of them, then that meant that this was probably as bad as it was going to get.

I went into the kitchen to make a pot of coffee. As I stood at the sink waiting for the coffee carafe to fill I felt the chill of the new tiles on the bottom of my feet. By the time I'd measured out the coffee, I was shivering. The old linoleum had never been more than comfortably cool, even in January. I flipped the switch on the coffeemaker and ran back upstairs for a pair of thick socks. Then I got the bird out of the refrigerator and proceeded to get to work. I wanted the house to be filled with the smells of Thanksgiving when Gordy walked through the front door.

By four o'clock I was dressed in my faithful Donna Karan. Parsley, sage, rosemary and thyme filled the air. But Gordy still hadn't walked through the door.

It wasn't that late, I told myself as I stood at the living room windows. It was a six-hour drive. Maybe they'd stopped at a truck stop for a burger. Maybe they hadn't gotten as early a start as they'd hoped.

This is silly, I told myself. Just call his cell and find out what's going on. Why was I so reluctant to do so? Okay, so the kid had a worried mother. It was unlikely to scar his psyche for life if I called and asked where the hell he was at four o'clock on Thanksgiving afternoon.

The cordless was already in my hand, of course, since I'd been wrestling with the urge for over an hour. But three wasn't four. I punched out his number.

No answer.

Okay, this was way worse than if I hadn't tried calling at all.

I decided to put on some music and set the table. Damn good thing I had guests coming, I thought as I folded the linen napkins I hadn't used in years, or I'd be chewing the woodwork about now. As it was, the sound of Johnny Mathis decking the halls and the simple pleasure of setting a beautiful table lulled me enough to stave off a panic attack.

Waiting, after all, was a mother's worst nightmare. Gordy hadn't kept me waiting very often but I knew the drill. Worrying wouldn't keep the worst from happening. So, generally, a good mother pretended not to worry.

I pretended not to worry while I checked for spots on the water goblets.

I pretended not to worry while I basted the bird and peeled potatoes.

I was still pretending not to worry when Stuart and Kelly arrived.

"My God, did Dolly Madison live on this block?" Stuart asked.

"Stuart!" Kelly admonished.

"Seriously, girls. I think I just saw Benjamin Franklin back his SUV out of the driveway next door."

"It's a great neighborhood," Kelly insisted as she glared at Stuart.

I laughed. "Don't be too hard on him, Kelly. One year the woman across the street actually served Thanksgiving dinner in a reproduction of a pilgrim costume."

"See?" Stuart said smugly.

I took their coats and hung them on the coat tree near the door.

"Oh, how cute," Kelly said when she saw the living room.

"Never mind cute. I'm following those divine smells to the kitchen. My yam and marshmallow casserole deserves to join the ranks of the well seasoned."

"I'm afraid my Jell-O mold didn't exactly unmold like it was supposed to," Kelly said with a grimace. She lifted the lid on the covered dish she was carrying. I tried to imagine what the mold had been.

"It was supposed to be a fish."

"Ah." It looked more like what usually got left on the dock. "Tell you what, why don't we just dump the whole thing into a cut glass bowl and forget that it's supposed to look like anything?"

Kelly looked relieved. "I knew you'd come up with something," she said as we swung through the kitchen door.

"Shush, Kell," Stuart said. "The girl will get a swelled head. Miss Dora couldn't stop singing her praises about that damned pink tree."

"You're just jealous cause you didn't think of it," Kelly accused as I handed her a crystal bowl that my mother had given Roger and me for our fifth anniversary.

Stuart flapped his hand. "Oh, who am I kidding. Guilty as charged."

As I listened to my coworkers, I started to glow inside. Praise and a paycheck. Here I was, over forty, and I was just starting to discover the satisfaction there could be in getting paid to do a job. I'd chaired plenty of PTA events, volunteered my time all over Whitefish Cove, and I'd felt good about it. But this was something totally different. It made me feel so—so adult.

And wasn't it about time? I thought, then burst out laughing at myself.

Stuart and Kelly looked at each other, then at me.

"Inside joke," I said between sputters.

"Speaking of inside jokes," Stuart said, "you know that guy Tony in men's better clothing?"

"No," I said.

"He's the one with that long ponytail that looks vaguely mobish," Kelly offered helpfully.

"That's the one," Stuart went on. "Well, last Thursday—"

Kelly and I were a rapt audience when the kitchen door swung open and Gordy came in, dragging an enormous laundry bag behind him.

"Gordy!" I exclaimed, leaving the huddle to throw my arms around him. "I've been so worried!"

"It doesn't look like it," he said.

"What? Well, I—" Hell, I was speechless. Wasn't he always telling me not to worry? And now he sounded, well, a little surly that I hadn't been dutifully at my post wringing my hands by the windows. "Gordy," I said when I'd recovered, "this is Stuart and Kelly. We work together at Grant's. Guys, this is my son."

"Hi," Kelly said.

"Pleased to meet you," Stuart added.

"Yeah. Hi," my son the scholar said as he turned to heave the laundry bag in the general direction where the breakfast nook used to be. He stopped midheave. "What the fuck happened to the breakfast nook?"

Stuart and Kelly looked at each other. "We'll be in the living room," Stuart said sotto voce.

"Well, that was a little rude," I said when they'd left.

"Ma, what did you do to this place? It doesn't even look like home anymore."

"Oh—just a little redecorating." Moira apparently was wrong. Some teenage boys did notice.

"What the hell for? And why didn't you at least warn me?"

"Well, you haven't exactly been easy to get a hold of lately, you know." Was this moody kid, with his hair on end like he'd just gotten out of bed, with his clothes looking like he'd slept in them, was this my son? "Look," I said, "why don't we start over? Come here and give me a hug."

He did, but with more reluctance than I seemed to remember in the past. He pushed away before I was ready to let go and went over to the refrigerator to open the door.

"I'm starving," he said.

"Well, we'll eat as soon as everyone's here."

"Everyone? Who else is coming besides Grandma? And who are those two people in there?" he asked, his chin jerking toward the door to the dining room.

"I told you—Stuart and Kelly. They're coworkers. They didn't have any place to go for the holiday, so I invited them here. Grandma's coming, too, and so is Quint Mathews—the guy who put in the new floor."

"What's he coming for? Something wrong with the floor—except for the fact that it's red?"

I folded my arms. "No. There is absolutely nothing wrong with the floor—including the color. I asked Quint to join us, that's all."

"Shit, I might as well be back at the dorm."

I was opening my mouth to ask him if that was the kind of language I was paying IU to teach him when the doorbell rang.

"I'm going to go get that. Please adjust your attitude by the time I get back."

It was Quint and, bless him, he was bearing wine. Four bottles of it. I quickly introduced him to Kelly and Stuart, then confiscated the wine and headed to the kitchen.

Gordy was in the refrigerator, trying to sneak some of the whipped cream off the pumpkin pie. This, at least, was recognizable.

"Hey, fingers out of that pie," I said.

"I gotta tell you, Ma, this doesn't taste as good as yours usually does."

"That's because I bought it. What with working, I didn't really have time to do all the things—"

"You couldn't bake a pumpkin pie but you invited all these extra people?"

"Well, they all brought things—"

He peeked under the covered dishes in the refrigerator. "Swell, weird dishes from weird people. What did I expect?"

I felt a jab of hurt. "They aren't weird, Gordy. They're my friends. And I expect you to treat them as well as I've always treated your friends."

The door came swinging open. Great. Bernice had arrived.

"Come give Grandmother a kiss," she said to Gordy, who obliged without the least display of surliness.

"Who are all those oddities in there?" Bernice asked after she'd hugged my son.

"See?" Gordy said.

I gasped again, but it was getting old. So instead, I went over to the junk drawer and started digging for the corkscrew. Seriously in need of a glass of wine, I was making enough racket, pushing batteries, old pocket calendars and cards of thumbtacks around for my mother to finally sigh loud enough to be heard.

"What *are* you looking for?"

"I can't find the damn corkscrew," I said.

I pushed open the kitchen door and yelled, "Has anyone out there got a corkscrew?"

Quint came to the rescue with one of those Swiss Army knives that do a hundred manly things. I downed the first glass of wine like someone was holding a gun to my head. When I sat the glass on the counter, my mother was already focusing on Quint.

"So you're I'm Your Handy Man," she said.

"Yes, ma'am," Quint said. "May I pour you a glass of wine?"

"Please," she said, her voice smooth as silk. Quint filled her glass and she put her arm through his. "Now why don't you tell me all about this painting technique you used?" she asked as she led him out of the kitchen.

Gordy rolled his eyes. "This is too surreal for me. I feel like I'm in one of those stupid family comedies about the holidays going all wrong." He took off out the kitchen door and I was left alone again.

I refilled my glass with wine, vowing to sip it this time. Maybe I was being insensitive to Gordy's feelings. Things were changing. And they were changing fast. And it was all my fault—it was my mistake. Maybe it was natural for Gordy to be angry. But, on the other hand, hadn't I raised him to be a better sport than this?

Kelly came into the kitchen. "Need any help in here?"

"Just hide the knives," I said.

"Your kid's kind of pissed that we're here, huh?"

"God, Kelly, I'm sorry. I don't know what's gotten into him."

"That's okay. Sullen is usually just a phase. Want me to flirt with him? See if I can improve his mood?"

The mother in me felt appalled at the idea. But the coworker/friend in me wanted to laugh out loud.

Stuart entered the kitchen. "Lauren, is there anything like a cocktail shaker in this piece of Americana you call home? The way things are shaping up, I could use a decent vodka martini."

I handed him a tall piece of Tupperware, showed him where the vodka and vermouth were, and told him to make do then went back to peeling potatoes.

"You look like you could use one yourself, girlfriend."

"I'm on my second glass of wine. If I switch to something stronger now, I may end up carving something other than the turkey."

"Oh, don't let it worry you. Kids are always a pain in the ass on holidays. At least, I know I was. Weren't you?"

I stopped midpotato. "I'm not sure I was allowed to be a pain in the ass," I said just as Bernice came back in.

"Baby, you were the biggest pain in the ass from the time you turned ten until—well, come to think of it—"

Stuart grinned from ear to ear while my mother commandeered a bottle of wine and went back to the living room.

"Your mother is a hoot. And what a dish. She looks really familiar, too."

I wasn't in the mood to discuss my mother's pedigree. I put the kettles of potatoes and carrots on to boil, wiped my hands, sent Stuart into the living room and headed up to Gordy's room.

I didn't bother to knock. He was sitting at his computer, just closing out a screen and signing off the Internet as I came in.

"Fuck, Ma, since when don't you knock?"

"Since when is 'fuck' every other word out of your mouth?"

"I've been living in a dorm full of eighteen-year-old guys. What do you expect?"

"I expect an apology."

He stared at me for a few, long defiant seconds.

Finally, I sat at the foot of the bed, where I'd sat so many times before under just as many circumstances. "Can you see at all how you're behaving like a spoiled brat?" I asked him.

He stared for a moment more, then looked away. "Things just aren't how I expected them to be, Ma."

I had a feeling he wasn't just talking about the kitchen floor or the breakfast nook. Maybe I seemed as changed to him as he did to me. There were new people in my life. A job. I was beginning to move on. Even more so than Gordy knew.

I felt a wave of love and protection wash over me. I'd intended to tell him about the house this weekend. If only he'd come home last night like he was supposed to, we'd have had time alone, a buffer zone in which we could have reconnected. Gordy was used to being the focus of my attention. Instead, I had a house full of people and a turkey in need of basting.

"Gordy, I've got to get back to the kitchen. Please come downstairs. Be nice to the people. In a few hours, it will all be over."

Matters improved once we were all gathered round the table, the tapers flickering, the hot food being passed. Kelly said that her family in Minnesota always said grace on Thanksgiving. Quint offered to do the honors and gave a simple prayer of Thanksgiving that he said had been in his family for generations.

My mother gamely took a portion of Kelly's Jell-O when it was passed her way, ditto Stuart's yam casserole, due mostly, I believe, to the fact that she was sitting between Quint and Stuart and getting plenty of attention. Gordy, I noticed, stayed with my mashed potatoes, gravy, stuffing and veggies. But he did make small talk with Kelly about college and music. By the time everyone was in the living room with coffee and pie, I started to clear the table and felt like we were home free.

I was rinsing dishes when my mother came into the kitchen to refill the silver coffeepot.

"Darling, your handyman is adorable. I still say—"

"Mother!" I hissed.

"Okay, I'll change the subject. Is Stuart gay?"

I almost dropped the gravy boat.

"Well, mother, I'm sure I don't know. I mean, I rarely discuss sex with my coworkers. Why do you ask?"

She shrugged. "Just curious. You don't get any gaydar from him?"

I thought about it. Did I even have gaydar? There wasn't much call for it on Seagull Lane. "I don't think I inherited that gene, mother."

"Well, you know, New York, the fashion industry, it's more of a learned trait than an inherited one."

"I'll ask Kelly. She might know if—"

Before I could finish my sentence, Stuart came rushing into the kitchen.

"I know who you are!" he exclaimed to my mother. "Bernie Blondell! *The* model of the late fifties and early sixties. Am I right?"

Bernice graced him with one of her more beautiful smiles. "You're right."

"I knew it!"

Stuart rushed out of the room again, seemingly to gloat to the rest of the guests that he'd figured out who Bernice was.

My mother and I turned to look at each other.

"Gay," we both said at the same time, then burst out laughing.

My mother and I, laughing together in the kitchen. Only one of the reasons, I thought, that this Thanksgiving would stay in my memory for a long, long time.

CHAPTER 9

At eight o'clock the next morning, I was eating toast while standing at the kitchen sink when Gordy came shuffling into the room.

"What's for breakfast?" he asked sleepily.

"Whatever you can find, sweetie. I've got to get to work."

"Work? But it's the Friday after Thanksgiving. Who works the Friday after Thanksgiving?"

"Temps at Grant's Department Store, that's who."

"I don't get it. Aren't you supposed to be pampering me or something? Your only child, home for the first time from the cold cruel world?"

My mommy antennae quivered. "*Is* it cold and cruel?"

"I'm kidding, Ma."

Suddenly, I wasn't so sure.

"It's just that after putting up with the crazy trio yesterday, I deserve some pancakes or something."

"Honey, I would love nothing better than to stay home and make you pancakes for breakfast, but I can't. I have to work."

His mouth dropped open like he'd never heard me say the word before. Which, in this context, he really hadn't. It's not like I'd been idle, but in my years of charity and community work, I would have been careful not to schedule anything on a day that Gordy had off school.

"Close your mouth, honey. I assure you, millions of women do it and their children—even ones younger than you—survive."

I meant it to be funny. Gordy didn't even crack a smile. I looked at the clock. My son had to pick the biggest shopping day of the year to lose his sense of humor.

I pulled out a kitchen chair and sat. "Gordy, the fact is, things have changed since you started school."

"You're telling me," he muttered.

"I now have to support myself. Which means I need this job." This wasn't the time, nor was there time, to tell him that the house was being sold. But I figured telling him that I had to work to support myself was a start. I explained that my spousal maintenance had stopped when he'd started college and that that had been part of his father's and my agreement. Then I pushed back my chair and stood. "I really have to get going, but if you've got questions, I'll be only too happy to answer them later. Meanwhile, you won't starve. There's cereal, there are bagels, and there are plenty of leftovers. What are your plans for today?"

He shrugged. "Probably call some of the guys."

I fetched my purse from the dining room table, took a couple of twenties out, and handed them to Gordy. "Have a good time, okay? I'll be home by seven. How about pizza and a movie?"

He took the twenties. "Sure. Thanks, Ma."

I kissed him on the forehead. "Gotta run. See you around seven."

I'd never been on the other end of the biggest shopping day of the year before. I was used to being one of the teeming masses. Now I had to hustle just to keep up with them. I divided my time between replenishing ornaments on trees as shoppers continued to denude them, wrapping ornaments in glittery tissue to stuff into Grant's signature gift boxes, and trouble shooting all over Winter Wonderland.

A seven-year-old girl busted a snow globe. An elderly lady nearly fell into the angel tree trying to retrieve a pink feather angel from a top branch. A man bought one hundred of the same ornament and wanted them all boxed separately. By quitting time, my feet were killing me and my Christmas spirit felt like it was going to take a holiday for the duration. But as soon as I walked out onto Wisconsin Avenue, everything changed.

The air was crisp and dry and there were still people milling about, looking at the display windows. Wreaths lit with fairy lights hung from the old-fashioned lampposts that lined the avenue and lighted garland was strung from lamppost to lamppost at every intersection. The sound of a Salvation Army bell ringer mixed with the sound of a group of singing carolers in front of the penguin window. There was a vendor selling roasted chestnuts and another selling hot chocolate. I heard the clop of horse hooves and turned in time to see a white carriage pulled by a white horse stop in front of the grand old Pfister Hotel across the street.

How I wished I'd asked Gordy to meet me downtown. I could have shown him some of the work I was doing. We could have looked at the windows together after buying bags of roasted chestnuts to keep our hands warm, just like we had when Gordy was younger—just as my mother and I had so many years ago.

Roger had been right when he'd said that I wanted one last Christmas in the house with Gordy for myself. I wanted Gordy to be standing next to me right now, his hand in mine, for myself, too. Gordy, I was pretty sure, wouldn't be caught anywhere near this spot on this night—especially with a mother who still wanted to hold his hand.

I was getting pizza and a movie with him. It would have to be enough.

But when I got home from work there was a note on the table from Gordy. He'd been invited out for dinner with his father and the aerobics instructor. And after that, he was meeting some of the guys from high school to shoot hoops.

My disappointment warred with the feeling that I was being punished for having to work that day—for being a less than perfect mother.

But hadn't Bernice just recently told me that her grandson didn't have a neurotic bone in his body? Gordy, as far as I knew, wasn't the passive-aggressive type. But what did I really know? If I was keeping things from Gordy, couldn't he be keeping things from me?

When was I going to tell him about the house?

When was I going to confront him with the lie he'd told his father?

Was I protecting myself as much as I was protecting Gordy? And did that come under the heading of illusion or delusion?

I decided it would be easier to tackle his laundry than wrestle with that question. But folding his underwear and matching his socks wasn't exactly the thrill I remembered. As the lonely evening wore on, I resisted the urge to jump in the car and head down to the high school's outdoor basketball court. Luckily, I wasn't yet desperate enough to humiliate my son in public.

I was still awake, pretending to read, when he came in around midnight.

"Hey, Ma."

"Hi," I said, trying to sound cheerful but not succeeding. Gordy didn't seem to notice.

"I'm starved. How about a turkey sandwich?"

I jumped up like a puppy eager for the attention of its owner, all the while thinking I should really be saying something sassy like "you know where the bread is." Fat chance. I even cut the sandwich kitty-corner.

"I can't get used to the kitchen being like this," he said when I put the sandwich and a glass of milk in front of him at the table then returned to the counter to make another sandwich for myself.

"Well, maybe if you spent a little time here," I said before I could stop myself.

Gordy groaned. "Don't tell me you're pissed that I met the guys?"

"Actually, no," I answered rather primly, as I sat across from him. "I'm *pissed* because you changed our plans about dinner without consulting me."

"Hey, when Dad called, I figured it was the lesser of two evils, you know? A short Friday night dinner as opposed to having to spend a bigger chunk of the weekend with him and his current bimbette."

"Gordy," I admonished, "that's no way to talk about a woman who is very important in your father's life."

"Yeah, she goes with the new Porsche."

Okay, I did laugh at that, but I felt bad about it, which I figured cancelled out the sin of merriment at Tiffany's expense.

"Does that mean that I'll see a little more of you tomorrow?"

"Ma," he said with the exaggerated patience one might show a mental patient, "it's not my fault you had to work today."

I decided not to point out that it wasn't my fault, either. Instead I said, perhaps a little too brightly, "Well, I'm not working tomorrow or Sunday so I hope we get to spend some time together. Maybe starting with some oatmeal pancakes for breakfast?"

I was treated to a sound of pleasure coming from Gordy's

throat, which in this time of drought was like an icy-cold soda. "You know what I'd really like to do tomorrow, Ma? I'd like to lie around in my sweats, eat home cooking, maybe play a few board games. You know, like we used to do when I was a kid and home sick from school? I guess that sounds kind of dumb, huh?"

"I think it sounds terrific. I could use a day like that myself."

"Cool." He ate the rest of his sandwich in one bite, washed it down with milk, and stood. "Night, Ma," he said as he came over to kiss me.

"Night, Gordy," I said.

After Gordy had gone to bed, I sat on in the living room, wondering if we'd gone around the block that quickly. Were things back to normal again? I heard the furnace kick in and saw the curtains at the windows stir slightly as the warm air was forced out of the old registers set in the baseboards beneath them.

I remembered Roger and I arguing when I'd been sewing those curtains. I'd wanted to make them long enough to cover the ugly metal grates, but he'd insisted on a shorter length because the longer ones would block too much heat.

I hoped that wasn't what I was doing with Gordy tonight— adding some window dressing so I couldn't see the imperfections.

Saturday morning brought a chilling winter wind and more snow flurries along with the oatmeal pancakes. Gordy watched cartoons while he ate. His appetite was good and so were his spirits. He even helped chop vegetables after we'd decided that some turkey dumpling soup would be good on such a cold, blustery day. While the soup simmered, we played a few games of Scrabble, which I won, and a couple of hands of poker, which I lost to the tune of twenty bucks. When Gordy fell asleep on the sofa after eating three bowls of soup, I baked a couple of batches of cookies and packed them for him to take back to Bloomington.

By the time Gordy's ride came to pick him up on Sunday morning, I felt we'd reestablished our old, familiar relationship. He still needed a haircut, and he still looked too thin but I felt "safe at home" once again.

Until, that is, I talked to Moira a few hours later. We were sipping hot cider in front of Moira's fireplace, she on one of the long, white sofas, me across from her on the other. I'd gone over there in a decent mood and the atmosphere should have enhanced it, but Moira's voice was drowning out the crackling of the fire.

"What do you mean you didn't get around to asking Gordy about the lie?" she demanded.

"Just that," I said with what I hoped was finality.

"In three days you couldn't find the time to, for instance, say 'Hey, Gordy, why did you lie to your father about asking me for that hundred bucks?'"

"Hey, for all we know Roger is the one who got it wrong. Maybe Gordy never said he'd asked me for the money first."

"And maybe Santa Clause really exists," Moira quipped.

"Like you never let anything go with your kids," I said defensively.

"Sure, I let a lot of things go. You pick your battles. But I was at least honest with myself when I decided to let something go. And what about the house? Did you tell him about that?"

Moira knew me well enough to see by the look on my face that I hadn't. She picked up a red, Chinese embroidered pillow next to her and tossed it at me. "You're hopeless, you know that?"

I caught the pillow and hugged it to me. "The house isn't going on the market until after the holidays. There's time," I insisted. "I'll tell him when he comes home for Christmas."

Moira looked at me dubiously, but like all great girlfriends, she knew when to change the subject.

After I left Moira's, I sat at the window seat in my bedroom, watching the sky as the evening came on and thinking about how little time left there really was.

The fog of my breath on the cold glass gave the houses and streetlights on Seagull Lane an out-of-focus look, distorted but in a beautiful way. Was that how I preferred to see things? Is that why I couldn't be honest with myself—or Moira? I just hadn't wanted to spoil my Saturday with Gordy by discussing the money or the house. I'd wanted the day to be as soft as the world looked through my fogged-up window.

I heard a car stop at the curb below. Curious, I wiped my breath off the glass in time to see Sondra the Hawk, draped in fur, getting out of her huge black car. A smaller, duller compact car pulled up behind hers and a couple in khakis and parkas got out. I knew that no amount of hot air on cold glass was going to do anything to help this particular vision.

I jumped off the window seat and went to answer the door.

"Ms. Hawk," I said as I threw open the door. "Something I can do for you?"

"Did Mr. Campbell call you? These are the Stouts from Cleveland. They're relocating in a few months and your house sounded a lot like what they're looking for. You don't mind if we come in, do you?"

Every nerve ending in my being wanted to just slam the door in her face but the Stouts were starting to look a little nervous so I answered, "Of course not," with abundant affability. After all, it wasn't their fault that Sondra was a bird of prey. "Why don't the two of you just wander around—kitchen's in the back—while I have a word with the—um—I mean Miss Hawk?"

Once the Stouts were out of earshot, I muttered fiercely, "This house isn't supposed to be going on the market until after the holidays. And even then, you're not supposed to show it without my permission."

"Roger said it would be all right," Sondra assured me, not even bothering to hide her smarmy smile.

"Well, it's not *Roger's* call," I pointed out.

"Look," she hissed, throwing back one side of her fur coat to put a hand on the hip of her bronze-colored trousers, "the Stouts are driving back to Cleveland tonight. They're hot prospects. It would be ridiculous to miss this opportunity."

The Stouts came out of the kitchen. "Will you be redoing the kitchen floor?" Mr. Stout asked.

The Hawk gave me a sharp look. "I understood that the work in the kitchen had been completed."

"It has," I assured her. "That *is* the new kitchen floor," I told the Stouts.

They exchanged a look.

"Hmm," said Mr. Stout.

"I see," said Mrs. Stout.

The Hawk threw a vicious leer then sashayed on her three-inch heels through the dining room and pushed open the kitchen door. I told the Stouts to feel free to check out the bedrooms upstairs, then followed Sondra.

"Red?" she asked in outrage. "Roger and I agreed on something neutral."

"Too bad you and Roger didn't do the shopping."

"This is unacceptable," she exclaimed as she poked the sharply pointed toe of her shoe at the tiles.

"What's unacceptable is you showing up here unannounced on a Sunday evening on a holiday weekend."

I could hear footsteps overhead and tried to remember what condition Gordy had left his room in. Then decided it didn't matter because Sondra the Hawk and her Cleveland clients were leaving. Now.

"Since the house isn't officially on the market until after the first of the year, I'd appreciate it if you'd collect Mr. and Mrs. Cleveland, Ohio, and leave."

She glared at me. "You're tossing me out?"

I put my hands on my hips. "If I have to."

Her eyes narrowed, then she spun around and marched out of the kitchen.

Every once in a while, I thought as I heard her call to her hot prospects from the foot of the stairs, you got to kick some butt when you needed to the most.

When I went into work on Monday, Dora was already sketching out Valentine's Day ideas at her drawing board.

"The display department at Grant's, along with the devil, never sleeps," she explained. "And, speaking of the devil, how was the yam and marshmallow casserole?"

"It was fine. Thanksgiving dinner was fine. Everything was fine—"

She looked up from her sketch. "Why do I have the feeling you're leaving out the word 'except'?"

"Except I had to kick a predatory Realtor out of my house last night—"

"All Realtors are predatory. Kicking one out of one's house could be pleasurable."

I took a moment to think about it. "You're right. It was the high point of my weekend."

"And the low point?" Dora asked.

An Important Message from the Editors

Dear Reader,

Because you've chosen to read one of our fine novels, we'd like to say "thank you"! And, as a special way to say thank you, we're offering to send you two more novels similar to the one you are currently reading, and a surprise gift – absolutely FREE!

Please enjoy the free books and gift with our compliments...

Pam Powers

Peel off Seal and
Place Inside...

THE EDITOR'S "THANK YOU" FREE GIFTS INCLUDE:

▶ Two NEW Harlequin® Next™ Novels

▶ An exciting surprise gift

YES! I have placed my

Editor's "thank you" Free Gifts seal in the space provided at right. Please send me 2 FREE books, and my FREE Mystery Gift. I understand that I am under no obligation to purchase anything further, as explained on the back and opposite page.

PLACE
FREE GIFTS
SEAL
HERE

▶ DETACH AND MAIL CARD TODAY!

356 HDL EE4T   156 HDL EE4H

FIRST NAME   LAST NAME

ADDRESS

APT.#   CITY

STATE/PROV.   ZIP/POSTAL CODE

Thank You!

The Reader Service — Here's How It Works:

I sighed. "That would have been when my previously charming son came home from college with a chip on his shoulder the size of a stump."

Dora gave me a look of distaste. "I know nothing of children. Never had one and, thanks to menopause, never will."

Stuart joined us. "We're not all here to procreate," he said as he unwound an impossibly long muffler from his neck.

"Amen to that," Dora said.

"But, actually," Stuart added, "Lauren did a pretty good job with it. Her rather adorable son Gordon shows every sign of becoming civilized as soon as he starts getting laid regularly."

Dora laughed, which covered up my slight gasp. The display department at Grant's wasn't exactly the PTA where, at a moment like this, all the other mothers would be murmuring reassurances that would have nothing to do with my son's sex life.

"Anyway, Dora, you'll never guess who this one's mother is," Stuart said as he jerked his thumb my way.

"Don't make me guess, darling. I drank a rather lot of gin over the weekend."

Stuart started to quiver with excitement like a Labrador retriever eyeing a squirrel on the backyard fence. "Are you ready?" he asked to heighten the drama.

"Never mind ready. In ten seconds I won't give a damn."

"Okay—okay." He took a deep breath. "Lauren's mother is Bernie Blondell!"

It took Dora a moment. "You mean that beautiful blond model from the fifties?"

"*And* early sixties," Stuart added.

"Really?" Dora looked me over. "How interesting."

I'd had years of experience with people's reactions to how little I resembled my mother. Dora's was certainly mild enough.

"And guess what?" Stuart asked.

Dora gave him a look.

"Oh, right," he said. "The gin. I got to sit next to her at Thanksgiving dinner! She is still divinely gorgeous and utterly chic. She was wearing this—"

The in-house phone on Dora's desk rang. She picked it up. "Yes?"

We watched her face change as she listened.

"You have got to be kidding?" she asked darkly. "Seriously? The whole thing? How many pieces do you think?"

We watched her squeeze her eyes shut as she listened to the answer.

"I knew there was a reason I hated children," she muttered. "All right. Give us a while. We'll come up with something." She hung up the phone and turned back to us. "You know that five-foot ivory ceramic tree with the gold leaf trim at the entrance near accessories and costume jewelry?"

We dutifully nodded.

"Someone's cute little brat just smashed it to smithereens. We've got to come up with something to replace it. Preferably something unbreakable."

"I've got a date with a half dozen cashmere sweaters in one of the display windows," Stuart hurried to tell us.

"And I'm due for my tedious yearly interview with the local press," Dora said. "Kelly, as usual, is late and Lola and Sienna have classes this morning."

They both looked at me.

"I'll take care of it," I said.

I had absolutely no idea what I was doing, of course. I decided the first thing I'd do was go visit the scene of the crime so I could get an idea of how much space I needed to fill. Maintenance was still cleaning up the area where the ceramic and gold leaf Christmas tree once stood. In keeping with the posh look of the accessories and costume jewelry department, the tree had been sleekly elegant. As far as I knew, there was absolutely nothing in the storeroom that could compare.

I took some measurements and headed back through the maze of halls to the display department. Kelly was just taking off her coat.

"Has she been in, yet?" she asked.

"Yes, and she commented on your lateness again. Kelly, if I were you—"

"Yeah, yeah. I know. But, honestly, if you'd seen the guy I picked up on Water Street last night—"

"You can tell me all the twisted details later. Right now, we've got a crisis on our hands."

I told her about the demolished tree and we took the elevator down to the subterranean level beneath the display department then set off on opposite sides of the huge, cluttered storeroom to search for anything feasible enough to consider.

I strolled among headless mannequins, opened countless cartons to peer inside and crawled around the leftovers of decades worth of display windows.

"Oh, my god," Kelly called out after about half an hour. "Lauren, you'd swear it was the nineteen fifties over here. Grant's must never throw anything away."

I wove my way to the far corner of the storeroom. "Holy cow," I said as I peered over Kelly's shoulder at a jumble display pieces.

"Plastic was so—" Kelly shuddered "—*plastic* then."

"Yeah, but I bet some of this stuff is worth money. Anything retro is in right now."

I moved a huge plastic light-up Santa out of the way. "Oh, look at this! Isn't he adorable?"

"Isn't he *dusty*," Kelly answered.

And he was, but still I figured he had potential. The snowman stood about five feet high and was made of stuff that looked like a cross between angel hair and cotton batting. One of his glossy black eyes was missing, as were half of the little black pieces of plastic coal that made up his smile. But his arms, long opaque plastic tree branches, were intact. Gingerly, I picked him up and stood very still. Nothing fell off.

"You're not seriously thinking what I think you're thinking," said Kelly.

"Just help me get him out to a bigger space so we can have a better look at him."

Kelly obliged, but it was clear that she wasn't seeing it. She looked at her watch. "Listen, I've got to call this guy from last night. See if we can hook up again later. Do you mind?"

"Go for it. But if I were you—"

"I know, I know. I'll watch out for Dora."

After she left, I took inventory of Dusty the snowman.

I preformed a sex change with a couple of coats of glitter spray paint then went to the accessories department where I got permission from the department manager to take what I needed.

"Just make sure the price tags show," she said.

I used jeweled broaches for Dusty's buttons, topped her off with a pink cloche adorned with a black sequined bow and hung scads of glittery scarves from her arms. Then stood back to see how she looked. I'd left her face blank for the elegance factor but I wanted to make sure she still had a personality.

"Bravo!"

I turned around to find Dora standing there, still in her tartan cloak.

"It's marvelous, Lauren. Just marvelous. I couldn't have done better myself."

My face heated and my heartbeat jumped. "I hope you don't mind that I went ahead—"

"Thank heavens you did. I could not seem to get away from the feature reporter for that weekly that nobody reads, anyway. She kept talking to me about inspiration and color wheels." While Dora talked she walked around Dusty, eyeing her from all directions, making an adjustment here and there. "I like it," she said succinctly. "As soon as the store closes, you can put your snowman in place. Now how about you and I going out for a cup of coffee. I think we need to chat."

I was nervous as we walked down the street together. But excited, too. It was impossible not to be a little buzzed being in the company of a woman who could pull off wearing a tartan cloak and who every other person on the street seemed to know.

We turned off of Wisconsin Avenue, walked a few more blocks, and went into a little diner.

"I hope this is okay with you. I loathe those pre-fab coffee houses that are all the rage now."

"This is great," I said.

A few waitresses called out greetings and Dora returned them.

An elderly woman, her hair the color of a copper penny, ambled over.

"How are the bunions today, Nell," Dora asked her.

"Don't ask. I swear someday I'm just gonna take that big butcher knife back there and have at 'em."

"Let me know when so I can plan to eat someplace else that day," Dora admonished with a smile.

Nell laughed. "And miss out on those big tips? Not on your life. Now what'll it be, I haven't got all day."

"I adore the grilled cheese here," Dora said to me.

"Sounds good." I was relieved that I wasn't going to have to do anything as strenuous as study a menu. I was far too nervous to decide what I wanted to eat.

"Two coffees and two grilled cheese sandwiches, Nell."

Nell scribbled on her order pad and ambled off again.

"Nell started working here right after I started at Grant's. She was straight out of high school—which I figure makes her about sixty. I was fresh from college—which makes me—let's just say a few years older."

"It's hard to imagine a woman having to work as a waitress all her life."

"I know. It's damn hard work. But lots of women make a decent living from it. I worked my way through college waiting tables. I have nothing but respect for career waitresses."

I was starting to worry about where this conversation was leading. Was Dora gently breaking it to me that even though she was giving me the ax there were still jobs that I could do? I was pondering whether bunions were a work hazard or if they were an inherited affliction when Nell came over with an insulated carafe of coffee, and a couple of thick cream colored mugs.

"Sandwiches will be up in a sec," she said as she poured with a steady hand.

"Thank you, Nell," Dora said.

I wasn't surprised that the coffee was excellent. I couldn't imagine Dora Reynolds putting up with anything less.

"So," she said once she'd taken a few sips, "what are you planning on doing with the rest of your life?"

"Excuse me?" was all I could say, the question was so unexpected.

"I mean for work—a career. You majored in education but

never finished college. You don't have much work experience. What is it you think you'd like to do if you end up working until you're Nell's age?" She smiled. "Or mine for that matter."

"Actually, I think I'd like to do what I'm doing now. Only for real—you know, not as a temp? Learn more about it. Maybe take some classes."

"You don't sound sure."

"Because I didn't really know I felt that way until you asked the question just now."

"Then I'm glad I asked it."

Our sandwiches came—along with a few more wisecracks from Nell—so it was a while before I could ask Dora why she'd asked the question in the first place.

"Because, I'd like to hire you permanently. But only if you're really interested in turning it into a career."

I put down my sandwich without taking a bite. "Permanently? Really?"

"Why so surprised? Surely you know you've got a certain flair for it."

I had a flair? Me? I think I might have blushed.

"You know, kid, that babe-in-the-woods thing is a little silly on a woman your age."

I grimaced. "Sometimes I feel like a babe in the woods."

She gave a bark of laughter. "That's another thing I like about you, kid. You're not easily insulted."

Thank you, Bernice, I thought.

I told her a little bit of my story while we ate. Why I was so inexperienced, why I'd never finished college. I decided to skip my stint in marketing.

"So," she said as she wiped her fingers on a paper napkin, "what do you think? Want to come on board permanently?"

"Yes! Absolutely."

"Great. I'll call your agency and find out the terms for hiring you," she said as she laid down a tip that was equivalent to the check.

We studied other store windows as we walked back to work. Dora pointed out her favorite buildings and took a verbal trip down memory lane. I relished every block, every word. And, later, when I placed Dusty in her new home, I felt the pride of a mother who had just given birth.

I pulled into my driveway that night, still floating from my conversation with Dora. The lights were on at Moira's so I went over and rang the doorbell. Moira answered almost immediately, but, considering what she was wearing, I had the feeling I was interrupting something.

"Come on in," she said as the silk kimono slipped off her shoulder to reveal the strap of a matching nightgown that showed plenty of cleavage.

"Are you sure? I don't want to…I mean, if you and Stan were—"

Moira laughed. "Don't worry. Stan and I weren't at it. At least, not yet. I have been considering shimmying down to the basement to seduce him away from his trains, though, but I've got time for a little conversation."

I followed her into the living room, admiring how she was able to walk in the matching brocade slippers with three-inch heels. "Cocktail? Glass of wine?"

"Well, this is kind of a celebration. I've got good news."

"Hallelujah! I'm going to break out a bottle of the good stuff. Be right back."

I slipped off my navy peacoat and threw it over the arm of a chair, then sank into the plush, white sofa. Moira had a fire in the fireplace. It felt cheerful and warm and good. Hell, I felt cheerful and warm and good.

Moira came back with an already opened bottle of white wine and a couple of glasses.

"Stan gets a case of this stuff from a client every year. It's absolutely heavenly. Just the right balance between dry and sweet," she said as she filled our glasses.

All I know is that the first sip tasted really good so I took another.

Moira sat on the other end of the sofa and curled her legs under her. She's one of the few women I know who really look good doing this sort of thing.

"Now, tell me—what's your good news?"

I took a deep breath. "I've been offered a permanent position in the display department at Grant's."

"Girlfriend, that is fantastic! Let's drink to it."

We clinked glasses then drained them.

"You accepted it, right?" she asked.

"Are you kidding?"

"Well, I wasn't sure. You've been taking all those computer workshops—"

"Which I royally suck at. To tell you the truth, until Dora asked me what I intended to do for the rest of my life, I really hadn't thought about turning this job into a career. But when she told me I had flair and that she wanted me—Moira, it was like it all suddenly became clear. *This* is what I want to be when I grow up."

Moira didn't look as pleased as I'd thought she would by my announcement. "Okay," she said, "let's drink to that because I think you're going to need more wine in you to hear my lecture."

I frowned. "You don't think it's a good idea?"

"I think it's a terrific idea. But I'm getting a little tired of all these self-references about you being immature or a child or something."

"But you know how I've been feeling since I screwed up my dates on the divorce settlement."

"Shit, girlfriend, everyone makes mistakes. So here is to *choices*—good and bad."

We clinked glasses again and drank some more.

"You know what Dora said over lunch? She said the babe-in-the-woods act on someone my age was a little silly."

Moira laughed heartily, her impressive breasts jiggling against the silk of her gown. "I think I like this broad. Let's drink to her next."

We did—and to several other things—then I decided that it was high time Moira got on with her seduction.

"Thanks for the wine—and the honesty," I said as she walked me to the door.

"Oh, look," Moira pointed out, "it's Amy and Bonnie, probably coming home from a crystal party."

Despite the fact that the night was not mild—and neither was Moira's lingerie—she stepped out on her front porch with me.

"Hi, girls!" she called out, waving in a way that she knew would make that kimono slip again.

"Hi!" Bonnie called back with a smile while Amy just stood there with her mouth open. Bonnie extracted a couple of bags from Amy's trunk, said something to Amy, then gave us a nod as she headed for her house.

Amy was still unloading the trunk when her husband Chuck came out of the house, ostensibly to help her with the packages, but since he wasn't known for his gallantry I had a feeling that he had seen Moira from the window and wanted a closer look.

"Well, hi there, Chuckie!" Moira sang out.

"Hi, neighbor!" Chuck returned heartily.

Moira stepped farther onto the porch steps and lifted her face—and her breasts—skyward. "Gorgeous night, isn't it?" she asked as the night wind tossed her lingerie and her hair.

"You bet," Chuck agreed. You could see his goofy grin in the glow of the streetlight.

"You're really terrible, you know that?" I said under my breath.

"Hell," Moira muttered, "someone has to be terrible on this godforsaken street or we'd all die of boredom."

Amy, apparently having had enough of this spectacle, shoved a huge box at Chuck and pushed him toward the house.

"Nighty-nite," Moira said with a little wave of her fingers.

Looking over his shoulder, Chuck nearly tripped on the steps. Amy's mouth started going but luckily we couldn't hear what she was saying.

"That should keep us from being invited to any more crystal, home decor or candle parties for a few months," Moira predicted when the couple had disappeared into their house.

"If you actually got naked, possibly we could skip the block party, too."

"Maybe when the weather is warmer," she said.

I had a terrible feeling she wasn't kidding.

CHAPTER 10

It was the tenth of December and as I opened the front door to get the morning mail, I was all too aware of the Christmas decorations on Bonnie's and Amy's houses across the street.

Amy's colonial could have only been inspired by Martha Stewart. Real pine swags were wrapped around the porch columns, genuine holly entwined in the cedar wreaths that adorned the front door and every window—even the second story ones. I'd tried for years to catch someone hanging those but Moira said that Amy simply rode her broom—handmade, of course—up to the second story on the first moonless night in November.

The decorations on Bonnie's Victorian were less Martha and more discount store. Plastic light-up Santa and snowman, plastic bells in the windows, plastic bow on the wreath on the door and on the lamppost next to the sidewalk. It'd been the same ever since her teenage boys had been little.

Even Moira had outdone me this year with an electric brass candle in every window of her Tudor and a huge wreath adorned with gold fruit hung on the front door.

I usually hired someone to hang lighted garland around the windows and porch roof but this year I'd decided I couldn't afford it. Every extra cent I made was going into a fund for the first month's rent and a security deposit on an apartment. My small, undecorated wreath looked a little lonely hanging all by itself on the front door.

I shut the door against the December freeze and shuffled through the mail. Catalogues. Requests for money. Hello—my credit card bill. I'd been good lately so I was feeling no sense of dread at all when I tore it open and pulled it from its envelope. My eyes ran over the usual—payment date—balance—payment—

Whoa. My gaze was pulled back to the balance like a couple of nails to a magnet. It was several hundred dollars more than it should have been. And the payment was twice as much as I'd budgeted for. I took the bill into the kitchen with me, and sat down at the table. I ran my finger along the list of charges.

Why would there be a charge of several hundred dollars from an Internet site that sold electronics?

I blinked. Oh no. Not Gordy. Please, I pleaded silently, don't let it be that Gordy took my credit card while he was home for Thanksgiving.

I bounced up and ran for my purse where it hung on the newel post in the front hall. I felt inside for my wallet, extracted it, opened it. My credit card was still there. I heaved a sigh of relief and took the credit card back with me to the kitchen. The fact that the credit card had still been in my wallet didn't change the fact that someone had used the account to do some Internet shopping.

Gordy could have taken the card out of my wallet and used it when he was home for the holiday. I checked the date. No. The purchase had been made only a week ago. Could someone at Grant's have gone into my purse and copied down my credit card number? The thought made me a little sick. I couldn't go into work thinking that. So, was it easier to think that it was Gordy?

No, I decided. It was just more plausible.

"Damn it," I muttered as I took a sip of my coffee. It had grown tepid and tasted bitter. Like the pot needed cleaning.

Just another of my mistakes, I thought. How could I be hard on Gordy when he screwed up if—

"Oh, fuck it," I muttered, startling myself out of my usual self-deception. "Not cleaning out a coffeepot isn't in the same league with using someone's credit card without permission."

I went into the living room, picked up the cordless and punched out Gordy's cell phone number. I knew he'd be in class and I'd have to leave a message, but I didn't care. I wasn't letting this issue go another minute.

Much to my surprise, on the fourth ring my son sleepily answered.

"Yeah?" he said with all the enthusiasm of a corpse.

"Why are you still in bed?" I asked him. "Are you sick?"

There was just a moment's hesitation and the faint rustling of bed covers before he answered. "Uh—no. My first class got cancelled. Prof has the flu. Uh—so I thought I'd, you know, sack-in."

It sounded reasonable enough, except that suspicion was running like adrenaline through my veins.

"Well, I'm glad I caught you," I said, trying to keep all anger out of my voice. "Because there's something we need to discuss."

"Yeah? Like what?"

"Like a little matter of a six hundred dollar charge on my account."

There was complete silence on the other end of the line. This did not make me feel any better.

"Gordy?"

"Shit," he muttered. More bed sounds and I imagined him sitting up while the springs of his too-thin mattress protested. "Listen, Ma—"

"Oh, believe me," I said stiffly, "I'm listening."

"Well, I bought some stuff—"

"Define *stuff*."

He grudgingly named a few high-priced audio toys and computer accessories.

"Gordy—" I began.

"Look, Ma, before you start, let me explain. I already sent the stuff back."

I pressed my fingers against my forehead. "You what?"

"I sent it all back. I mean, I knew I'd done the wrong thing, so when the stuff got here, I sent it all back. The credits will probably show up on your next bill."

For one second I was so relieved, but this conversation wasn't over, yet. "Gordy, how did you get the account number in the first place?"

"Oh—off a receipt that was in my wallet. From some shirts and stuff."

At least he hadn't been riffling through my purse, but still—

"Gordy, don't you think you should have discussed these purchases with me before you made them?"

"Of course, Ma—I mean, it won't happen again. It was just a Saturday night and I was bored and kind of homesick and started to surf the web—you know how it is."

I smiled a little. He was homesick. "Yeah, I know how it is. When do you think you'll be able to come home for Christmas?"

When we got off the phone I felt a lot better. Although, I wasn't sure why. The fact remained, Gordy had used my credit card without my permission. And he'd basically done it to make himself feel good on a bad night. I was sitting at the kitchen table, chewing on the situation instead of toast when I heard the front door open.

"Anybody home?" Roger yelled.

I groaned. Just what I needed.

I got up to meet him halfway.

"I'd appreciate it if you'd ring the doorbell, Roger," I said, halting his progress in the dining room.

"Since when?"

"Since always," I said, deciding not to add that I'd never had the nerve to tell him. But now I knew I had spunk. "So I'd appreciate it in the future if you wouldn't just let yourself in."

Roger sighed. "Fine. Whatever. You won't be living here much longer, anyway."

The remark did not make me feel any more charitable toward him, no matter what the season. I crossed my arms. "What do you want, Roger?"

"I wanted to see how the kitchen turned out and to let you know my plans for the holidays—" he'd skirted around me and had been walking toward the kitchen while he talked. Now he stopped in the doorway and said, "Jesus Christ, Lauren. What the hell were you thinking?"

I saw no point in pretending that I didn't know he was talking about the tiles. "They were on sale," I said defensively. "Besides, I like them."

"I thought we'd decided on something neutral."

"No, you and Sondra decided on something neutral."

"Is this some kind of girlish scheme to stay in this house longer by making it as unappealing as possible? Because if it is—"

"Roger, I happen to like the red tiles and when have you ever known me to pull girlish schemes, anyway?"

I could see him thinking that over while he ran a hand over the wall. "I suppose this cost more than a mere paint job, thus eating up what you saved on the tiles."

I shook my head. "Nope. Not only that, but I got a discount for letting Quint keep the booth from the breakfast nook."

He actually looked slightly impressed.

"This type of paint finish is very trendy right now," I said, pushing my advantage. "And any discerning buyer will certainly recognize the quality of the tiles. Besides, the color red is far more adaptable than people think. And it's very in right now. Neutrals are—um—passé."

He gave me one of his looks—the one that was supposed to make me feel stupid. "I think that job decorating Christmas trees at Grant's has gone to your head."

I grinned. "Actually," I said proudly, "I've been hired to work permanently in the display department and am planning to take some classes next semester."

"I hope that means you got a raise because this house is going on the market right after the holidays. The housing market is at an all-time high, but the boom can't last forever."

What had I expected? *Congratulations?* A hearty *well done?*

Delusional, as usual. That's what Roger had said that awful day in his office.

I hated that he'd been right.

Well, I was delusional no longer. I was worried. About our son. And Roger was about to become the benefactor of my latest dose of reality.

"Before you get into the state of the stock market, Roger, there's something we need to discuss."

"Joke all you want, but if I hadn't paid attention to these things, our son would not be enjoying the education he is today."

"Yes, well, that may be true. But the thing is, Roger, your son may need some attention of another kind right now."

He looked at his watch. "If this is about what to get Gordy for Christmas, I've already bought him something."

I knew I couldn't compete so I didn't bother asking him about the gift. Besides, there were more important things at hand.

"We might have a problem," I began. Roger listened while I told him about my conversation with Gordy that morning.

"You're overreacting, as usual, Lauren," he said.

"You really think so?"

Roger shrugged. "He already knows he did the wrong thing and returned the items. What more could you ask for?"

"A little honesty, perhaps?"

"Since when does our son lie? Hasn't he always been a good kid?"

"Yes. But he's never been on his own before. Sure, he's bound to make some mistakes. Still, I think he might have lied when he asked you for that hundred dollars."

"Will you lighten up on the kid? You've certainly made your share of mistakes since I've stopped covering your ass. Now what's with this kitchen floor."

My mouth dropped open. "*Covering my ass?* That's how you saw it?"

"That's how it *was*. You sat in this house like nothing had changed. Like nothing ever would. You were so in denial that you even forgot some very important details. Like that you were supposed to be building your way to independence."

I wanted to wring his neck—even if he was right. Or maybe especially because he was right.

"The kid's eighteen, Lauren. Cut him some slack. It's not like the same hasn't been done for you. You're still here, aren't you? Now let's talk about a real problem—this floor," Roger said.

"What's wrong with the floor?" Quint asked from the doorway.

Neither of us had heard him come in. I felt my face go hot as I wondered how much he'd heard.

"And you are?" Roger asked.

"Quint Mathews," Quint said as he came forward, holding out his hand.

Roger shook it. "Roger Campbell."

"I'm the man who installed this floor. If you have a problem with the work I've done, you should talk to me."

"Are you the one who talked Mrs. Campbell into these tiles?"

The corner of Quint's mouth quirked. "No. *Lauren*—" okay, I admit it, I liked the way he emphasized my name "—talked me into them. She can be pretty persuasive."

Roger stared at Quint but seemed to be speechless—a side of Roger I had never seen before. Finally he said, "Why are you here, anyway? Do you visit all the tiles you install?"

"I brought bagels for coffee," Quint said in that deep voice as he held up a white paper bag. "Lauren likes the sesame ones with honey cream cheese spread."

I managed to hang on to my laughter until after Roger left, then I couldn't seem to stop.

Quint grabbed me around the waist as I walked past him to retrieve some mugs for our coffee. "What's so funny?" he asked, his mouth quirking again.

"Just the way Roger looked when you said 'Lauren likes the sesame ones with honey cream cheese.' I thought I'd die. I mean, I was married to the guy for almost nine years and he couldn't even tell you what my favorite ice cream flavor is."

"Chocolate marshmallow swirl with almonds," Quint said.

"Well, yes—but, how did you know?"

"I pay attention to women I'm interested in," he replied.

I smiled. "You know, I'm glad you stopped by."

"Why is that," he said as he let go of me and sprawled into one of the kitchen chairs.

"Because I was having a lousy day," I said while I tried not to notice the way his jeans tightened on his thighs. "And I don't want to have a lousy day. It's too close to Christmas."

"What would make you happy?" he asked.

The question startled me. But the answer, surprisingly, came readily. "I'd like to go out and buy a real Christmas tree. I haven't had a real tree in years. But this is the last Christmas I'll be in this house. It seems appropriate."

"Then let's do it."

For such a mundane chore, picking out a Christmas tree turned out to be a treat. Quint seemed to think nothing of driving from lot to lot until I found one that I fell in love with. On the way, we made trips through various fast food places, scarfing down fries and burgers and Chicago-style hot dogs and listening to Christmas songs on his truck radio.

When we got home it was nearly time for me to go to work.

"Thanks," I said. "That was fun."

"Yes, it was," he said in that serious way of his. Then he bent his head low, his lips hovering close to mine. I quickly turned my head and offered my cheek. The kiss was sweet but the look on his face when it was over was puzzled.

"I have to get going," I blurted.

All the way to work I wondered what might have happened if I hadn't turned my head. Would Quint have kissed me on the lips?

"Don't be ridiculous, Lauren," I muttered to myself at a stoplight. "Where else do you think his mouth was headed?"

And what would it have felt like? A little jolt went through me as I wondered if his lips would be firm or soft or moist or—

I pondered until the cars honking behind me made me realize the light had changed to green.

I was turning onto Wisconsin Avenue, into heavy traffic, and my body was reacting like a co-ed in heat.

"Get real," I told myself firmly. After all, I reminded him of his mother. I *had* to be mistaken about his intentions. By the time I parked my car in the lot where I now rented a space by the month and walked the few blocks to Grant's, I almost had myself convinced that turning my cheek was exactly what Quint had expected me to do.

Dora was waiting for me when I reached the display department.

"I need you to go up to men's designer apparel and dress a mannequin."

"But—I've never dressed a mannequin before," I said.

"They put on their pants one leg at a time like the rest of us," Stuart assured me.

"Very funny," Dora said without a trace of amusement. "Now, as I was saying. Some woman came in and bought the entire ensemble off the mannequin and it was the last of the collection so you'll need to choose something different. And if the props need changing due to the new outfit, take care of that, too." She studied me for a moment. "What's that 'deer-in-the-headlights' look for? I'm certain that you're up to the task."

"Yes, of course," I told her, deciding not to mention that if I looked wide-eyed and startled it was because of a real live man, not a mannequin.

I took the elevator up to the first floor, then the escalator up to the second floor and the men's designer apparel department and threw myself into choosing a new outfit with as much fervor as possible. Still, Quint stayed on my mind. I couldn't help but wonder what he'd look like in this sweater or that shirt or that sport jacket. It wasn't until I started to actually try to dress the mannequin that my mind was totally taken up with the job at hand.

The fiberglass brute refused to cooperate. We'd just become tangled enough to do the tango when I noticed the blue-eyed man with the cane coming up the escalator. I had just seconds to consider if wrestling with a naked male mannequin was even less dignified than passing out yogurt samples while dressed like Little Miss Muffet. I decided it was a no-win situation and buried my face in the mannequin's neck like he was my date at the ball. Unfortunately, he wasn't much of a dancer and had no idea how to lead. Which, I guess, is how I ended up tumbling to the floor with him landing on top of me.

"Ahhheeiii!" I yelled in surprise at the sudden change in position.

To my horror, the blue-eyed man was suddenly standing over me. "Are you all right?" he asked.

"Fine, thanks," I said.

"Oh—you don't care to have this naked man removed from you?"

"Well, yes, I do, but—"

He hung his cane on a nearby clothing rack, picked up my dance partner and set him aside before he held out his hand. I put my hand in his and he pulled me to my feet where I landed much too close to him.

Maybe he didn't shave often but he sure smelled good.

"Thank you," I said, deciding it was probably best not to gushingly call him my hero again.

"The pleasure was all mine," he said, then he retrieved his cane and limped off toward men's outerwear.

By the time I got my fiberglass boyfriend dressed the blue-eyed stranger was nowhere to be seen. But the sightings were starting to unnerve me. He seemed to be everywhere, as if he was invading my life. Except to be accurate I suppose I'd have to say that I was invading his, since what I'd been living until recently certainly hadn't been my real life.

The thought stilled my hands as I was straightening the mannequin's collar. This was my real life now, wasn't it? I belonged on the sidewalks, in the diners, in this store. I was creating a new life—a real life—with complexities, problems, triumphs and failures. Damn, it was scary but it sure felt good. And it sure felt real.

The next day I decided it was high time I did some Christmas shopping so I invited Moira along. We hit several stores and I took liberal advantage of my employee discount at Grant's. We stopped into a restaurant for lunch and the harried hostess seated us at a minuscule table that wouldn't even hold all our packages. We stuffed them under the table and chairs and sat down to hear the daily specials.

"Never mind the specials, sweetie," Moira instructed, "just bring us a couple of Cosmos."

"I have to work tonight," I said.

"So have some regular coffee with dessert. You'll pee the vodka out of your system in no time."

"So—um—that's two cosmos?" the waitress asked.

"Yes—now run along and get them, dear, or I'll give your tip to the Salvation Army."

I decided to hide behind my menu for a while.

"You want to split the bruchetta and the Gorgonzola tortellini?" Moira asked.

"Absolutely."

The waitress came back with our drinks and took our order then disappeared again in a hurry.

Moira took a healthy sip of her drink, breathed a long sigh, settled back in her chair and asked, yet again, "So what's new?"

"Roger met the red tiles."

"Bet I can guess how that went over."

"He also met Quint."

"I miss all the good stuff," she pouted. "So, who got the worst of it?"

"Well, I got fresh bagels and my favorite cream cheese spread so I don't think it was me." I decided not to mention the kiss on the cheek that might have been directed at another part of my face entirely.

Moira laughed. "Marvelous. I take it Roger didn't partake?"

"More like he took off."

"Then why so glum?"

I sighed. "You really want to hear this?"

"If you want to tell me, of course."

"I think Gordy might be having some problems."

"What kind of problems?"

"I wish I knew." Moira already knew about his behavior at Thanksgiving, and about the lie he'd told his father, so I told her about the unauthorized charges on my card.

She took another sip of her drink.

"Well?" I asked.

"Do you think he could be into drugs?"

I almost knocked my glass over. Drugs? I hadn't even thought of that. "Moira, you're supposed to make me feel better about this, not worse."

"Well, sweetie, I know that's my usual MO, but let's be realistic here. IU has a pretty good rep as a party school. Gordy is on his own for the first time. Smoking a little pot wouldn't be unheard of."

"If you add it up, we're talking seven hundred dollars here."

"True. But I can't see him starting on the harder stuff like cocaine or—"

"Moira! For heaven's sake. Couldn't he just have turned into an electronics junkie?"

She shrugged. "I suppose so." She thought about it for a few moments, then nodded her head. "IU is loaded with wealthy kids. He might be just trying to keep up."

Of all the possibilities, I liked that one the best. "He did say he knew he'd done the wrong thing and that he'd already taken the stuff back."

"Simple enough to check, then. Just call your credit card company and get the latest activity on the account."

Yeah, I thought as our waitress brought our food. Simple.

Moira leaned forward. "Listen, Lauren, I know you think Gordy is special, but it wouldn't be the first time a college kid smoked a little weed."

"Did your kids do drugs?"

"I suspected it a few times."

"What did you do?"

"I searched their rooms. Surprisingly, Gina was the one with the stash, not Kenny."

"Did you confront her?"

Moira shook her head and grinned. "No. I just took it and waited to see what she'd do."

"What did she do?"

Moira laughed. "Absolutely nothing. She could hardly ask me if I'd taken it without admitting that she had it. She might have accused Kenny, but if she did they kept it between themselves.

I've always suspected that she knew it was me, though, because we never had any trouble after that."

"What did you do with it?" I leaned in closer to the table. "The pot, I mean?" I whispered before taking a bite of the bruschetta.

"Stan and I smoked it. We had some pretty wild nights thanks to Gina."

I had to gulp water to keep from choking on the bruschetta. I had no problem envisioning Moira inhaling, but Stan? I surreptitiously looked around to see if anyone was listening.

"Don't worry Sweetie, I'm not carrying any contraband in my purse. That was many years ago. I am currently crime free—unless you consider tantalizing boring neighborhood men by wearing lingerie on the front porch a crime."

"To be on the safe side, we better check the village ordinances. In Whitefish Cove, you never know."

CHAPTER 11

For days after my lunch with Moira, I thought about searching Gordy's room. But it seemed like such a violation. Besides, what did I expect to find? Gordy wasn't stupid enough to leave evidence in his room when he knew he wasn't going to be home until Christmas and he also knew that it was the one time of year I usually cleaned like a maniac.

I called the credit card company to see if the returns had been made but they had no record of them. I was told that they might show up on my next statement, which meant I had another few weeks to wait.

Luckily, those were frantic days at work and that helped keep my mind occupied. We'd already started designing the Valentine's Day windows even though we still had to deal with Christmas displays. Every time an item on display sold out, we had to rethink and rework.

Evenings, I poured over the course catalogues for local colleges, making notes of what courses looked the most valuable, which ones I thought I could afford. I wrapped presents, wrote Christmas cards and decorated the house with baskets of pinecones, candles and wreaths. And, of course, unwrapped all my little ceramic snowmen and Santas from their tissue paper and placed them carefully in their designated places.

"This is it, kiddies," I told them. "I can promise you a home next year, but it won't be this one."

Okay, here I was talking to the Christmas decorations. Moira was right about me. I was truly one of the domestically demented. But I loved my little seasonal knickknacks. Each one had been chosen for its smile or the jauntiness of its hat or some other endearing peculiarity. One I'd even bought just to rescue it from being the last one on the shelf when I'd made a mad dash for a last minute gift one long ago Christmas Eve.

Quint hadn't stopped by since that awkward kiss and I admit I was missing him almost as much as I was missing Gordy—the old Gordy. The one who brought his friends around to pillage the Christmas cookies while they made up nonsense—and often hilariously offensive—lyrics to traditional songs of the season. So on a blustery day roughly a week before Christmas, with a low hanging sky of steely clouds that promised snow, I decided that decorating the tree might be just the thing I needed to ignite my Christmas spirit.

The spruce was still out on the front porch where Quint had left it. I'd managed to find the old tree stand up in the attic but as I wrestled with trying to fit it onto the trunk of my lovely spruce it was more incomprehensible to me than a spreadsheet. No wonder I'd switched to artificial trees after the divorce. This was one of those manly things that I am ashamed to admit in the age of feminism that, along with lighting a charcoal fire in the Webber, I had never learned to master, so when Tommy Williams hailed me from across the street with a "Hi, neighbor! Need some help over there?" I breathlessly accepted.

He had that tree standing tall in no time.

"Wow," I said in honest awe.

"Bonnie insists on a real tree every year. I've been through just about every stand known to man. I gotta tell you, though, Lauren, I've got better ones down at the store than this one of yours."

"I'll keep that in mind for next year," I said, unwilling to inform anyone in the neighborhood yet that in all likelihood I'd be living in a place next year that outlawed real Christmas trees.

"Neighbor discount always applies," he added jovially.

He was as sweet as his wife, Bonnie, who was presently trotting across the street with a thermos in one hand and a small stack of plastic cups in the other.

"It's freezing out here, you two. I brought you hot chocolate."

I could have cried. Some of my neighbors on Seagull Lane were really wonderful. Like Tommy and Bonnie who never wore anything that quite matched and who had a barbecue for the neighbors every July Fourth. I was going to miss them.

"How are the boys?" I asked after a few sips of hot chocolate drowned the tears in my throat.

"The boys are good," Bonnie said.

"Eddie is still a pain in the ass sometimes," Tommy added.

Bonnie laughed merrily. "He's our rebel, that's for sure."

"Thinks he can make a living as a tattoo artist," Tommy muttered.

Bonnie shoved him good-naturedly with her mittened hand. "It's a phase. Meanwhile, Kyle graduates from college next year and once Brian leaves for college next autumn, we'll be real empty nesters."

They looked at each other with the kind of gleam in their eyes that told the world they couldn't wait. They'd probably buy an RV and have sex in every national park in the country.

"Want me to haul this thing in for you?" Tommy asked.

"I'd be forever grateful."

He set it up in the corner by the window while I got some cookies to go with the hot chocolate.

"Oh, no, hon—we've gotta run," Bonnie said.

"Choir practice," Tommy added.

"Well, thanks for the help—and the hot chocolate."

"Oh, hush!" Bonnie said. "What are neighbors for?"

I shut the door behind them and started to work on the tangle of lights for the tree. It was two days of failure and triumph, of swearing and laughing, before the lights were in place and every one was actually lit. Okay, I still couldn't put the tree in the stand or light a fire in the Webber but, damn it, I'd managed to string the lights on a Christmas tree. The bonus was that in the two days of frustration I forgot to remember that this was the last Christmas I'd be spending in my little clapboard cottage.

The lights on the tree suddenly blurred as I fought to hold back the tears. Images filled my head. Gordy on his first Christmas, looking bewildered among the wrappings and ribbons. The year he'd gotten his Big Wheel and had insisted on taking it outside even though it was snowing. His first ten-speed bike.

So many memories. I hoped that memories—the good ones at least—were packable because I didn't intend to move without them.

"I better buy a lot of bubble wrap," I murmured with a sniff and a grin. Because all those precious fragile things—the bits and pieces of life that really mattered—I intended to take with me, no matter where I ended up.

The display department at Grant's had Christmas Eve off so Dora had declared the day before Christmas Eve as "food day." We feasted on deviled eggs (Kelly), Brie with apples (Stuart), pâté from a local specialty shop (Dora) and an assortment of homemade Christmas cookies (me and Lola and Sienna who, being art majors, had brought the fancier ones). I tried not to think of the force-fed goose as I spread pâté on a slice of crusty baguette.

The eggnog in the ornate silver punch bowl, a relic unearthed in the storeroom, was spiked with brandy and everyone was feeling mellow and pleased with themselves.

"So, kids," Dora said, "we've pulled off another holiday. And may I say, I couldn't have done it without each and every one of you." She held her silver punch cup high. "Here's to us," she said.

"Here's to us," we all agreed heartily.

"I think we'll all remember this as the year of the blown-glass pickle," Dora said.

"I'll never forget Dusty the snowman," I murmured affectionately.

"To Dusty!" Stuart exclaimed and we all raised our cups and drank again.

"I intend to try to forget that this is the year that Snow White over there got me singing Christmas carols," Kelly groused.

"Behave," Dora said, "or I'll make you sing a chorus or two."

Everyone laughed and I felt warmth spread in the pit of my stomach that had nothing to do with the spiked eggnog. There was a camaraderie here that I hadn't felt since I was in school. And a sense of the kind of accomplishment that I don't think I'd ever felt before in my life. We'd done something together, something we were proud of. These were my colleagues, my peers. My friends.

I took the silver ladle and refilled everyone's cups before raising mine to the group. "I just want to say, that I'm glad to know each and every one of you. I've learned so much from all of you and I—"

Stuart groaned. "Somebody feed this woman more pâté before she starts to gush."

Okay, so I had a tendency to gush. So what? Everyone was laughing at Stuart's joke and I laughed right along with them.

I was still trimming the tree at six on Christmas Eve. And Gordy still wasn't home. At least this time he'd charged his cell phone and was keeping in touch. They'd run into some snow south of Chicago and were taking it easy but he promised to be home in time to help finish the tree.

I was listening to an old Sinatra Christmas album, happy that I'd never parted with my old turntable, sipping wine and refusing to feel sorry for myself for being alone on Christmas Eve. Gordy would be home soon enough and my mother was coming for a late dinner. There were pork chops with apricot and raisin stuffing baking in the oven and wild rice with mushrooms simmering on the stove. Add the scent of fresh spruce and it was impossible not to feel some Christmas spirit.

Suddenly, I heard childlike voices that I knew weren't coming from Frank. I turned down the stereo and went to the window. A light snow had started to fall and Amy Westcott had once again gathered some of the children of Seagull Lane for caroling. A woman who can do that year after year can't be all bad, I thought, even if she insisted the ABCs, who were always dressed like angels, be in the front row. I went out onto the porch to hear them better, clapped when they were finished, and offered cookies all around. They were just leaving, their angelic voices wishing me a merry Christmas, when Quint Mathews pulled to the curb in his truck.

"Well, well," Amy said, "he certainly is a handyman to be making house calls on Christmas Eve."

"Merry Christmas, Mrs. Westcott," Quint called heartily as he got out of the truck.

They stuck around for another carol, probably so Amy could assess the situation in her gossip-loving mind, I thought glumly. It didn't help that Quint bounded up the stairs and came to stand close to me while we listened.

"Let's go inside," Quint said when the angels had moved on to Moira's house. "You must be freezing."

"Mmm, it smells awesome in here," Quint said once we were inside.

"Thanks. I'm just waiting for Gordy to get home to help me finish decorating the tree and then my mother is coming for a late supper." I reflexively started to brush snow from the shoulders of his jacket and his hair, then realized what I was doing and stuck my hands in the pockets of my gray trousers.

His face was flushed with cold and he was grinning down at me as he held out a small present wrapped in gold paper with silver ribbons. "Merry Christmas, Lauren," he said.

"Oh, Quint—how sweet—you shouldn't have. I've got one for you, too."

"Then why shouldn't I have?" he asked me in that serious way he had, head tilted, staring at me like I was a cipher.

I didn't like his scrutiny. Didn't like this feeling of uneasiness I had. I still wondered, if I hadn't turned my head that day—

"We're friends, right?" he asked softly.

And just like that he put me at ease. I smiled. "Of course we are. And since we're friends, you could help me decorate the tree."

"I'd like to."

He shrugged out of his jacket and hung it on the coat tree by the front door while I went over to the turntable to put on another album. A compilation this time.

Brenda Lee started singing about rockin' around the Christmas tree.

"Hey," Quint said, "my mom had this record."

I took a long, slow breath. Yes. I reminded him of his mom. We even liked the same Christmas music. Okay, now I was in familiar territory again.

"Want a beer or a glass of wine?"

"A beer would be great."

I went out to the kitchen to fetch him a Miller and top off my glass of white wine. When I got back to the living room, Quint was hanging a big, striped glass ball on the tree.

"That's one of my favorites," I said.

"Then come over here and we'll hang it together."

Since I had to deliver his beer, I thought, why not? He took the beer and set it down on the table next to the sofa, then he took my hand in his—the one that held the ornament— and moved it slowly to a strong branch. I didn't notice that his arm had gone around my waist until I looked up into his eyes. I admit that I don't have much experience with these things, but I didn't see anything familial in the way he was looking at me. Those soft brown eyes were pure seduction. Or was it me and the wine and the night? Was it my loneliness that was making me see something that wasn't there? Could I be *that* lonely?

"Show me some of your other favorites," he said, his gaze on my mouth and not on the tree.

"Well, I've always loved the clip-on blown glass cardinals." I cleared my throat, hoping some sort of physical action would make me break from his gaze. "Cardinals in the snow are so— um—beautiful. Don't you think?"

Brenda stopped rockin' and Luther Vandross started to sing "The Christmas Song."

"This song is for dancing," Quint said. Then he took my wineglass out of my hand, put it down next to his beer, and drew me into his arms.

It was easier to dance cheek to cheek with him than look into his eyes. And could he dance. His face might have a stillness all its own but his body moved with a sensuality that you'd never guess he had if you'd only watched him wield a hammer.

"Relax," he whispered into my hair.

"Aren't I relaxed?" I whispered back.

"I get the feeling that your mind is going a mile a minute. Give in to the music. Give in to my body."

If this was a line, I thought, it was a killer. And it worked. I laid my head on his shoulder and gave myself over to the enjoyment of being in a man's arms again. In fact, I was so relaxed, I didn't even hear the door open.

"Ma—I'm home."

I jumped back from Quint like I'd been doing something wrong.

"Gordy! Merry Christmas!" I ran to him and threw my arms around him. He was cold but I was pretty sure that didn't have anything to do with the stiffness of his body. "You're just in time to help finish trimming the tree. Come on, take your coat off. You're covered in snow. Would you like some hot chocolate? Some hot cider, maybe? And I bet you're hungry. Dinner isn't ready yet, but I've got—" I started to rattle off a list of dips and cheeses and assorted munchies when Gordy stopped me.

"Ma, chill, will ya? How much wine have you had?"

"What? Just a sip or two. Why?"

"'Cause you're acting like you're on speed or something."

"Lauren is just excited that you're home," Quint clarified.

Gordy glared at him. "And what the hell are you doing here? Laying another floor?"

"Gordy!" I admonished. "Quint just stopped by to drop off a present."

"A company calendar?" Gordy asked with enough sarcasm to put a chill in the room.

"I think I better go," Quint said.

While Quint put on his jacket, I gave Gordy a look that I hoped would suffice until we were alone, took a present from under the tree, and followed Quint outside.

"I'm sorry, Quint," I said as I handed him his gift. "I don't know what's gotten into him. He's changed so much lately."

"College can be tough," Quint said. "Besides, I doubt he expected to come home and find his mom in the arms of a man."

"But we were only dancing."

He tilted his head. "Were we?"

I stared after him as he bounded down the front steps and walked through the thickening snow to his truck. Before he climbed in, he blew me a kiss and called out, "Get inside. You'll freeze!"

I felt hot enough to melt every snowflake on Seagull Lane. I put my hands on the porch rail and leaned out far enough to catch snowflakes on my tongue. I needed cooling off—both inside and out—before I went in to face my son.

He was waiting for me in the living room.

"What was he doing here?"

"I told you. He came to deliver a present."

"Right. And just stayed for a few dances."

"Yes, as a matter of fact."

"And if I hadn't come in when I had?"

"Well—he probably would have been gone. Gordy, what's gotten into you?"

"The question is what's gotten into you. Ma—that guy is a handyman—and he's a hell of a lot younger than you."

"I don't know what his job has to do with anything, but his age doesn't matter because we're just friends, Gordy."

"Yeah, I bet you have all kinds of shit in common."

"Gordy, if you're accusing me of something, why don't you just say it."

He hung his head for a moment and I noticed how much longer his hair was since he'd been home for Thanksgiving. How much more unkempt he looked. When he looked back up at me, his eyes were hard but I could still see the boyish hurt in them.

"I think you hired that guy to put that stupid kitchen floor in just so you could hide the fact that you're—"

"Gordy!"

"You don't think other people think the same thing? I could see you dancing together from outside."

"I'm not concerned with what other people think at the moment. I'm concerned with what you think." I walked up to him and took him by the shoulders. "Look at me."

He was still boy enough to obey.

"Nothing is going on between Quint Mathews and me. In fact, I hadn't even seen him in weeks until he stopped by tonight. We're casual friends, that's all."

He looked shamefaced enough for me to let him off the hook. After all, this was new territory for both of us. One day I might actually be interested in another man again. But for Gordy—or anyone else—to think it could be Quint Mathews was absolutely crazy.

"Now, why don't you take your things upstairs to your room

while I put some appetizers out and then we can finish trimming the tree. Your grandmother should be here soon."

The rest of the evening went as planned. We finished decorating the tree, telling each other stories about special ornaments as we always did. But I sensed Gordy's heart wasn't really in it. Bernice arrived, looking gorgeous in a bulky white sweater and a long, slim white skirt.

"I knew that pale sage sweater would look lovely on you, dear," she said, "but you really must do something about your hair."

"Merry Christmas to you, too, Mother," I said as I kissed her on the cheek.

"Now where is that handsome grandson of mine?" She took one look at him and frowned. "Is there a boycott of hairdressers that no one told me about?"

"Aw, Gran," Gordy said.

She ran a manicured hand through his hair. "You know, I think I have just the thing in my purse for you."

Sure enough, she rummaged in her enormous winter-white leather purse and came up with a tube of something. I grinned as I watched her work a potion into my son's hair thinking that no one else on earth would get away with that.

"Now, go look in the mirror. You look older and positively European."

For the first time since he'd walked in the door, Gordy looked pleased.

Dinner was a success—which meant that Bernice only had a few criticisms. But Gordy was still oddly subdued, only responding to his grandmother's flirting. We opened the gifts from Bernice after dinner. Some kind of trendy watch that Gordy was thrilled with and a dress for me in a drapey fabric of pale green. It was beautiful, but I couldn't imagine where I'd wear it.

Bernice was almost impossible to buy for. This year I'd found one of her old *Vogue* covers on the Internet and had it framed. She was thrilled with it.

"You're still as beautiful now as you were then," I told her.

"That's why I'm always telling you to take care of your skin, Lauren. You're never too young to worry about what the sun can do to your face."

Classic Bernice, but I didn't mind. I was too busy watching Gordy and trying to pinpoint just what was so different about him this year. And why.

After Bernice left I got out the VHS of *Miracle on 34th Street*, but Gordy started up to bed before I even had a chance to load it into the VCR.

"Aren't we going to watch the movie?" I asked. It had been a Christmas Eve tradition for us ever since Gordy had been four years old.

He shook his head. "I'm not a kid anymore, Ma."

After he'd gone upstairs, I sat in the living room, lit only by the Christmas tree, and watched the snow falling and wondered—with the way things were going between Gordy and me—how I was ever going to tell him the truth about the house? I wondered, too, why I was still being so protective of him. Hadn't he just told me he wasn't a kid anymore? Surely he could handle the fact that we were going to have to move.

Tomorrow, I promised myself. Tomorrow over breakfast I would tell Gordy that the house was going up for sale.

The doorbell woke me at eight on Christmas morning. It was Roger.

"I thought you and Tiffany were going to some island for the holiday."

"We're on our way to the airport. Just wanted to drop Gordon's present off."

Well, this was something new, I thought as I climbed the stairs to wake Gordy. Roger had been taking trips to tropical places at Christmas for years and he'd never stopped on Christmas morning to deliver Gordy's gift himself.

"Ma, I'm on vacation," Gordy moaned as I shook him awake.

"Your father is here."

"I thought him and what's her name were going to some private island for Christmas."

"They are. He wants to see you first, I guess. To give you his present."

This seemed to wake him up. I wasn't sure I liked the idea that seeing his father hadn't roused him but the idea of seeing his father's present got him out of bed in a hurry. He threw a robe over his boxers and started downstairs.

I followed and watched him hug Roger. The picture made me smile and gave me a burst of unexpected holiday goodwill.

"Why don't you and Tiffany join us for breakfast," I asked Roger. "Then Gordy can open your present?"

"No time. Besides," Roger said with the kind of grin I'd rarely seen on his face, "it's not wrapped."

"Where is it?" Gordy asked sleepily.

"Right outside, son."

Gordy stumbled over to the door and looked out, then looked back at his dad, a question clearly on his face. For answer, Roger threw him a set of keys. Gordy caught them easily with one hand.

"She's all yours, Gordo. Merry Christmas."

"Holy shit!" Gordy said before he burst out the door, barefoot.

I gave Roger a wary look, then walked over to the door myself.

There at the curb sat a shiny new black Honda Civic. And if I knew Roger, it was the model that had all of the bells and whistles.

"Are you crazy?" I asked my ex.

"Look at him out there," Roger said. "He loves it."

"Well, of course he loves it, Roger. That's not the point. The point is shouldn't parents discuss something this momentous in a child's life?"

"I don't recall you letting me in on what you got Gordon for Christmas."

"But I didn't give him a car! Do you realize how this is going to change things?"

"Yes, I know how it will change things. For you, Lauren. It will change things for you. And, God forbid anything should change for Lauren."

"What does that mean? I've been going through changes right and left lately."

"*Lately* being the operative word here. And only because you've been forced to."

Suddenly, my son's car roared to life. He was sitting behind the steering wheel, revving the engine, while Tiffany the aerobics instructor leaned against it wearing so little clothing I couldn't understand why she wasn't frozen solid.

"I just don't think Gordy is ready for this, Roger. Lately, there have been some changes that—"

"The kid is eighteen. He needs a car. And you're just going to have to deal with it."

He went out the door and I stood there, wiping steam off the glass of the storm door, watching Gordy, barefoot in the snow, hug his father and the bimbette enthusiastically before they got into Roger's Porsche and drove away.

Gordy hurried back to the house.

"I'm gonna get dressed, Mom, and take her for a ride," he said while he ran past me and up the stairs.

I sighed. Of course he'd want to take the car out right away. Who wouldn't? It was asking the impossible to expect him to want to stick around for the traditional Christmas breakfast of waffles and ham. Besides, this was just the ghost of all the Christmases yet to come.

If my life was changing at the age of forty-one, imagine all the changes Gordy's life was going to go through? There would be times in the future when he might be too far away to come home for Christmas—or too busy with his own life. There would be times that a young woman might be important enough for him to spend the holidays with her family instead of his own.

But there was no reason that I couldn't have waffles and ham for Christmas breakfast. Just like there was no reason that the digital camera that was wrapped under the tree couldn't wait until Gordy came back from taking his new car for a spin.

CHAPTER 12

At four that afternoon, the camera and I were still waiting. So much for a wonderful last Christmas on Seagull Lane.

Gordy had been in such a hurry to get out the door, he'd forgotten to take his cell phone with him. So, I spent my time tidying up, looking out the window and channel surfing. So far, I'd seen three different versions of *A Christmas Carol*, but it was going to take more than the prospect of Tiny Tim walking again to get me back into the spirit of the season.

Where the hell was he? And what the hell had Roger been thinking? This was no time to give Gordy this kind of freedom. This kind of responsibility.

And it was no time for me to have to spend Christmas Day all alone. Moira and Stan were in New York with their kids. Everyone else I knew would be busy with their own families. Other years Gordy's friends had filled the house, coming and going, eating all the leftovers, keeping me busy in the kitchen. But those other years, his friends had been the ones with the cars.

I'd never felt so alone in my life.

I looked at the phone. What about Bernice? What about calling my mother for a little support? What's the worst that could happen? Bernice always held a brunch for her friends on Christmas Day, catered by the restaurant in her building. Surely everyone would be gone by now.

Bernice answered on the third ring.

"Mom? I'm a little worried about Gordy."

There was a pause, then a sigh. "What now?"

I told her about Roger giving Gordy a car and about how he'd been gone since nine o'clock that morning.

"Lauren, what do you expect? The boy gets a car, of course he wants to show it off. He's probably out joyriding with his friends."

"You know, I'm really pissed at Roger over this."

"Are you out of your mind? You should be glad you've got an ex-husband who takes an interest in his son and can afford to buy him things like a new car. What did your father send you this year?"

I rolled my eyes. Why did she have to bring this up now? "He sent me a seashell," I said. "One of those big ones that sounds like waves when you put it up to your ear."

Bernice sighed again. "And you're complaining about Roger? Not that I don't still think he's an asshole, but at least he knows how to give his child a Christmas present."

"Dad said he found the shell himself when he was snorkeling. I thought it was very sweet."

"You would."

"Okay, so it's not the kind of gift every woman dreams of getting from her father," I admitted.

"Still," Bernice went on, "I suppose it's better than the carved coconut he sent you last year."

She was certainly right about that, I thought as I tried to hold back a sputter of laughter. "Okay, maybe I'm a little protective towards Dad—"

"Understatement of the year," Bernice muttered.

I couldn't argue. I'd been a lot easier on my Dad than I'd ever been with my mother.

"Nevertheless," I went on, "my point is the car gives Gordy

too much freedom. He's been gone all day. Anything might have happened to him."

"You're being ridiculous. He carries identification. If something had happened to him you'd have heard by now."

"You know, Mother, the least you could do is listen to my fears, offer a little support."

"I think you're wrong to worry. I'm not going to offer support when I think you're wrong."

"But it's not just the car, Mom. Can't you see that Gordy is changing? I think something might be wrong. Seriously wrong."

"The only thing that's wrong is he's adjusting to being on his own, something you should try to do, as well. Give the boy some room. You're trying to smother him just like you tried to smother me when you were little."

I pulled the phone from my ear and gasped at it—and then I hung up on her.

"What a bitch," I ranted as I started to pace the living room. Smother her? All I'd wanted was a little attention. A little time. The same thing every kid wants.

"Oh, what did you expect, Lauren," I muttered to myself.

Just as I was settling back down in front of the television, car lights swooped across the living room wall. I rushed to the window. It was Gordy.

Okay. How to handle this? Be cool and offer him a sandwich? Go off on him and tell him how hurt and worried I'd been all day? Tie him to a chair for the rest of Christmas vacation and force him to watch *It's a Wonderful Life* over and over again? The last solution held the most appeal, since I'd at least know where he was at all times.

But what if my mother was right? What if my overripened maternal devotion was smothering him?

Gordy bounded in the door with a big grin on his face. The cold radiated from him but his smile was pure Yule log. "This has been, like, the most awesome day of my life, Ma! All the guys just think it's so cool that Dad got me the Honda. First I drove over to Mark's—"

He took off his gloves and jacket while the story of his day tumbled out and filled the room. Call me a doting mom, but by the time he was through I couldn't bring myself to be mad at him.

Instead, I asked him if he was hungry.

"Starving," he said.

So we went to the kitchen and I got out the fixings for sandwiches and the rest of the dips and cheeses. We assembled a feast, put it on a tray and took it into the living room.

"Why don't you open the rest of your presents while we eat," I suggested.

He took a huge bite of sandwich then went on his knees in front of the tree and grabbed the box that held the camera.

"Cool!" he said after he'd torn off the paper. "Oh man, I can take some pics of the Honda and send them to Dooley in an e-mail. Cool gift, Ma. Thanks." He took the camera out of the box and looked at it for a while, took another bite of sandwich, then he looked at me. "You know what's even cooler? The fact that you're not even mad that I was gone all day."

That did it for any lingering anger I might have been feeling. I was putty in his hands as he held out his gift for me. I opened it and found a gorgeous pair of leather gloves. "These are beautiful," I said as I tried them on.

Gordy opened a few more things I'd picked up for him—a sweater and some socks. He put a pair of the socks on right away. Maybe it was only because his feet were cold, but it made me feel good. And it made me know that at least I'd done one thing right. At least Gordy and I would never have a relationship like I had with my mother.

I started to gather the discarded wrapping paper and ribbons when Gordy said, "There's one more present under the tree."

"There is?"

He reached for it and read the tag. "It's for you," he said as he handed it to me.

Gold paper and silver ribbon. I'd almost forgotten. It was the gift from Quint. I unwrapped it to find a small gold heart-shaped locket on a thin gold chain. I carefully opened the locket. There was a picture of the old breakfast nook inside. Tears rose in my throat. I swallowed them down by taking another bite of my sandwich.

"Not exactly a company calendar," Gordy said.

I shrugged, trying my best to make light of it. "He just knew how much that booth meant to me, that's all."

I easily steered the conversation back to the car while we finished eating. Gordy said he was beat, kissed me goodnight and headed up to bed. I sat on in the living room, opening the locket every few minutes to look at the picture inside. Finally, I slipped it over my head. It felt warm in the hollow of my throat.

When I went to bed that night, I lay awake a long time. But I wasn't thinking of the fight with my mother or of the car that had kept my son away from me all day. Instead, I held my palm over the locket and thought of dancing in Quint's arms on Christmas Eve.

Decidedly non-motherly feelings coursed through my body. Could a forty-one-year-old have a crush? And, if so, was there anything she could do about it? I grinned in the darkness. Not that I wanted to do anything about it, of course.

Or did I?

* * *

The rest of Gordy's vacation buzzed along with such speed that I wished I could have put on an emergency break. My schedule at work was erratic and since Gordy now had wheels there was no telling if he'd be there when I got home or not. I spent a lot of time waiting. Until, one evening, I finally got sick of it. Was I building a new life for myself or not? It was the holiday season and I was fifteen minutes away from a city full of festivities. I picked up that day's newspaper, turned to the entertainment section, and scanned the pages.

Ten minutes later, I was on the phone asking Moira if she wanted to go to a jazz club with me that night.

"Who is this?" she demanded.

I laughed. "All right, all right. I know it's not like me, but that's the point. Now do you want to go or not?"

"Are you kidding? What time should I be ready?"

About an hour later, I in my never-fail Donna Karan and Moira in a tulip shaped skirt, a low-cut, sparkly tank top and a tiny little cashmere cardigan were squeezing ourselves into a smoke-filled club. The jazz trio was already playing, something I vaguely recognized even though I'm generally jazz handicapped. The crowd at the bar was two deep and all the little tables were taken. Moira shouted over the bodies and managed to secure us two vodka martinis. We took our drinks and hugged the wall alongside a few other people waiting for seating to open up.

A couple at a nearby table started showing signs of leaving. Moira grabbed my arm.

"Get ready to dash for it," she said into my ear so I could hear her above the noise.

I started to protest that some people had been waiting longer than we had but before I knew it she was dragging me toward the newly vacated table. I felt like a baserunner sliding into home when I landed on the chair.

"Moira, really," I said, trying to ignore the glare of the other people waiting.

She flapped a hand at me. "You've been waiting too often lately." She took a sip of her martini. "You know, the books don't tell you that that's where the real pain of motherhood comes in. Giving birth is nothing. Waiting is the hard part."

What she said was true. "I bet we spend half our lives waiting. We wait for our men to come home from work. We wait for our kids to come home from school."

"We wait for the hemlines to come down to something sensible again," Moira added as she eyed a tall blonde in a skirt that looked like it contained less than a yard of fabric.

I downed the rest of my drink. "But the worst waiting," I announced as I caught the eye of the cocktail waitress and held up two fingers, "is waiting for a teenager who has a car to come home."

"Tell me about it. Especially if it's a boy."

"You never had to wait for Gina?"

"Gina knew I wouldn't accept that kind of behavior from her."

The waitress set two fresh martinis down in front of us.

"Are you saying that you expected more from your daughter than you did your son?"

Moira plucked a skewered olive from the vodka and took a bite while she thought. "Yeah, I guess I am saying that—much as it appalls me to admit it."

I pointed my finger at her in triumph. "I knew it! I've been thinking a lot lately about how women accept behavior from men that we would never condone from a woman. And I think it starts the minute they wrap that pink diaper around you in the hospital nursery."

"Nah, it goes further back than that. Happens in the womb. We hear our mothers doing it."

I laughed. "That theory won't wash. You're forgetting Bernice."

"Imagine forgetting Bernice," Moira quipped as her eyes swept the bar. "Whoa—don't turn around now but take a look at that guy with the black hair at the end of the bar. Very dishy."

I casually turned my head, like I was studying the hammered tin ceiling above us. By the time my gaze settled on the end of the bar, I knew which guy she meant right away. He was movie star handsome and wearing a cashmere turtleneck that looked so soft it made my fingers itch.

"Beyond dishy," I said when I'd finished my sweep of our setting.

"I think he's alone, too. And you're in luck, there's a bowl of peanuts on the bar just to his right."

I frowned. "How does that make me lucky?"

"Because when you casually stroll over and get them, you can introduce yourself."

"Oh, right. I can so see me doing that."

"Oh, why not?"

"Because women like me don't do things like that. Women like you do."

"Listen, hon, I've got an unlimited supply of peanuts at home and it's way past time you became that kind of woman."

I took a gulp of my martini. "Don't be so damn pushy. Can't you be satisfied that we're actually out at a jazz club on a weeknight and it was my idea?"

"Fine. Then I'll go talk to him myself."

I watched her walk over to the bar wishing I had that kind of confidence when it came to men. Maybe if I tried on a less stellar specimen? I started to scan the place but when the door opened my eyes were drawn to it. And guess who limped in?

It was him and here I was sitting at a tiny table all by myself, an empty chair across from me. He looked around, his gaze stopping on the vacant chair. I swear he was about to come over. At last, I thought, we're really going to meet. And then, just as he started to move his cane, Moira rushed back to the table with tall, dark and handsome in tow.

"Lauren, this is Melvin Hobbs. He's—"

Well, I never did hear what he was. I was too busy watching blue eyes limp over to the bar and take Melvin's seat.

"Listen, how was I to know he was married?" Moira asked in the car on the way home. "Besides, what's the harm. We got a free drink out of it, didn't we?"

Big deal. I'd gladly pay for my own damn drink just to have found out if the man with the cane was meant to join me at my table.

Finally, the evening before New Year's Eve, I corralled Gordy and talked him into ordering Chinese delivery and watching a DVD with me.

I was munching on cashew chicken and watching John Candy trying to sell shower curtain rings as jewelry to appease a royally pissed Steve Martin when Gordy said, "I guess you're never going to take that thing off, are you?"

"What thing?" I asked, my eyes still on the screen.

"That locket. It means something to you, doesn't it?"

My hand went to the locket. It felt warm from my skin. "I told you, Quint knew how much the breakfast nook meant to me. I think it was a sweet gesture on his part."

"Yeah. Sweet. So tell me, Ma, if the damn booth meant so much to you, why did you have him rip it out?"

"Well—" I hadn't anticipated the question. And I still hadn't found the right moment to tell my son that the house was going on the market.

"Was it because he just looked so damn good while he was painting the walls?"

I was so taken aback that I actually felt my body jerk. "What? Gordy, what are you talking about?"

"Something's going on between you two, isn't it? And he's— what? Maybe six years older than me?"

"Of course nothing's going on." Okay, a kiss or two on the cheek. A dance to an old Christmas song. But it really was nothing. Or at least not the something Gordy was insinuating.

"Then why the hell did you have all that work done in the kitchen? When I was home for Thanksgiving you said you now had to work for a living, that money was tight. I mean, I got socks for Christmas! But you sure found the money to pay him, didn't you? Just to keep him around. Just so that you—"

"I think you better stop right there," I said. I switched off the movie and stood. "It's time I told you a few things. I don't know why you're so angry or where you got the idea that anything was going on between Quint Mathews and me—"

"I've got eyes. Besides, that creepy trio from across the street are telling everybody that he's here all the time."

"Amy Westcott is a huge gossip, and you know it. The fact is, I remind Quint of his mother. She died of cancer a few years ago. That's why he stops in sometimes. And I'm sure that's why he gave me the locket."

The explanation didn't erase the sullen look on my son's face. "That still doesn't explain why you hired him in the first place. Why you spent money doing stuff to the kitchen when we always liked it just the way it was."

So the time had finally come. It was now or never. I would

have preferred never but if I waited any longer, Gordy might very well come home for spring break and find some other family living in our house.

I took a deep breath. "The fact is I had the work done in the kitchen on the advice of a Realtor. Gordy, the house—it's going up for sale right after the holidays."

He jumped to his feet. "Selling the house? But why? I thought you loved this house."

"I do—but it belongs to your father and he wants to sell it."

"That's a fuckin' lie!" he spit out. "Dad wouldn't do that."

I was too alarmed by his outburst to even care that he'd sworn at me and called me a liar. I reached out and put my hand on his arm. "Gordy, calm down."

He shrugged off my hand. "I'm calling him right now."

"You can't call him—remember? He's on some private island where there isn't any phone service."

"Huh, that's pretty convenient."

"Convenient for who? Certainly not for me! Don't you think I'd like him here to back me up on this?"

"But why would he sell the house from under us? Why, after all these years—"

"Gordy, I'll explain it all to you if you'll just sit down."

Reluctantly, he lowered himself to the sofa. This wasn't going to be easy. But it had to be done. All I could do was hope he would understand.

"When your father and I decided to get divorced," I began…

Twenty minutes later, I could see that he didn't understand.

He shoved his hands into his hair and looked at the floor. "Christ, no wonder I'm such a loser."

I frowned. "What does that mean?"

He ignored the question. "You sound like you pretty much

screwed up on the divorce, Ma. Like you neglected a little detail like our life was going to turn to shit as soon as I graduated from high school. Nice move, Ma."

"Our lives haven't turned to shit. And, yes, I know I wasn't very on the ball when your father first left. I've felt like a fool more times than I care to remember. Why do you think I put off telling you for so long? Why do you think I've been working my ass off at Grant's?"

I squatted down in front of him and put my hands on my knees. "But things aren't going to change that much for you, honey. The worst of it is that we are going to move, that's all. You're still going to be able to go to college. Your dad still has to pick up the tab for that."

"Yippee. And when I come home on holidays, where is that gonna be, Ma?"

"Well—I don't know. Not yet, anyway." I refrained from telling him it might be little more than a hovel—at least for a while. "But wherever it is, Gordy, I promise to make it a home for us."

"Nothing is ever going to be the same again," he muttered.

Something he'd said kept niggling at me. Something I found scarier than the prospect of trying to find an apartment I could afford. "Gordy," I asked, "why did you call yourself a loser? Is everything okay at school?"

"Oh, right. Get on my ass now. Great timing, Ma."

This time it was me who pushed my hands into my hair. This was my fault. I'd never taught Gordy to handle changes because I'd never learned to handle changes. I'd created Fantasy Island right here in the middle of Seagull Lane.

"Look, I know I made a lot of wrong choices. But I thought I was doing the right thing for you. I know you're angry with me right now, but I hope you'll remember what I just said and try to understand. I need your understanding and acceptance right now as much as you need mine."

He made a noise—a snort. Its message was clear. He almost pushed me over as he shot off the sofa and ran upstairs. I heard his door slam and I knew that he was right. Nothing was ever going to be the same again.

I gave him half an hour and then I went up after him. I knocked on his door, waited a moment, then opened it. He was packing.

"What are you doing?"

"I'm going back to school tonight."

"But—I thought you weren't going back until after New Year's."

"Some guys I know are throwing a party. As long as it looks like everyone else is doing exactly what they want to with their lives I might as well, too. Why should I miss the party of the year?"

"Gordy, I don't want you to leave this way," I said as I followed him down the stairs.

"Tough," he said as he reached the door.

"Gordy—wait—"

But he didn't wait. I went out onto the porch and stood in the bitter wind, my arms wrapped around me, watching the Honda's taillights disappear as I cursed Roger for buying Gordy the car. And cursed myself for letting my son down.

"Honey, why don't you come to the country club with us?" Moira asked me over the phone the next day. "You can't spend New Year's Eve all alone after what happened with Gordy."

"I'd feel like a third wheel."

"Not to worry. Stan is only partially inflated."

I laughed despite my misery. "Well, I'd be totally flat."

"Like those duds at the club would notice."

"Moira, thanks, but, really—no, thanks. I'm planning on

getting into bed with Humphry Bogart tonight. Maybe I can help him pick up the pieces after Ingrid gets on that plane."

Moira laughed. "Well, if you change your mind, we're not leaving until nine."

"Thanks," I said. "But don't expect to hear from me."

We wished each other a happy New Year and I hung up the phone.

I hadn't heard from Gordy since he'd left the night before. He wasn't picking up his cell phone and hadn't responded to any of my messages. I finally called his dorm room and managed to catch his roommate Dooley who told me that he'd seen Gordy that afternoon and was planning on seeing him again that night. So at least I knew he was alive.

I thought about giving my mother a call to wish her a happy New Year, but what she'd said about me smothering her was still too raw.

In the end, I decided that this was as good a time as any to give the living room a good cleaning. I vacuumed up a few pounds of tree needles and dusted. Then I moved on to the kitchen and mopped the new tiles. As long as I was intending on spending the evening in bed with a DVD, I decided I might as well spruce up my bedroom, as well. I changed the sheets, dusted and vacuumed and lit a few scented candles just to make things less gloomy.

The dress my mother had given me for Christmas was still hanging on the hook on the outside of the closet door. I ran my hand down the fabric. Soft and expensive. My mother might be missing the mommy gene but you couldn't fault her for her taste.

What the hell, I thought, I might as well wear it. It was, after all, New Year's Eve.

I took a long, hot scented bubble bath, shaved and moisturized, blew dry my hair and put on some makeup just to make myself feel better. I slipped the dress over my head and felt a chill as it slithered over my body. When I looked in the mirror, I was surprised at how good it looked on me. It had a wide scooped neckline that was within an inch of falling off my shoulders and a draped bodice that gathered to one side with a jeweled pin that took the emphasis off my hips. It was simple yet exquisite. It made me feel special.

I dug in my closet and pulled out a pair of silver sandals with three-inch heels that I'd bought on sale years ago. Just one of those purchases that seemed too good to pass up but that never got worn. I slipped them on and went downstairs. There was wine left from Christmas. I poured myself a glass, put Sinatra on the stereo and took some shrimp and some twice-baked potatoes out of the freezer.

I was a woman alone on New Year's Eve but, damn it, I wasn't going to bed with Bogart. I was going to celebrate.

Okay, dancing by myself had its drawbacks, plus I couldn't help but think back to that night that Quint and I had danced and that made me wonder where he was tonight. What he was doing.

I looked at the phone. I could just call him and wish him a happy New Year, couldn't I? I'd probably get his machine anyway.

I was pretty sure that his number was still under a magnet on the refrigerator so I took the cordless out into the kitchen. I found his card under a little plastic elf and dialed.

He answered on the second ring. "I'm Your Handy Man."

I bit my lip, feeling a little unsure. Honestly, I had expected to get the machine, and now here was Quint's deep voice on the other end of the line.

"Hello?" he said.

"Hi!" I blurted.

"Lauren?"

"Uh—yes. I'm just calling to wish you a happy New Year. I

thought I'd leave a message. Figured you'd be—you know—out partying or something."

"I've never been much for fighting the drunken hordes. Seems like a silly way to end a year and begin a new one."

I leaned against the kitchen wall. "I know what you mean. I'm a big believer in staying home, too," I said, as if I'd ever had much choice.

"So, you're home by yourself tonight?"

"Yes. Gordy went back to school last night so I'm defrosting dinner and listening to music."

"Sounds nice," he drawled deeply. "Can you defrost enough for two?"

"I think so," I answered.

"Want me to come over?"

I squeezed my eyes shut and slid a little way down the wall. He wanted to come over. "Sure," I finally managed to get out, "if you'd like to."

"Great. See you in a few."

I was still pondering the wisdom of this turn of events when the doorbell rang. I opened the door to Quint Mathews standing on the front porch, holding a bottle of champagne.

"Gosh," he said, "you look beautiful."

I'd totally forgotten about the dress. I felt a little foolish and wished I'd thought to change into something more casual. "Oh—well—it's New Year's Eve. I decided I'd get a bit—you know—dressed up."

We stood there staring at each other until he finally put his hand on the doorjamb and leaned in closer to me. "Are you going to invite me in?" he asked softly.

"Oh, of course. Please," I said, as I stepped aside. "Come in."

He walked past me, slipped out of his leather jacket and hung it on the coat tree—just like he always used to do. It felt good to see it hanging there again.

"I see you're wearing my present," he commented.

My hand immediately went to the locket. "Oh, Quint. I love it. I should have called and thanked you for it, but things with Gordy haven't been so hot and my mother and I are fighting."

He put a finger on my lips. "I'm glad you love it. And I love the sweater. See? I'm wearing it tonight."

I hadn't noticed before, but he was. And now that I'd noticed he was, I noticed how really wonderful the fine gauge black knit V-neck sweater looked on him. He definitely had the chest for it—and the stomach.

And I definitely shouldn't be noticing.

"Come out to the kitchen. I think I've got a couple of champagne flutes somewhere. Unless you want to wait until midnight to pop the cork."

He looked at the clock over the refrigerator. "It's nine o'clock. If we pop it now, we're sure to have a happy New Year."

"I think I like your logic."

The flutes turned out to be on a top shelf. Even with the heels I couldn't quite reach them.

"Here, let me give you a hand," he said.

My breath caught in my throat when I felt his hands at my waist as he came up behind me and lifted me a few inches straight off the floor. I grabbed the flutes and clutched them to stop my hands from shaking.

When he lowered me back to the red tiles, the back of my body slid all the way down the front of his.

"Um, these are kind of dusty. I'll give them a quick wash."

I couldn't look at him as I went over to the sink and turned on the hot water. What I really needed was cold water. Plenty of it.

What was wrong with me? How could I react this way to someone who was practically a boy, who had told me I reminded him of his mother? I felt almost incestuous. And something else—

Well, I did say *almost*, didn't I?

The something else was the sudden awakening of parts of my body that I'd long ago stopped thinking of as anything but equipment to facilitate motherhood. As I washed the glasses, I peered downward, wondering if my nipples were visible beneath the thin, drapey material of my dress. Something I hadn't had to worry about for quite some time—drapey fabric or not.

I turned off the water and dried the glasses, wondering if I'd morphed into one of those middle-aged female lechers overnight. What did they call them? Tigers? Cougars?

Behind me, the cork popped and I nearly jumped out of my skin.

"Better hurry with those or we're going to lose half our champagne."

What could I do? I turned around and held out the flutes. He poured.

"Let's go back into the living room," I suggested. It was darker in there, nothing but Christmas tree lights. I could hide my condition easier while I got myself under control.

I felt him following me. I didn't dare turn around. But I didn't have to. I already knew that he looked fabulous in the sweater. I already knew that his straight black hair shimmered from the lights on the tree.

"Mind if I put some more music on?" he asked.

"Please do," I answered as I sank to the sofa and tried to look nonchalant while hiding my breasts with my arms. Not easy to do when you're also trying to drink a glass of champagne.

I hoped that he would go for Mannheim Steamroller or

maybe something religious. But the next sound I heard was Luther Vandross.

Oh, my god, I thought as he walked toward me and held out his hand.

"I've been thinking about dancing with you to this again ever since the last time I was here."

"Uh—why don't we just sit and talk. How was your Christmas? Did you—"

"It's New Year's Eve," he said with that engaging grin of his. "Dance with me."

I put down the champagne flute and took his hand.

In the heels we were nearly eye to eye. In the thin dress and the fine knit of his sweater, we were nearly skin to skin.

"I've been fantasizing about being this close to you again for days," he said. "And I've been wondering what might have happened if you hadn't turned your head that day."

I pushed out of his arms. "Wait a minute—this is just wrong."

He tilted his head. "You haven't thought about it?"

"Of course I've thought about it!" I burst out. "But you don't remind me of my mother!"

One side of his mouth cocked as he frowned in consternation. "*What?*"

"You said I reminded you of your mother. So, I'm sorry, but it just seems way too weird to—"

He came up to me and placed his palm gently over my mouth.

"Hush," he said.

I hushed. Not because I'm all that obedient but because the warmth of his hand on my mouth had taken my breath away.

"I never said you reminded me of my mom. I only said there were certain ways you were alike."

"Isn't that the same thing?" I mumbled against his hand.

He shook his head as he slid his hand behind my neck. "No," he said softly. "Because if you reminded me of my mom, I wouldn't have been thinking about doing this for the past two months."

This turned out to be a kiss. And what a kiss. I thought I was going to melt at his feet by the time he was through.

"Do you understand now?" he asked.

I nodded.

"Do you understand that I've wanted you from the first time I saw you?"

"I was wearing sweats," I pointed out.

He grinned. "You look absolutely beautiful tonight, Lauren, but I've wanted you in your sweats, in your flannel pajamas, in your little sweaters and trousers and in your superhero costume." He paused. "Maybe most of all in your superhero costume."

I laughed.

"I love it when you laugh. Now come back over here and dance with me."

I went back into his arms and no matter what the song was, from "Jingle Bells" to "Silver Bells," we danced and kissed. His lips on my throat, my earlobe, my mouth. My lips on his chin and his cheekbone and his neck. And his mouth. Oh, yes, his mouth over and over again.

He danced me over to the coffee table where we dipped to pick up our glasses and drank more champagne, our bodies still in contact, still swaying to the music.

"I can't believe we're doing this," I said.

"Why not?"

"Well, it can't be right. Can it? I'm forty-one and you're—" I frowned. "How old are you, anyway?"

"Twenty-two," he murmured as he skimmed his lips over my temple.

I jumped away from him and put my hand over my mouth. My God, he was even younger than I'd thought.

He grinned. "I'm legal," he said as he came toward me. "And I want you. And I think you want me. Why shouldn't we give each other a happy New Year?"

Personally, I couldn't think of one damn reason.

The lovemaking was slow. More dances. More kisses. And touching. Ah, yes—the touching. I couldn't seem to get enough of running my hands up and down his back and around to his shoulders and arms. His hands traveled to just as many places. My back, my buttocks, my waist, but always just missing my breasts. Always just brushing the sides of them with his thumbs until I thought I'd go mad.

The guy might be only twenty-two but he knew exactly what he was doing.

When the last song played he asked, his voice husky now, his gaze traveling my face, his breath moving quickly in his chest, "Take me up to your bedroom, Lauren."

Man, was I glad I'd cleaned.

I took his hand and we went up the narrow staircase together. The candles I'd lit earlier were still flickering.

"It's just like you are," he said. "Warm, feminine—I want to make love to you, Lauren. Tell me you want it, too."

Was he going to make me sign a contract, was that how it was done these days? I mean, I hadn't been this horny since 1986, so what did I know?

He got that little half grin again. "Do this for me. I want to hear you say it."

"I want to make love to you, too," I said.

He pulled his sweater over his head and started to unzip his jeans. I stared at his chest, which was smooth and strong, and his belly, which rippled slightly with muscles while I wondered if I was supposed to get undressed, too? Were there other rules I should know about? I started to pull the dress off my shoulders, but he said, "No—let me."

In black boxers, the kind that are tight to the thigh, the kind that showed exactly how much Quint Mathews had to offer a woman, he walked over to me and slowly peeled Bernice's Christmas present off me. Frantically, I tried to remember what kind of bra and panties I had on. But it didn't seem to matter because he had them off of me in no time and then he was on his knees before me. My head fell back and I cried out when his lips touched my stomach. As he kissed his way downward, I shamelessly parted my legs, shamelessly put my hands into his hair. And then I felt his tongue on me—between my legs—and an orgasm slammed through me with dizzying speed.

When it was over, he pulled away and looked up at me. "Wow," he said.

"It's—um—been a while."

He got to his feet and took my hand. "Then come over here, baby, and let's do this right."

He lowered me to the bed and for the next two hours he did everything right.

When we were finished, I was sated. I was languid. I was wet and loose all over.

And I was hungry.

Unlike Roger, Quint hadn't immediately fallen asleep. He was holding me, my head on his chest, while he brushed his thumb back and forth on my shoulder. It felt luxurious. But I was afraid my stomach was going to growl at any minute.

"Want something to eat?" I asked him.

"Absolutely," he said.

He put on his boxers, I put on a robe and we went down to the kitchen.

We microwaved, then ate and talked and laughed and when we looked at the clock, we realized that we'd missed it. It was almost one in the morning.

"Happy New Year," he said, toasting me with a shrimp.

"Happy New Year," I returned.

"After we eat, let's go back upstairs and—"

"No—absolutely not. You've got to get out of here before dawn. My neighbors can't see you leave."

He laughed. "Then let's eat fast because I think there's a thing or two we can accomplish before dawn."

He wasn't kidding. And to save time, we accomplished them all on the living room rug.

A few hours later, Quint was upstairs getting dressed while I peered around the living room curtains, hoping no late-night revelers would suddenly return home. I left my post when I heard Quint come down the stairs.

He immediately drew me into his arms and kissed the top of my head.

"Lauren," he said, his voice muffled against my hair, "we are going to be able to do this again, aren't we?"

I took a deep, shaky breath. "I loved being with you tonight, Quint, but—"

"Oh, oh," he said, pulling back to look into my face, "I'm getting the brush-off."

I slapped him playfully on the chest. "Very funny. I bet your heart is just breaking."

He laughed softly. "Okay, so there's no future. So what? Why can't we indulge ourselves occasionally? Just a couple of undulating, consenting adults."

I shoved my hands into the pockets of my robe and shook my head. "Would you settle for friendship?"

He reached out and ran a finger down the side of my face. "If I have to."

"Thanks for last night," I said.

"Shut up and give me one last kiss," he said.

So I did. By this time the sky was lightening, the dawn of the first day of a new year breaking.

I pushed him toward the door. "Now get out of here before my neighbors find out what a fallen woman I've become."

He chuckled as he opened the door and checked to see if the coast was clear. Then he turned back to look at me.

"You know how to find me if you need me."

"Likewise," I said softly.

He slipped out and closed the door behind him.

I decided to stay up and watch the rest of the sunrise. I ran upstairs, pulled on some sweats, came downstairs and pulled on boots and a parka and let myself out the back door. I couldn't see the actual sunrise, but looking east toward Lake Michigan the sunny glow was crowding out the rest of the night, slowly turning the day's hue to pink. I breathed in the cold, sharp air, my head flung back, until the bowl of sky above me turned blue.

Another year. And I had no idea what it would bring with it. Had no idea of where I'd be living or what would happen next between me and Gordy. And yet, once again, just as I had when I'd started out at Temporary Solutions, I felt hopeful.

CHAPTER 13

It was a bright, cold day in February when I started to pack. The house had gone up for sale the first week in January. So far, there were no takers—apparently I'd permanently scared off the Ohio Stouts—but after so many years in this house there were a lot of things to sort through. I wasn't sure where I was going but it was certain to have even less space than my cottage on Seagull Lane.

I walked through the rooms, legal pad in hand, and tried to decide what I absolutely had to keep and what I could manage to part with. When I reached Gordy's room, I got a little misty eyed. His bookshelves with all his favorite books. His bulletin board that still held drawings he'd done last summer when he'd kicked around the idea of getting out his paints again.

We'd always been so close. The problems between us were so foreign to me that I just couldn't believe that they wouldn't straighten out eventually.

I'd talked to him only once since he'd left in such anger the day before New Year's Eve. The one good thing about the conversation was that I found out that Gordy had been in touch with his father since Roger returned from the islands and that Roger had, thankfully, backed me and admitted that he was the one who had decided to sell the house. But Gordy obviously wasn't ready to accept the situation yet or forgive me for making such a mess of things. And I couldn't seem to bring myself to be tough on him for his rudeness and anger. I was still too busy being tough on myself for creating the situation in the first place.

Thank the lord for Grant's. I don't know what I would have done if I hadn't had my job to go to every day.

I now had my own workstation, complete with drafting table, file drawers and a telephone. We'd just finished work on the designs for the Easter windows and were starting on the spring fashion show with the special events department, so I was now working days. I'd been assigned to scout for props and consult on accessories, which really meant that they told me what they wanted and I ran all over the store looking for something to fit the bill.

I was still pinching pennies and I had decided that taking any courses would have to wait until I'd found an apartment. So far, I'd only found three I could afford. One involved taking on several cockroaches as pets, another involved *becoming* the landlord's pet and the third was a basement apartment that smelled like it'd be a great place to grow mushrooms.

But I was learning something new every day at work. And sometimes there was even excitement to be had.

"Did you hear yet who the featured supermodel in the show is going to be?" Stuart asked one day while we were studying the sketches for the runway.

"Nope. They say nobody knows," Kelly said. "Except, of course, for Dora and Monica Lisbon."

Monica Lisbon was head of special events.

"I heard it was Elle McPherson," Stuart whispered.

"Get real," Kelly said.

"Well, they're saying it's someone huge—someone international."

"Last rumor I heard they were saying Naomi Campbell," I put in.

"Either would be to die for," Stuart decided. "And by the way, teacher's pet," he said to me, "I've got a little info you might be interested in. There's an apartment for rent in a building I used to live in. A friend of mine just vacated. Hasn't even been listed yet."

Now this was the kind of talk that made my heart race faster than the prospect of meeting someone who was six feet, weighed a hundred pounds and looked good in clothes. "Is it a two bedroom?" I asked eagerly.

I needed two bedrooms. Because Gordy had to have a space of his own when he came home. I had to give him at least that much.

"Yup. Two bedrooms," Stuart said. "Right on Prospect Avenue."

I groaned. If any street was out of my budget, it was Prospect Avenue with its high-rise condos and converted mansions. "How much is the rent?" I asked despite the fact that I knew this conversation wasn't going to get me a new roof over my head.

But when Stuart told me, I thought I'd misheard him. "How much did you say?"

He repeated the number again and my mouth dropped open.

"Girlfriend, there are still some bargains to be had. It's kind of small and it's not in a high-rise, but if you lean far enough out your window you can practically see downtown."

"Worth a look," Kelly said.

"When do you think I can see it?" I asked Stuart.

"I'll give the super a call. Wait until you meet him. He writes a pretty popular sci-fi series. Totally fascinating character."

And so I found myself rounding the block for the fourth time, looking for parking on Prospect Avenue during rush hour to meet Stuart's idea of a totally fascinating character.

This was the insane thing about living downtown or on the east side—the parking. But, the store was only about a mile and a half away so I could actually walk to work. Maybe give up the car all together. This was the kind of lucrative city neighborhood that had cafés, coffee shops, grocery stores and drug stores all within walking distance.

Finally, a BMW pulled away from the curb and I neatly took its parking spot. It was a windy, wet night, and I pulled the collar of my peacoat up against my neck as I walked the block to the apartment building with the inexplicable name of The Coronet. It was six stories, probably built in the late sixties or early seventies. No doubt an op art gem in its day, it now looked a little shabby and shrill, giving the eye a stumbling block amid the tall, spare and glassy high-rises that surrounded it.

There was a small, well-lighted outer lobby. I buzzed the super's apartment.

"Yeah?"

"Lauren Campbell. I'm here to see the apartment."

There was the sound of a buzzer and I pushed the door open and went up the two wide, shallow marble steps to the lobby. The walls were painted the same shade as the medicine I used to give Gordy for stomachaches. There was a black leather settee on chrome legs against one wall that reminded me of the backseat of a car and an enormous framed poster from an Elvis concert above it. The effect was more funky than tacky, which was a good sign.

I found the super's apartment around the corner, across from an elevator that looked like it was the size of a closet. I knocked on his door and waited.

"Come on in!" he yelled.

The miniblinds were closed and the apartment was dim, lit by only one lamp and the spillover from a computer screen on a desk on the far side of the room. The super was sitting at the computer, clicking at the keys, his back to me.

"Take a seat. I'm almost done," he said.

I sat down on a decent leather sofa but the *almost* turned into fifteen minutes.

"Excuse me?" I ventured.

"One second," he answered.

One second turned into another ten minutes.

"If you'd rather I came back—"

He stopped his clicking and stared up at the ceiling, shaking his head slowly. "It really bugs the hell out of me when they expect me to actually act like the building superintendent."

He swung around in his desk chair, jerked to his feet and grabbed a cane hanging off the arm of the chair.

It was the man with the blue eyes.

"Well," he said, staring at me under lowered brows, "you've got my attention now. So what do you want?"

Apparently, I didn't make much of an impression even without my bonnet and braids because he was giving no indication that he recognized me as the woman he'd rescued from a naked mannequin or the woman from the jazz club.

"I came to see about the apartment—the two bedroom. I'm Lauren Campbell."

"Jack Neuhouse," he said. "Stuart sent you, didn't he?"

"Right."

"Well, it's up on the fifth floor so let's hope the elevator is working. If I have to limp all the way up, you might as well plan on spending the night."

I stared at him.

"That was a joke."

I followed him as he limped over to the elevator and pushed the button. The door immediately slid open.

"We're in luck," he said dourly.

I followed him inside. The walls were filled with graffiti. A few of the drawings made me blush. I tried not to look at him. But it was so hard not to meet those blue, blue eyes.

"Disgusting, I know," he said in a voice that implied just the opposite. "Management has given up trying to correct the problem," he said. "I suggested they just let the denizens express themselves and it's worked out quite well as you can see. We frown on four letters words, of course, but it's much harder to censor pictures."

I let out a giggle that embarrassed me in its girlishness.

He gave me a look from under his brows. "Fetching, aren't you?"

Luckily, I didn't have to answer because the elevator doors opened.

"Watch your step," he said. "It never quite reaches this floor."

"Is it—um—is it safe?" I asked.

"We haven't lost anybody yet."

I climbed up the six-inch gap between the elevator floor and the hallway. Someone was cooking—something spicy and deliciously aromatic.

"Puerto Rican lady lives there." He pointed at a door with his cane. "She's a great cook. Whenever she's late with her rent check, I get a pot of this fabulous stuff she makes with beans and rice and chicken."

We went around the corner and he unlocked the door to 5C and stood by to let me walk in ahead of him.

Stuart was right. It was small. There was a galley kitchen to the right, separated from the living room with a breakfast bar. The living room was narrow and long with two windows at the far end. I took a walk over to check out the view. Below me, Prospect Avenue ran five lanes wide, one way, heading north from downtown. It was just getting dark and the march of headlights glistening on the rain washed street was as beautiful as any parade. All around me were tall buildings, most of them with enough glass to make me feel like I was watching one of those huge walls that held multiple television sets, each playing a different channel.

"Beautiful," I said.

"Funny. That's not usually the reaction we get."

I turned away from the window. "Okay if I just take a look around?" I asked.

"I believe that's what viewing an apartment means," he said dryly.

The biggest bedroom was small. The smallest bedroom was tiny. But the carpeting was decent and the windows opened in both bedrooms.

It was workable. Definitely workable. And, much as I hated leaving it, the idea of moving out of the house on Seagull Lane before I absolutely had to really appealed to me. I felt like I was taking hold of the reins of my life. Being proactive at last.

"Hardly a palace, as you can see," Jack Neuhouse said.

"No. But it could be a home. Can I paint the walls?"

"Any color but black." He studied me for a few seconds. "I bet you're the type to put curtains on the windows."

I grinned at him. "You're absolutely right. I am."

"Probably make them yourself, too," he mumbled.

"Of course. I also loom the cloth. That's why I need the second bedroom. For the loom."

His eyes quickly went to mine. I thought I detected a small look of appreciation in that sea of Caribbean blue.

"We don't allow goats or sheep," he said.

I sighed. "What a shame. Nevertheless, I think I'll take it."

He raised a brow in surprise and I got to see how really handsome he was. Not in any conventional way. His hair was shorn fairly close to his head but still managed to stand up here and there. His craggy face held a five o'clock shadow that looked like it had decided to stay for cocktails. He was both rakish and scruffy and probably pushing fifty, but the years looked good on him.

"The elevator breaks down a couple of times a week," he said.

"Are you trying to talk me out of it?"

He shrugged. "Just a little truth in advertising. I don't want you slipping nasty notes under my door if you come home and there's an out of order sign hanging there."

"I've never written a nasty note in my life," I said.

"Somehow, I believe that. Well, come along and fill out the forms so I can get back to work."

I filled out forms and gave references. He looked at me a moment too long when I handed him the check for the first month's rent and security deposit and I thought he was going to say something about the mannequin episode. But he seemed truly not to recognize me. I decided I liked it that way.

I told Moira about Jack Neuhouse that night while she helped me pack.

"And you just keep running into this guy?"

"Yeah. He seemed to be all over the place."

She put a hand on her hip. "And why, may I ask, did you never mention this man to your best girlfriend?"

"Really, Moira, I spoke to him once when I was handing out yogurt. He was incredibly rude to Bernice, who was nagging me about the milkmaid gig. He was just so sarcastic but in that charming way, you know? Bernice was totally indignant and I was so grateful to see someone put her in her place for once that I gushingly called him my hero and then offered him a free yogurt. Not one of my most alluring moments."

"I'm sure it went with the braids, sweetie," Moira said.

"Thanks. I feel better now. Anyway, after that I saw him a couple of times around town. And then one day at Grant's, he rescued me from beneath a naked male mannequin."

Moira stared at me. "I'm beginning to think you live a whole other secret life."

I laughed and kept on wrapping dishes.

"What I like most about this whole thing—"

"Other than living above the man with the blue eyes?" Moira asked.

"Will you get your mind off him."

She gave me a wicked grin. "You first."

I decided I wasn't touching that crack with a ten-foot curtain rod.

We wrapped dishes and knickknacks in silence for a few minutes and then Moira asked, "What are these?"

I looked up. She was holding up a few small canvases. "Oh, those are Gordy's."

"You mean he painted them?"

I nodded. "He was really into art for a while—just before he started high school."

"So, you're saying he painted these when he was like fourteen, fifteen?"

"Yes. But he started drawing when he was around eight years old. We used to do watercolors together."

"Lauren, I don't know if you realize this or not, but these are pretty amazing for a kid that age."

I moved closer so I could look over her shoulder. "Well, I always thought so—but I'm his mom."

"Well, I'm not, and I'm telling you, as an art lover and collector, we might have something here."

"Seriously?"

"I may be flighty, hon, but I never kid about this sort of thing."

"I was thinking I might get a few of them framed for the apartment."

"I sure would if I were you," Moira said.

"Will you help me chose which ones to hang?"

"Are you kidding? I'd adore it." She stared at me for a moment. "What?"

"I was just thinking about how far you've come."

"Funny, I keep thinking about how far I have yet to go."

"But it's only been a few months since you were bribing Roger with pork loin for a roof over your head and wearing a cape to work. And now you've got a real career and your own apartment."

"What apartment?"

My head jerked up. Gordy, a duffel bag hanging over his shoulder, was standing in the kitchen doorway, bedraggled and angry.

"Tell me something, Ma—were you planning on sending me your forwarding address?"

"Gordy—honey—I just got the apartment this afternoon. I

haven't really had time to tell anybody yet. And if you'd return my calls once in a while—"

He tossed his head. "Right, all my fault again."

I looked helplessly at Moira.

"I think I hear Stan calling me," she said. "Probably needs help with his caboose or something."

At the back door she mouthed *Call me*.

"Is there some kind of school holiday I didn't know about?" I asked Gordy hopefully after I'd shut the back door.

"No." He threw his duffel down. "School's over for me. I dropped out."

While I tried not to go into shock he went over to the refrigerator and pulled out the milk, defiantly drinking it right from the carton.

"You dropped out? Why? I mean, wouldn't it be better to finish out the term, at least?"

He slammed the refrigerator door. "Forget it, Ma. I'm not going back."

I held my breath and counted to ten. I knew I had to tread softly or I'd never get the information I needed.

"Are you hungry? I could make you a sandwich."

He shrugged as he stared at some spot on the wall—some point he'd invented in his mind to keep from having to look at me. He seemed so tired—the skin of his face drawn tight like there was nothing there but flesh and bone. It was hard to tell if he'd lost weight in his baggy clothes but I was betting on yes.

I made him a turkey and provolone sandwich, poured him a big glass of milk and handed them to him. He started over to the corner where the breakfast nook had once been, then stopped and just stood there for a moment before taking a seat at the table. I sat across from him while he wolfed half of the sandwich down in two bites.

"Gordy, have you talked to your father about this?"

He snorted. "Yeah—right. He calls me every day."

"Gordy, I call you. You never return my calls."

"Well, there are no calls to return with Dad. Nothing to ignore."

"Still, I think he'd agree with me on this, Gordy. If you finish this first year, you'd have credits that could be transferred—"

"Ma—just knock it off, okay?" He finally looked at me. His cheeks were red like they'd always gotten when he was being defiant as a little boy. "I didn't quit," he said. "I got kicked out."

I would have bet my next week's paycheck that I never would have heard those words from my son. Good thing I'm not into gambling, because we wouldn't be eating next week if I were.

"Kicked out?" I repeated.

He was slumped in his chair, chewing down the last of his sandwich. He didn't bother to answer me. We both knew I'd heard it right the first time.

"But, Gordy, why? Is it drugs?"

He pushed his chair back with such force it slammed against the wall and nicked the new paint.

"Don't you know me at all, Ma? Would you have asked me that six months ago? Or is thinking I'm smoking weed or shoving some powder up my nose easier than knowing the truth?"

For a moment, I was too stunned to even speak. Gordy turned around, picked up his duffel, and headed toward the front door.

I hurried after him. "Gordy, what truth? Gordy! Where are you going?"

"To Dad's."

"But—but you belong here!"

"Not anymore, I don't."

"What do you mean by that?"

He stopped and turned to face me. "There's a for-sale sign out there on the lawn. You *rented* an apartment already and I didn't even know you were looking." He stopped and shook his head in bewilderment. "It's like I don't even have a home anymore."

"But—" I wanted to tell him that I'd make a home for him wherever I was. But he didn't give me the chance. He turned around again and headed for the door.

"Gordy, please, we need to talk. Wait until morning—Gordy!"

"I don't want to talk. And at Dad's, I know I won't have to."

He slammed the door in my face and all I could do was stare at it. I didn't know what to do. Didn't know how to stop him. He was no longer a little boy that I could take by the hand and lead to safety.

But I needed answers. Shit, who was I kidding. I didn't even know all the questions, yet. Not knowing what else to do, I reached for the phone and called my credit card company. It was a place to start.

I went through the five thousand numbers I had to punch in to finally get the recording of the latest transactions on my card. There had been no returns posted. The six hundred Gordy charged was still on the card.

The money had to be the key, I thought as I hung up the phone. Add the six hundred to the one hundred he'd gotten from Roger. Seven hundred bucks. If he wasn't buying drugs, what was he doing with it? And how did it figure into the reason he was kicked out of school, into his changed attitude and appearance?

I made myself wait a half an hour, then I called Roger.

"Is he there?" I asked.

"Yes. He's already sleeping. He looks like hell. What's going on?"

"I don't know what's going on. All he said was that he'd been kicked out of school."

"That's crap. He told me he dropped out."

"Well, he's lying to you, Roger."

There was a pause, then a tightness in his voice when he said, "My son doesn't lie to me."

"Your son has been lying to everyone."

"This is going to be one hell of a day," Dora dourly predicted as she swept past us on her way to her office.

I was feeling a little dour myself. I was still trying to make sense of what had happened with Gordy the night before. I'd lain awake most of the night wondering what the hell had gone wrong and how I was going to handle the situation.

"What's bugging her?" Kelly asked after Dora had shut her office door behind her.

"It's rumored that the supermodel who was supposed to be the surprise attraction of the fashion show has backed out," Stuart said.

"Well, that should make for a fun morning," Kelly grumbled.

I wasn't worried. I figured my day couldn't get any worse than it already was.

A few hours later, it got worse.

Dora poked her head out of her office. "Lauren, can I see you for a moment?"

I'd been putting together a book of fabric samples so Dora and Monica could choose one for the skirt of the runway that was being set up in the room with gilded crown moldings that used to be the tea room at Grant's. I put it aside and walked over to Dora's office.

"You wanted to see me?"

"Shut the door, kid, and take a seat. We've got problems."

"What's up?"

"Well, I don't know if you've heard the rumors or not, but

they're true. Our so-called secret supermodel appearance is off. The bitch backed out on us and now we're in a fix. Milwaukee isn't exactly New York. Supermodels aren't knocking on the door begging to walk the runway at Grant's."

I made sympathetic noises but I didn't really see what this had to do with me.

"We thought we might actually have to cancel. Imagine— no spring fashion show for the first time in sixty-five years. And then I remembered that your mother is Bernie Blondell. When I mentioned this to Monica she practically started swinging from the chandeliers."

"Oh?" I said cautiously. Suddenly I had a gut feeling I wasn't going to like this conversation.

"We were thinking of how in vogue older models have become and about how much publicity might be generated by her having local ties. So, we've decided that we want her to be the star of our fashion show."

My mouth went semidry, like cheap champagne. "Um—" I cleared my throat. "You want my mother in the fashion show?"

"Yes, kid, that's what we want. We want Bernie Blondell to replace that bitch who dumped us."

"Are you sure? I mean, she hasn't modeled in years, and—"

"But, I hear that she's just as gorgeous as ever."

"Well, true, she is, but—"

"But what, dear?" Dora asked as she interlaced her fingers and leaned across her desk to scrutinize me.

"Well, it's just that—"

"It may not have occurred to you, Lauren, but helping to save this fashion show would be quite a feather in your cap as far as a career at Grant's. It'll make you look good to the company."

She smiled. "And don't let's forget that I hired you with no experience, no training—"

I laughed. "Yes, yes—and I'll be forever grateful," I said. "And, of course I'll talk to my mother about being in the show. I'm sure she'll be thrilled at the invitation."

She slammed her hand on her desk. "Now we're talking! Tell her we'd like her for at least three outfits and that—"

I sat there and barely heard a word. All I could think of was that my mother was going to invade my work world. A world where I was thought of as talented and competent. I mean, it was one thing to have my mother criticize me in front of strangers, but to have her cluck over me in front of Dora—my insides cringed at the thought.

By the time I left Dora's office my stomach was in knots. Work was one of my few refuges these days. If Bernice got involved in this project, I could kiss any peace of mind goodbye.

But I loved this job. And if the show was a success, it would be a boost to my fledgling career.

Unfortunately, there were more problems with the plan than me not wanting my mother to invade my work world. Bernice and I were still in semifeud state about Gordy's behavior during the Christmas holidays. I had no idea how she was going to take the fact that her perfect grandson was no longer in college and appeared to be moving in with his father.

When I got back to my workstation, I did some deep breathing and thought fondly of Chocolate Suicide and lamented the fact that so few restaurants delivered these days. Feeling no calmer, I picked up the phone and called my mother to ask her if we could get together for dinner.

"I thought we weren't speaking," she said.

"I thought we just hadn't spoken," I countered.

She sighed. "If this invitation is for the purpose of discussing my grandson, then we might as well hang up right now."

"It's more business than personal."

I nearly choked on the words, considering that if this dinner went well, it would mean that business was going to get uncomfortably personal for a while.

"All right. But I've got a dinner date already. Why don't we meet for a drink at my hotel around seven?"

"Seven it is, then," I said.

As I drove to my mother's, I considered my options. It was hard to see me coming out a winner in this situation. If Bernice said yes, I was facing several weeks of possible humiliation at work. But if she said no, I'd be letting Dora down. I might even have to crawl back to Temporary Solutions to pass out samples in silly costumes by day and try to figure out a spreadsheet by night.

By the time I found a parking spot on a side street in Yankee Hill, I was rooting for possible humiliation because I owed Dora a great deal. Now I just had to decide whether to tell Bernice about Gordy before or after I proffered Dora's invitation.

I was still wrestling with that one when I walked into the lobby. Bernice was already seated on one of the sofas, sipping an old fashioned. She was wearing a gray wool sheath and patent leather slingbacks that would have done Audrey Hepburn proud.

"Mother," I said when I'd walked across the lobby. "You look beautiful."

Her smile curved softly. "Thank you. You look very nice, as well. Although, that sweater shouldn't really be worn with a shirt under it. And, if I were you, I'd rethink the shoes."

To seethe or not to seethe? This became the question. And then it hit me. I could use this to my advantage. Like Quint had once told me, it was up to me how I decided to take the things my mother said to me. This time I was going to grab the silver lining and hang on for dear life.

"You know, Mother, I think you're probably right. Maybe we could go shoe shopping sometime and you could help me pick out a few pairs."

Bernice looked a little surprised, but she hid it by taking another sip of her old fashioned.

A waiter in a white shirt and black pants came over to see if I wanted anything to drink. "I'll have what she's having," I said.

"Why do I get the feeling I'm being buttered up for something?" Bernice said after the waiter left.

"Just because I suggested some shopping?"

She looked at her watch. "Let's get on with it. I don't have much time."

"Well, before we get down to business, there are a couple of things I need to tell you. First, I've signed a lease on an apartment."

"Really? Where is it?"

I told her and she knew the building.

"I had friends living in that building years ago," she said. "It's not a bad place to start out. And I must say that I'm pleased that you're not leaving it up to Roger to decide when you have to move."

I didn't even get a chance to bask in her pleasure a little before she asked, "And the other thing you wanted to tell me?"

"Well—Gordy has left school and is temporarily living with his father."

She stared at me for a few heartbeats. "How temporarily?"

"I'm not sure—until he can stand the sight of me again, I suppose."

"Children can be so selfish and self-absorbed," Bernice said and I nearly dropped my drink. "Really," she went on, "you're the one who's raised him. It wouldn't hurt for him to show you some respect for your hard work and sacrifices."

Okay, I knew she was projecting a little, but, what the hell, I'd take the support. "Thank you, Mother," I said.

She looked at her watch again. "Now if there really is business to discuss, we better get to it."

"I'm here to make you an offer." I'd decided the word *offer* might work better than the word *favor*.

Her brow went up. "What kind of offer?"

"Grant's would like to hire you for their spring fashion show."

She just stared at me for a moment. "You mean, they want me to do the announcing or something?"

I shook my head. "No. They want you to be the featured model."

She tilted her head. "Really? And whose idea was this? Are you involved?"

"My boss, Dora Reynolds, and Monica Lisbon from special promotions cooked it up. The only way I'm involved is working on props and accessories." I could see she was getting interested. Looking flattered, even. So I pressed on. "Dora practically begged me to ask you. They'd like you to do three outfits, at the very least."

Now she was really smiling, that wide smile that got her her first modeling job in a toothpaste ad when she was sixteen. It suddenly made me feel ashamed of myself for being so reluctant to ask her.

"So, can I tell Dora that you're interested?"

"Yes. Do that." She started to put on a pair of black lambskin gloves. "I have to run, dear. I'm meeting my date down the street for dinner. Please, stay and finish your drink. They'll just put it on my tab."

She kissed my cheek, then stood and with one graceful move, threw a full-length fur coat over her shoulders where it settled like a finely trained animal.

"Tell your Dora Reynolds to give me a call," she said. "And tell Gordy I am not at all pleased with his choices."

I watched her walk across the lobby—as did just about everyone there. She still had that model's walk that always mystified me. When I was younger, I used to try to emulate it only to either trip over my own feet or lose my balance completely and fall flat on my butt.

After all these years, my mother was still a mystery to me that I'd never been able to crack. And now, it looked like I was going to be working with her.

As long as it was going on my mother's tab, anyway, I decided I could use another drink.

With two old-fashioneds under my belt, I drove over to Roger's. I couldn't just let this go. I needed answers. And I needed my son back home with me. Even if the home was soon going to be a tiny two-bedroom apartment.

"He's out," Roger said when I got to the condo.

"Out? Are you crazy? He shouldn't be out with what's going on. He needs guidance right now. Living with you, he might as well be living alone."

"Lauren, if I were you I wouldn't throw stones. Your glass house isn't looking so good right now."

"Meaning?"

"Meaning our son got this way on your watch."

"But I've been telling everyone that something was wrong with Gordy, and no one wanted to listen."

"And that's exactly why he's chosen to stay here with me. He doesn't need a hysterical mother on his back when he's going through a tough time. Now I'd appreciate it if you'd leave."

I bit my lip and looked down at the floor for a second. "No," I said, lifting my head, "I don't think I'm ready to leave yet. Not until I point out to you that we really don't know what tough time Gordy is going through. Doesn't that bother you at all? Because it sure as hell bothers me. I think it's time our son stood up and told us the truth."

"I really wish you would stop accusing our son of lying."

"Roger…" But then I realized he and I had never been on the same page where Gordy was concerned. Why would I expect Roger to listen to me now?

I left him standing there while I stalked back to my car.

CHAPTER 14

At Grant's, things were bubbling. Dora was overjoyed to have Bernice come on board. And Bernice was overjoyed to be working as a model again. She was stunning to watch at the preliminary rehearsals. She was still so polished. Still such a presence. And, alas, still so opinionated.

Bernice had sent me scurrying to find some accessories for a pale turquoise suit and I'd returned with black shoes and purse.

"Honestly, Lauren, even a novice should know that one never wears a black shoe with a delicate color."

Should I have been surprised? No. Because I also always picked the wrong length of pearls, couldn't tell the difference between mauve and pink, and was told I had better start carrying a ruler around because if I thought those shoes had three-inch heels I must be blind.

After three days, I was concerned about becoming one of those older single women who stop for martinis all by themselves after work. The kind that hang around hotel bars just so it looks as if they might be staying there and not looking for a pick-up.

To everyone else, my mother was sweet, gentle, kind and witty. Even when Kelly brought her coffee with cream when she'd requested it black, Bernice handled it with grace and the utmost of care for Kelly's feelings. Everyone loved working with her.

Everyone but me.

* * *

The situation with Gordy wasn't so hot, either. I kept trying to get him to come over to the house to go through his belongings but he remained obstinate so I packed it all up and what wasn't going to the apartment, Moira agreed to store in her attic.

I moved into my apartment on March first. It was a blustery day, but sunny enough to feel almost warm. Quint insisted on helping with his truck. With Moira's car, my car and Stuart helping to load, we decided I didn't need to hire movers. The furniture company had moved my new sofa and entertainment center in but the rest of it had to be transported in the tiny elevator—which often meant we sent up entire loads on their own and raced up the staircase to meet them on floor five.

"Some of the tenants aren't pleased," Jack said while I waited in the lobby for the empty elevator to return.

I grimaced and twisted my hands together. "I'm sorry. We should be finished soon."

He shook his head. "Do you ever give up being the good girl?" he asked. "Someone forgot to teach you the delights of being a nuisance."

The remark, given my history, intrigued me. But the elevator doors opened just then and I didn't get a chance to pursue the subject. We already had a stack of stuff in the lobby ready for the next trip up.

When we were finished, Moira ordered pizza for everybody and Quint ran down a few blocks to a store for cold beer. We sat on boxes and my sofa, still wrapped in plastic, groaning about aching muscles and admiring the view.

"This place is a voyeur's paradise," Moira said.

"No kidding," Stuart agreed. "You should get yourself a pair of binoculars."

Stuart was the first to leave, then Moira, who became teary-eyed at the door.

"I'm gonna miss you so much, honey."

"Stop that. Your mascara will run. Besides, I'm only a few miles away."

We sniffled and held each other for a few minutes and then she left.

Quint, sprawled attractively on my new sofa, didn't show any signs of leaving.

"Don't make me kick you out of here," I said.

He tilted his head. "So the answer is still no?"

"Find yourself a nice girl your own age, Quint. You deserve her."

"But until I find her," he said, one corner of his mouth quirked in that way he knew I found irresistible, "couldn't we just engage in infrequent, meaningless sex?"

"I did that once," I said. "It was called marriage."

Quint laughed at that, got off the sofa, kissed me sweetly on the forehead and left.

I was tired but too keyed up to sleep. I sat in my darkened living room, watching the traffic, watching the images of people working at desks, working out on treadmills, filling dishwashers and watching television.

It occurred to me that I should have had Quint and Stuart put the bed up for me before they left. How hard could it be? So about half past midnight, I tried to put the frame together myself, but every time I got one side of the bed rail into its assigned slot on the headboard, the other side would fall out. I was making so much noise, I nearly missed the knock on the door.

I tiptoed over. "Who is it?" I asked.

"Look in the peephole," a voice said.

Oh, right, I thought. I was in an apartment now. They had peepholes. I squinted one eye shut and pressed the other to the hole.

It was Jack.

What could he want this time of night?

And would I give it to him if he asked for it?

"I'm here in an official capacity," came his voice muffled through the door.

Of course he was. What had I been thinking? I took the chain off the door and unlocked it. "Come in," I said.

"The tenant below you thinks you've murdered your parents and are now building coffins to have them carried away in."

I blinked. "Excuse me?"

"You're making a hell of a lot of noise for a new tenant."

"Oh—oh, I'm sorry. I didn't think—it's just that I was trying to put my bed together so I could get to sleep."

"I assure you that nearly everyone on this side of the building would love to see you get to sleep. Is there anything I can do to help?"

"Well, I'm having trouble getting the frame together— maybe, if you could just—"

"It's what I'm here for," he said.

He followed me into the bedroom and I was flabbergasted at how insanely easy it became when there were two people working at it. He helped me hoist the box spring and mattress into place and before I knew it, he was helping me make the bed with my sprigged green sheets.

It seemed an intimate thing to be doing with a man I barely knew.

"There," he said when the last pillow had been stuffed into its case. "Now the building can sleep. Good night, Ms. Campbell."

He started for the door and I suddenly asked, "Would you care for a cup of hot chocolate?"

I grimaced at my question. Hot chocolate? Right. He was a scruffy writer. He probably had a half-empty bottle of bourbon on his desk that he couldn't wait to get back to.

"I'd love some," he said to my surprise.

We perched on a couple of stools at the breakfast bar, sipping our chocolate.

"Do you have trouble sleeping?" I asked him.

"I think insomnia goes with the profession."

"Stuart told me that you've written a series of sci-fi books."

"Stuart talks too much."

"Why sci-fi?"

He gave me a look. "Not easily deterred, are you?"

"I used to be a fund raiser for the PTA."

"Ah, and here I thought you all went into the CIA once your kids went off to college."

I laughed. "So, why sci-fi?"

"If I buy a hundred pizzas from the soccer team will you stop asking questions?"

"No," I said.

"Didn't think so. I chose sci-fi for the usual reason. Escape. I had a—lonely childhood. We lived on a farm and I hated it. Hated the smell of hay and manure. Hated the endless chores and the monotony. I'd hide out in the woods and make up little worlds of my own. This, of course, didn't make my parents happy or make me very popular with my siblings. So, when I was about sixteen, I hopped a freight and got the hell out of Kansas." He drank more of his hot chocolate. "I bummed around for a while and the stories just kept coming. When the notebooks got too heavy to carry on my back anymore, I settled in Milwaukee."

Stuart was right. He was a fascinating character. But hadn't I known that the first moment I'd laid eyes on him? "So are you still escaping?" I actually had the audacity to ask him.

He shook his head. "No. Now I'm punishing myself for my success as a hack by writing something *literary*, as they say. The free apartment is the draw here. I hate the interruptions but I'm hanging on to enough money so I won't have to compromise my soul. For a few years, anyway. And you? What brings you to The Coronet?"

"Nothing quite as interesting. Just divorce, financial ruin. The usual."

"How long have you been divorced?"

"Ten years."

His eyebrows shot up. "And it's taken you that long to find an apartment?"

I laughed. "It's a long story. Let's save it for another time."

I thanked him for helping with the bed. He thanked me for the hot chocolate. We stood in the doorway, staring at each other for a few seconds and then he turned from the door and I shut it.

"Honestly, Moira, I don't think I've ever been so interested in a man in my life," I told her over the phone the next day.

"What about Quint?"

"No comparison. Quint was a boy, charming, sexy, but didn't you ever notice how his face was sort of a blank slate."

"He's gorgeous, nuff said."

"But with Jack, you get the sense that every line on his face tells a story, every wrinkle on his forehead stands for a problem grappled with or—"

"Oh, brother. Honey, have you got it bad. And after only one hot chocolate, too."

"I'm pretty sure I'm not his type."

"And that, girlfriend, makes it all the more interesting."

Interesting turned into scarce for the next few days. I managed to forbid myself from lingering in the hallway by the elevators and I only thought of purposely plugging up the kitchen sink once or twice before I came to my senses.

Meanwhile, when I tossed and turned at night, the emphasis was still on my son. My mind only occasionally wandered to the man with the blue eyes on the first floor. It was after just such a night when I finally gave up trying to sleep at six in the morning.

I was about to make myself a big breakfast when I remembered those huge muffins at the coffeehouse where I stopped for my morning latte on the way to work. I'd become one of those people who walk to work in the mornings drinking overpriced coffee. Today, I actually had the luxury of time to sit and have a four-thousand-calorie muffin.

Freshly showered and wearing one of my mother's picks—pale yellow cardigan with a pale green skirt—I left the building around seven. True spring had finally arrived. The trees were well-budded, daffodils and hyacinths were bursting through the earth of the gardens surrounding the converted mansions. There were some pleasures that even worry can't take away from you.

The coffeehouse was packed. I stood in line for a good ten minutes to order my latte and muffin. I smiled as I wondered what Moira would make of this kind of waiting. It seemed to have nothing at all to do with gender this time, and everything to do with how many people ordered something with whipped cream on it.

I turned around to find a table and there he was. Just sitting there like he was waiting for me. Which, of course, he wasn't. But, since tables were in short supply and his had an extra chair, I thought, why not?

"You know, you're the only person I've ever met who has a smile while waiting in line for their morning coffee," Jack said as I sat down across from him.

"I was just remembering something a friend of mine said about women always waiting."

"Ah—well, this place would seem to be an equal opportunity irritation."

I laughed.

"Do you always laugh in all the right places?"

"Is that bad?"

"Not when it's me trying to be droll, it isn't. What are you doing up so early? You usually just stop in for a takeout."

"Have you been spying on me?"

He gave a little shrug. "Of course. I find you a fascinating specimen of your species."

"What species is that?" I asked.

"Dislocated suburbanite," he answered.

"What happened to your leg?"

He laughed softly. "I take it yours was one of the few houses in the neighborhood that had no bushes to beat around."

"If you can reduce my life to a cliché," I said primly, "I can certainly ask you about your leg."

He looked down at the table for a moment and when he looked back up, his face was sober. "Actually, I appreciate the forthrightness. Most people just stare and hint."

"Then tell me," I said.

"Only if you promise not to cry," he said with the kind of grin the devil might envy.

"I promise," I said as I started to eat my muffin.

"It was that freight hopping that got me out of Kansas that also did me in. One day in Southern Illinois, I missed. Broke my leg in three places. Of course, being out in the middle of nowhere, I didn't know that at the time. Another rider of the rails helped me splint it up. Never did heal right."

"How old were you?"

"Seventeen."

"Does it hurt?"

"Some days are better than others."

I sniffed.

"Now don't get all misty eyed on me," he said.

I gave myself a shake. "I guess I was thinking of my son. He's eighteen and I couldn't sleep last night for worrying about him and he's living with his father. I can't imagine what your mother must have gone through—not knowing where you were."

He toyed with a napkin. "I think they were just fine with not knowing where I was. Still are."

"You mean, you haven't been in touch with them since you left Kansas?"

He shook his head. "It wasn't likely we would suddenly begin to like each other."

I dug in my purse for a tissue.

"You promised not to cry," he said.

I blew my nose. "Sorry. I'm a sucker for a sad childhood story."

"Maybe someday, you'll tell me yours," he said.

That afternoon, we had a meeting in Monica's office to choose the final outfits for the show. Monica should have been in charge, along with the buyers from the various departments, but it was Bernice who'd taken the floor.

"Who on earth chose this necklace to go with this outfit?" my mother asked.

"I did," I answered with a sigh.

"Are you insane? These amber beads are far too long to wear with this neckline. Any idiot should be able to see that—"

Okay, I'd just had breakfast with a guy who lived what he believed. A guy who'd left home at sixteen rather than take any shit. A guy who was still resisting convention. Maybe it was about time I stood up for what I wanted, too. I cleared my throat. "Um—Bernice—excuse me, but I'd like to speak to you alone for a moment."

"Now?" she asked like I'd just made a request for her to cover herself in whipped cream and stick a cherry on her head.

I, however, remained calm. "Yes, please, now."

As I walked back to the display department, I could hear her heels clicking behind me. Once we'd entered the department, I turned to face her. She was seething.

"What in heaven's name could be so important that you had to interrupt a meeting to tell me?"

"Me, mother. *I* am more important at the moment than a meeting about costume jewelry."

"Well, what's the matter? Have you been to a doctor? Are you sick?"

"Oh, I'm sick, all right. Sick and tired of the way you treat me. Sick and tired of being yelled at and belittled in front of my colleagues. I work here, Mother—you are a guest. So quit treating me like shit!"

Bernice actually looked dumbfounded. "Treating you like shit?"

"Yes—and I think you know what I'm talking about. You don't talk to Dora, or even Kelly, the way you talk to me."

"But you're my daughter. Of course I'm going to think I can take liberties."

"Well, Mother, guess what? You can't. I deserve as much respect as you give anyone else. If I make a mistake fine, tell me, but don't treat me like I'm a little girl who just spilled on her velvet pinafore!"

She fumed and tapped her foot for a few seconds. "Okay," she finally said, "fair enough. But I also have a request. I'd like you to acknowledge that I might know a thing or two about this business and stop acting like a petulant child every time I correct you."

"You correct me like I'm a child! At work, at least, can't you just treat me like everyone else?"

"Do you think you can take suggestions and direction from me like everyone else?"

All right. She had a point. This wasn't a one way street. And if we were going to walk it together, we were going to have to give each other respect and space.

"All right," I said. "If you can do it, I can, too."

And that was the beginning of a truce between my mother and me. We both worked hard at it. I really listened when she made suggestions, she really did her best to treat me with respect if I didn't get it right the first time. To my surprise, after a few days I discovered that we weren't just learning to work together, we were actually starting to like each other, too.

"You should just chill and let Roger have Gordy for a while," Moira said as she dipped her paintbrush into a gallon of white paint.

I'd decided to paint all the rooms of my new apartment white—sort of make it a blank canvas to display my new life on. Moira had generously come over to help. I'd finished painting my bedroom last night and we were now working in what I hoped would someday be Gordy's room.

"Who knows," Moira went on, "maybe the shirt is right. Maybe the kid just needs a little time."

I was silent long enough for Moira to say, "Well, I guess that suggestion went over as well as a thunderstorm at an outdoor rock concert."

I sighed and put down my paintbrush. "I'm sorry. It's just hard to accept this, that's all. I mean, I raised him, I was the one who was there for him. And now when he's in real trouble, he turns to his father."

"I don't think he's so much turning to his father as he is turning away from you, sweetie," Moira said.

I picked up a can of diet cola from the floor and took a swig. "Is that supposed to make me feel better?"

"Well, you know him pretty well, you love him, he loves you. You've been close, maybe closer to him than anyone else who's ever been in his life. He's not ready yet for you to see whatever his demon is right now. It means too much."

Who knew I'd get that kind of parenting advice from Moira?

"You know, that almost makes sense," I said as I picked up my paintbrush again.

"Don't sound so surprised—after all, I did raise two of my own."

"And they're both thriving so I guess you must have known what you were doing," I conceded.

"Ha! I wouldn't go that far. I made my share of mistakes. But you learn as you go. Therefore, at this point, I am the expert and you are the novice."

I hooted as I slapped more paint on the walls. "I don't know about that, but I'll tell you one thing, you've given me some terrific ideas for this place."

We'd already finished the living room. My new, smaller and more colorful sofa—a geometric print in blues and purples—had finally been stripped of its protective plastic and was in place on the wall perpendicular to the windows. One of Gordy's largest paintings was framed and hanging on the wall above it. Moira had found me a slipper chair in deep purple velvet at a closeout sale. A padded bench that opened for storage stood before the sofa in place of a coffee table. Since the apartment was so small, I'd gone minimalist and I found it was suiting me. Gone were the chintz, the ruffles, and the Americana that I'd clung to as if having a maple coffee table would insure that life would remain steady.

When we finished painting Gordy's room, Moira helped me decide where to hang a few more of his paintings.

"If you don't talk this kid into picking up a paintbrush again," Moira commented as she studied an impressionist-style still life, "I'm going to go after him myself."

"When the time is right, I'll broach the subject with him. I promise."

Moira sighed. "Ah, yes. Women and waiting. They go together like chicken wings and blue-cheese dressing. Which reminds me. I'm hungry. Got any takeout menus around here?"

I took Moira's advice and tried to give Gordy time. I didn't push, but a couple of times a week I called him and asked him to come over for dinner. The answer was always no. Finally, I decided that neutral territory might be the answer. He wasn't ready to see me living as a person yet and not his mom. So maybe we could have lunch in one of his favorite places, instead. Lunch wasn't all that big a commitment. It might work.

To my surprise, he said yes.

We made plans to meet at a microbrewery on Water Street that wasn't far from Grant's and had fantastic burgers and terrific views of the river. I got there first and spent a worried fifteen minutes wondering if he was going to show. But, right on time, the hostess showed him over to my table. There was a stoop to his shoulders that I didn't remember, but his father seemed to have succeeded in talking him into a haircut.

I kept the conversation going, telling tales of my job, and what it was like working with his grandmother. I wasn't sure he was listening at first, then he said, "I can't imagine you and Grandma working together."

"It hasn't been easy. I finally had to tell her off."

"No kidding? I'd like to have been a fly on the wall for that one."

The waitress came for our order. After she left, I told him about some of the courses I was thinking about taking next year. He seemed interested. Asked questions. The waitress came back with our burgers and when she left I decided to take the plunge.

"Sometimes I wish I could be a fly on the wall in your life, too," I said.

He gave an impatient move of his shoulders. "Don't start."

"Why not start?" I asked. "Don't you think I have a right to know what happened?"

He stared out the window for a long time. "Yes," he said tightly, in a way that reminded me too much of his father. "I think you have the right to know. But please don't ask me."

"I'm asking, Gordy. Why did you get kicked out of school?"

A fine rain had started to fall. It splashed jaggedly on the window next to us while I nearly held my breath, waiting.

"I can't do this," he said and then he took off, leaving his burger untouched.

I sat there stunned for a second then muttered, "Hell with this." I grabbed the burgers, wrapped them in napkins, threw money on the table and took off after him.

I caught him halfway down the block. He was just getting into his car. I jumped into the passenger side.

"We're having this out," I said. "Here and now. Why did you

get kicked out of school?" I asked him. "And if it wasn't drugs, what did you do with those electronics you charged to my account? What did you do with the hundred you asked your father for?"

He lowered his head until his forehead was against the steering wheel. "Let it go, Ma."

"No. I've let too many things go. No more Fantasy Island. No more window dressing. I want the truth."

When he brought his head up, I could see that he was silently crying. "You sure you can handle it?" he asked.

I gently pushed back his hair with my hand. "Gordy, one thing I've found out lately is that I can handle just about anything."

He laid his head back against the headrest. "Ma, I just wasn't making it. I mean, you get down there and you think *freedom*. But freedom also means there's nobody there to tell you when to study. Nobody there to tell you when to go to bed. When to get up. When to eat. I got lost, Ma." He shook his head. "Somewhere I got lost. I got into the crowd that parties, but some of those guys—" he turned his head to look at me "—they're really smart, you know? They can tap a keg one night and still ace a test the next day. I couldn't hack it. I kept falling further and further behind."

"Couldn't you have pulled back on the partying?" I asked.

"No—see, Ma, I'd already chosen sides. I was one of the cool guys. One of the dudes. Without partying, I'd have no friends. And it was way too late to change crowds. I was already known as one of the campus assholes."

I laughed a little at that. It was hard to picture my son as he was portraying himself. This was a Gordy I didn't know.

"Gordy, why didn't you come to me? Why didn't you let me know you were in trouble?"

He shrugged. "I guess a guy doesn't want to admit to his mom that he's a loser. Besides, when I came home for Thanksgiving and Christmas, things had changed so much. You suddenly had this life that had nothing to do with me."

"You'll always be the most important thing in my life. Don't you know that? And you could never be a loser in my eyes. You screwed up. Just like I screwed up. We both made some wrong choices. But it's not the end of the world."

"Maybe not," he said. "But it sure feels like it."

"Huh—tell me about it," I said.

He actually laughed. I fished some tissues out of my pocket and handed them to him. After he blew his nose, I handed him his burger, then unwrapped mine. We sat in the car, the rain coming down all around us and ate cold burgers. There was more I needed to know, more I wanted to ask. But I didn't want to risk pushing him away again by pushing too hard. We had begun. That had to be enough for now.

That night I prowled around my apartment almost wishing I had something to dust. This minimalist lifestyle didn't leave a restless woman much to putter with. Maybe I'd have to get some plants so I had something to water.

It was past eleven and I should really have been in bed, sleeping. We were swamped at work and I needed to be alert so I could keep on my toes around Bernice. But my mind couldn't stop thinking, speculating. I felt good about the progress Gordy and I had made that day. Now, if only he'd tell me everything— because I knew there had to be more to the story—then I could deal with it. It was this uncertainty that was driving me crazy.

I'd considered calling the university to see if I could get any information, but it seemed important that Gordy tell me himself.

Whatever he'd done, he had to both own up to it and own it in order for him to move past it. I'd learned that much in the past few months. Gordy had to take responsibility for himself, just like everyone else did.

I lay down on the sofa and tried to get interested in a book. Next thing I knew, the sound of a car alarm woke me. I peered at my watch. It was just after one. The evening had been mild so I'd left the windows open. Now the chilly night air was drifting in and I got up to close them. It was a slow night on Prospect Avenue. Not much traffic and most of the high-rises that surrounded my apartment were already dark.

I had a sudden urge to go outside, see what my new neighborhood felt like at this hour. I slipped a thick hooded sweatshirt over my drawstring pajama pants and ribbed tank top and left the apartment. In the stillness of the building, the elevator sounded loud with disapproval. When I reached the lobby, I passed quickly out the door and lowered myself to the top step. We were close to the lake here, closer than the Cove had been, and I could feel it on my face and in the tossing of my hair. I could be happy here, I thought, if only Gordy was all right. If only he were here with me.

I suddenly heard a noise. Footsteps and a thumping. I looked to the left.

"Another wanderer in the night?" Jack asked.

I was absurdly pleased to see him coming down the street. "I'm more of a sitter on the stoop in the night person," I said.

He lowered himself next to me. "What won't let you sleep tonight?"

I sighed. "My son. He's going through something that he won't let me in on." I told him a few of the details, ending with, "And it almost kills me that he's chosen to live with his father and not me. Now you tell me what won't let you sleep tonight?"

"Plots. Characters. A woman on the fifth floor."

I laughed, maybe to cover up the sound of the somersaults inside my belly. "I'm not the kind of woman that men lose sleep over."

"Who says?"

And then he leaned over and put his mouth on mine.

I jerked my head back. "What are you doing?"

"It's called kissing. Or do they use a different term in the suburbs?"

"No, I believe the terminology is the same. I was just wondering why you would—um—"

"'Cause I want to," he said. Then he did it again.

This time I let it happen and sooner than you can say *Does the bus stop on this corner* we were in each other's arms, necking. Right there on the steps of The Coronet, on Prospect Avenue, in the middle of the night.

His stubble was rough on my skin as he kissed my neck, nibbled my ear, kissed my nose and then took my mouth again. The flavor of him was intoxicating and I felt myself drifting into a state of bliss that was making my limbs heavy and my joints weak.

A taxi went by and the driver honked his horn and whistled out his window at us.

I pulled away and blinked. "Um—I guess we better go in."

"Your place or mine?"

I took a breath. "I'm not ready."

He sighed and squinted up at the sky. "I knew you were going to say that."

"Sorry—I didn't mean to—"

"Quit being nice. A lady has a right to say no."

"Thank you," I said sincerely.

"But a man has a right to try again."

"I knew you were going to say that," I said.

He laughed heartily and when I finally crawled into my bed—
alone—I fell to sleep with the sound of it still in my heart.

"You know," my mother said the next day, "losing sleep never
changes the outcome of anything."

"What makes you think I'm losing sleep?"

"I know you. Besides, you've got dark circles under your eyes
that could pass for a lunar eclipse."

I was obviously too old to stay up until three in the morning,
necking with a man I barely knew, on the front stoop of my
apartment building. But that was a secret I was keeping to myself
for now. After all, like Quint, there was no future in my involve-
ment with Jack. He might be losing some sleep over the woman
in 5C, but I was hardly the one for him.

CHAPTER 15

The truce with Bernice was going well at work, so one night I decided to celebrate and actually cook for myself. I'd been haunting the frozen dinner section of the small grocery store on the way home from work for too long. Tonight I felt like pasta. Something simple, with veggies, a little olive oil and some freshly grated Parmesan cheese. As I walked the rest of the way home, the scent of the narrow, crusty French baguette sticking out of the top of my shopping bag kept me company.

I was sautéing mushrooms and peppers and garlic when someone knocked on my door. I looked through the peephole. It was Jack.

"I know you're in there," he said. "Open up."

"Geeze, give a girl a chance would you?" I said as I opened the door.

"I don't know if you know this or not, but it's customary for new tenants to invite the super for dinner."

I put my hand on my hip. "Really? Funny—I don't remember reading that in the lease."

"Always read the fine print. Now, are you going to invite me in or are you going to risk having me ignore you when your drain clogs or your air conditioning goes out?"

"Threats like those will get you food anytime. But how did you know I was cooking?"

"Are you kidding? A hungry writer always knows when someone is cooking within five miles."

I went back to the stove to stir my mushrooms and Jack perched on a stool at the breakfast bar.

"Did you get a lot of work done today?" I asked him.

"It flowed, baby, absolutely flowed."

I tried to tell myself that calling someone "baby" was probably customary for a hard-boiled writer, but I liked the sound of it anyway.

"Can you tell me what the book's about?"

"No. I'm not ready to talk about it yet."

"Fair enough."

When I passed him to get the pasta pot out he grabbed me and kissed me. It was quick and hard and it made my belly do a flip-flop. "Do you know," he asked, "how many women would be willing to just accept that answer?"

"How many?"

He thought for a moment. "One and a half. But the half woman lives in Des Moines so she barely counts."

I laughed, shoved the pasta pot at him and told him to fill it with water.

While we waited for the water to boil, Jack prowled around the living room, reading book titles on shelves, checking out what magazines I read. He stopped in front of the painting above the sofa and squinted at the signature.

"Relative of yours?" he asked.

"My son."

He looked around the room. "They're all his, aren't they?"

I nodded. "Gordy used to paint a lot. He gave it up a few years ago."

"Probably when he reached high school," Jack muttered.

I thought about it. "You're right. That is when he stopped."

"Peer pressure, need for acceptance," Jack muttered as he studied another painting. "Too bad. This is interesting stuff."

I knew I was grinning like a fool. "I always thought so," I said.

"Proud Mama bear," he said as he limped over to me and brushed the pad of his thumb over my bottom lip, then bent to kiss me.

"What was that for?" I asked breathlessly.

"I like kissing you. Haven't you noticed?"

He was homing in for another one. I held him back with my hand. "I think the water is boiling," I said.

"Coward," he muttered.

"Hungry," I corrected.

When the food was nearly done, Jack excused himself to go into the bathroom. I was getting out a couple of plates when there was another knock on the door. I looked through the peephole. It was Moira.

I opened the door. "Well, this is a surprise. What are you doing here?"

"I left my sunglasses over here the other day. You know—the teal ones?"

"Right. They're in the bedroom. I'll get them."

When I got back to the living room, Moira was sitting on a stool, nervously tapping her fingernails on the breakfast bar. Moira wouldn't threaten a manicure for nothing.

I handed her the glasses. "Something's up," I stated.

She stopped tapping. "Honey, I hate to tell you this, but there are rumors floating up and down Seagull Lane about you and Quint Mathews."

I looked quickly at the closed bathroom door.

"Moira—" I began, but she was undeterred.

"I was standing in line for some lox at The Market in the Cove and these two women behind me—can't think of their names but we've seen them at those excruciating crystal parties Amy always throws—anyway, these two women were talking about how you'd even lost your house for having an affair with a guy who was barely legal."

"Quint is twenty-two!" I exclaimed.

Just then the bathroom door opened and Jack came out.

"So you like younger men, huh? No wonder I can't seem to get to second base with you."

"Oh, Christ," Moira said. "I had no idea anyone else was here."

I sighed. "Jack Neuhouse meet Moira Rice."

"No wonder you never sleep at night with all this carrying on," Jack said.

"It's not what you think," I said primly as I went to drain the pasta. "It was one night, that's all."

The food was ready, so I invited Moira to stay.

"Who's this Amy you mentioned?" Jack asked while I cut the baguette into hunks.

"Amy Westcott," I explained. "Lives across the street from my old house."

"And she's the village gossip," Moira noted.

"I just thought of something." My fork was halfway to my mouth. "Quint's truck was parked outside my house till nearly dawn. Amy must have seen it."

"So what?" Jack asked. "Why get so fired up about it? You're divorced. So you had a fling with a twenty-two-year-old? If I was unattached and had a younger chick in my bed, I wouldn't care if the whole world knew."

"Typical male reaction," Moira drawled.

"No, really," Jack said. "What's the big deal?"

So I told him about Gordy accusing me of hiring Quint to put in a new kitchen floor to hide an affair.

"So that's how to get to third base with you. I have to lay a new floor."

Moira burst out laughing. I gave them both a stern look, then went on.

"As I was saying, I swore to Gordy that nothing was going on between Quint and me—and at the time, nothing was. If this gets back to him, he'll never believe that I was telling him the truth. He'll think I lied and he'll never trust me again and we're just now starting to communicate again and this could just wreck the little progress we've made."

"Preemptive strike," Jack said. "Tell the kid yourself. You've been divorced for ten years. You've got a right to get laid once in a while—not that I'm biased on the subject or anything."

Moira looked at me. "What is it with you and handymen?"

Jack sat straighter on his stool. "Please—I'm a building super."

"Mind if we get back on the subject?" I asked.

Jack raised a brow. "I thought we *were* on the subject. Your sex life."

I opened my mouth to protest, but then realized that that's what we were talking about. My sex life.

"Okay—look," I said. "The thing is, mothers get judged differently than other people."

Moira nodded. "She's right. Especially by their sons."

"I can't argue with that," Jack said. I thought back to that morning at the coffeehouse—Jack had probably been as hard on his mother for not being what he'd needed as I'd been on mine.

"This is just not a good time for Gordy to have to deal with something else. Hell, I don't want to deal with it, either."

Moira nodded. "It's a potential mess, all right. And God only knows what the shirt will have to say."

"The shirt?" Jack asked.

"That's what Moira calls Roger, my ex."

"He has his shirts custom made," Moira added.

"Scary," Jack said with a shudder.

"I always thought so," Moira agreed.

"Will you two shut up? I'm trying to think what to do about this."

"Well," Jack said, "so far we only have rumors and a parked truck. Could this Amy possibly have any real proof?"

Now it was my turn to shudder.

"*Is* that possible?" Moira asked.

"Well, we did start out in the living room—"

"Hmm, I had no idea you suburban ladies could be such hussies."

I gave Jack a look and turned back to Moira. "Someone could have seen something through the windows, I suppose."

"But then it would be just her word against yours," Moira said hopefully.

I groaned. "We both know how the gossip chain works on Seagull Lane. Everyone listens to Amy. Especially Bonnie."

Jack held up his fork. "Wait a minute, who's this Bonnie?"

So we told him.

"In other words, you think that if Amy has proof, this Bonnie will know all about it?"

"Right," Moira and I both said.

"Then I say get hold of this Bonnie and put the screws to her. It sounds like she's the kind of woman who would spill pretty easily under the right conditions."

"He's right," Moira said. "Except with Bonnie we don't need screws." She looked at me. "A pan of your killer brownies should do it."

And so we made a plan. Moira would call Bonnie and tell her I was coming over for coffee and I had mentioned that I missed Bonnie so could Bonnie come over, too?

"You know, she always liked you best of anyone else on Seagull Lane," Moira told Bonnie.

So, of course, Bonnie accepted the invitation.

We plied her with coffee and brownies and asked endless questions about her three sons. I could see Moira's eyes starting to glaze over as she tried to stifle a yawn.

Bonnie took her third brownie and I poured her fresh coffee. I figured she was probably buzzed enough on caffeine to loosen her tongue on a subject other than how Brian was doing in chemistry.

"You know, he could even turn out to be a doctor," she said with motherly awe and pride.

"Doctors are generally trustworthy people," Moira said, giving me an opening.

I seized it. "Speaking of trustworthy, Bonnie, I know I can trust you. So could I be perfectly candid?"

Bonnie tittered and blushed at the compliment. "By all means," she said as she took another bite.

"It's come to my attention that someone is spreading rumors about me."

Bonnie dropped her brownie. "I think I better be getting home. I have to put a roast in the oven for Tommy's dinner."

Moira moved more quickly than Bonnie and was standing in the kitchen door blocking her way by the time Bonnie reached it. "We think you know something, and if you do, I think you better tell us. You know how Tommy hates you listening to Amy's gossip. One call from me, and—"

Bonnie got a look of horror on her face. "All right. All right! I told Amy to keep her mouth shut, anyway. Lauren, you know I've always liked you. I hated what she was doing, but—"

Moira cut to the chase. "Just tell us, how does she know what she thinks she knows?"

So far the three of us had managed to avoid any and all words pertaining to sex.

"Why, she saw the pictures, of course," Bonnie said.

"Pictures?" Moira and I cried in unison.

"Yes. See, Amy gave Chuck one of those newfangled digital cameras for Christmas this year. I've never been able to figure out how to work a regular camera, let alone one of those new ones."

Moira rolled her eyes.

"Yes," I prompted, "so Chuck got a digital camera—"

"Oh—well, you know how Chuck gets on New Year's Eve. Champagne," Bonnie said with a giggle. "He gets real funny and hyper, like a kid on too much sugar."

"Right," Moira said impatiently, "old Chucky was drunk on New Year's Eve. So tell us about the pictures."

"Oh—well, he was out there at midnight clicking away with the new camera at the Banyons down the street setting off fireworks. They do it every year, you know, despite the fact that it's against the law. Anyway—" she lowered her eyes "—some of the pictures show you and a certain young man silhouetted in the window in somewhat compromising positions."

I could just imagine Amy's glee when she saw those photos mixed in with the Banyons' fireworks.

"You don't happen to know where Amy is keeping these pictures, do you?" I asked.

"Well, no, I don't. And, as far as I know, I'm the only person—besides Chuck and Amy, of course—who has seen—"

I jumped up from my chair. "*You've* seen them?"

"Oh, dear. I think I better go."

Bonnie shuffled out of the kitchen, glancing warily at Moira, but Moira made no move to stop her this time.

"Stupid cow," Moira said after we heard the front door shut.

"Pictures, Moira! My, God. Gordy still has friends on this street. What if—" I couldn't even complete the sentence.

"Shut up," Moira said as she grabbed a brownie. "I'm thinking."

I figured another brownie wouldn't hurt anything at this point, so I took one and started to eat. "How do we get hold of those pictures?" I asked with my mouth full.

"I don't think the pictures are the key here. I mean, the chances of finding them in that house of hers with its two hundred antiques with four thousand drawers—some of them probably secret—is one in, say, five million."

I had no idea how Moira had arrived at these numbers, but who was I to argue?

"So what is the key?"

"I'm not sure. Why don't we call Jack?"

"Jack?" I asked in alarm. "Why Jack?"

Moira heaved a sigh of frustration. "Because he's a writer. Which means he's got an imagination. Maybe he'll come up with something that'll help."

I also wasn't going to argue with Moira on the subject of deviously imaginative minds. I figured if she thought Jack's was better than hers, we definitely needed to contact Jack.

"Moira's right," he said and I felt a juvenile stab of jealousy.

"The pictures aren't the key. Besides, Chucky has them on disc or a memory card. He could print out a few hundred in no time if he wanted to. Or post them to an Internet site."

At this point, I was having a hard time keeping my brownies down.

"Okay," Moira, who was on another extension, asked, "then what is the key?"

"You need to get the goods on this Amy," Jack said.

"Jack," I said, "Amy Westcott could win mother of the year hands down. All she does all day is cart her multitalented daughters to their various meets, lessons and performances and putter around in that little gift shop she owns."

"That's it!" Moira screamed on the other line.

"I think I just went deaf," Jack said.

Moira didn't bother apologizing. "Amy's Ambience is the key!"

"Huh?" Jack said. "I still don't think I'm hearing right."

"Amy's Ambience," I explained to him, "is the name of Amy Westcott's gift shop in Whitefish Cove. But, Moira, I don't see how the gift shop fits in."

"Haven't we wondered how she manages to stay in business? I mean, the place is always empty and yet year after year there it sits."

"So?"

"So, I bet the Westcotts, one of Whitefish Cove's golden couples, are doing something funny with the books."

"I'd say Moira is right again," Jack said. "It's plausible."

There went that stab of jealousy again even though in reality I knew I had nothing to worry about. Moira had married Stanley for his silence and calmness. Jack was like the anti-Stanley.

"However," Jack said, "finding something like that out isn't going to be easy. And, even if it could be done, it would take time and money and—"

"Actually," Moira said, "all it would take is a key to the front door of their tax accountant's office."

Jack snorted. "Yeah—right. Do you know him?"

"In the biblical sense, hon. He's my husband."

Jack volunteered to be driver/lookout. We chose a weeknight. Stanley often worked nights—especially during tax season—so no one would be suspicious if they saw lights. We knew for sure that Stanley wouldn't be there since he'd taken Amtrak down to Chicago for a model railway show. Moira was supposed to pick him up around eleven that night.

Jack had borrowed an old van from someone. One of those huge ones that are impossible to see around. At nine o'clock, he parked it in front of Stanley's little storefront office. It was practically as long as the office was wide, great cover for Moira and me as we slipped out, both wearing all black, and ran up to the front door. Moira had it unlocked and the alarm system shut off in just seconds. We went inside and quietly closed the door. The van needed a new muffler, so the signal for someone coming was simply for Jack to start the van. Believe me, there wasn't another bad muffler in all of Whitefish Cove. We'd hear it. The noise would make great cover to get back out of Stan's office. Anyone around would be too busy staring at the scruffy looking guy in the driver's seat of a van too noisy for their quiet streets.

Now inside, we took our little flashlights out of our pockets and started to look around.

"There's a lot of file cabinets in here," I whispered. "Does he keep hard copies of everything?"

"I think he does."

"You know more about computers than I do, so why don't you check that out while I check out the file drawers."

Moira nodded and headed for Stanley's desk.

"Ouch!" she squealed and then I heard a thump. I turned the beam of my flashlight on her. "Damn heels," she said from where she lay on the floor.

"It might have occurred to you to wear something more sensible on your feet for this caper."

"Nothing doing," she said as she got to her feet. "My ass looks wide as a bus in these pants if I don't wear heels."

Classic Moira. "Just get to work, all right?"

I heard her power up the computer as I scanned the file cabinets for the Ws.

"Damn, he's got a password."

"And the file drawers are locked."

"Oh—I bet I know where he'd hide a spare key," Moira said.

I watched as she checked under the philodendron on the desk. She grinned when she held up the key. "That's my Stanley, no imagination at all."

We opened the Ws, found Westcott and pulled the file, then sat on the floor with our flashlights.

"Holy write-off, Batman," Moira said after a few minutes of reading.

"They charged that trip to Tuscany to the gift shop!" I said in disbelief.

"She probably bought a couple of vases or something. You know, I'm not sure, but it looks like every couple of years they make a profit. Just enough to keep the IRS off their backs."

I crawled over to look over her shoulder while she thumbed through pages.

"There," I said and jabbed my finger on the page. "Look at the year."

"Christ, isn't that the year they put in that patio with all that junk—fountains, a pond, a—"

"Right. And that's one of the years they made a profit. Amy bought it from herself. She's her own best customer. How is she getting away with this?" I asked.

"Ha—I know how. The Westcotts have a very clever tax attorney. And if I have anything to say about it, as soon as we confront Amy with this, Stanley is dumping them as clients or he can sleep in the basement with his trains for the rest of his life."

We liberally used the copying machine, then put all the papers and documents carefully back where they'd been in the file. Once we'd locked the drawer and replaced the key, we turned off our flashlights and got out of there.

As planned, Jack starting the van took any attention off of us as we jumped back in.

"Well?" Jack asked.

"Success!" Moira yelled. "It turns out that Amy Westcott with her perfect strand of pearls is the Leona Helmsley of Whitefish Cove. Probably furnished her whole damn house as a write-off!"

"Oh, my god," I said, between pants. "My heart is still racing. I can't believe what we just did! Do you think it's a federal crime since we broke into an accounting office and looked at someone else's tax returns?"

"I couldn't do time. Bad hair days. I'd have to run for the border—and I'm not talking tacos," Moira said.

"Ladies," Jack interrupted, "as much as I might enjoy the idea of helping to raise the suburban crime rate, let me remind you that you had a key to the office."

Moira and I looked at each other.

"You know, the business is in both our names, too," Moira told us.

"You mean, we probably didn't even commit a crime?" I asked with a modicum of disappointment.

"I wouldn't say that," Jack answered. "I think the IRS probably frowns on peeking at your neighbor's tax returns and then using them for blackmail."

"Well, I don't give a damn," Moira said. "It was a rush. Now let's get over to Amy's."

"Now?" I asked. "It's ten o'clock at night!"

"What? You don't want to inconvenience her after what she's been doing? We're going over there. Now."

My heart raced while Moira gave directions to Jack. When we pulled up in front of Amy's house it was dark.

"I think maybe we should wait," I said.

"Is she always the nice girl?" Jack asked Moira.

"Yup—unless, of course, you lay her a new kitchen floor."

Jack laughed and I punched him in the arm.

"Which is one of the reasons," Moira explained, "that I think you two should wait out here while I go do this by myself."

"Moira, I can't expect you to—"

"Believe me, hon, the pleasure is all mine."

She got out of the van and as I watched her swagger across the street, I sort of understood the four-inch heels. If you had to blackmail someone, power shoes definitely made a difference.

"So which one was yours?" Jack asked.

"Huh?"

"Which house did you live in before you were brought low enough to seek refuge at The Coronet?"

"Oh—" I pointed. "That one." It was weird. I was looking at the house I'd thought I couldn't leave. And there wasn't one stirring of sadness or longing inside me. It was just an empty house. Not a home anymore.

"I bet you had the cutest curtains on the block and that the window decorations changed with the seasons."

"I have not now, nor have I ever denied, being a suburban soccer mom," I said.

"Well you can kiss any aspirations of being block watch captain goodbye. Now you're just an outlaw like the rest of us."

I laughed.

"You know, it's kind of a turn-on watching a good girl go bad. I think, as a man, I'd be remiss if I don't try to take advantage of the situation."

He pulled me to him and kissed me. This time it wasn't hard and quick. Nor was it the playful necking on the front stoop. This time it was long and leisurely. In fact, we barely came up for air before we were at it again. Deep kisses. Wet kisses. The kind of kisses that make you ache.

His hand started to creep up my black sweater. And I wanted it where it was going, believe me. My nipples were at attention and growing more impatient by the second. I should stop him, I thought. But then I remembered what Moira had said. If it happens in a car, it doesn't count.

I moaned into Jack's mouth and helped his hands get where they were going. He slid his hand into my bra and found my nipple and I gasped and tore my mouth from his.

"Maybe we shouldn't," I said.

"I thought you were ready to embark on a life of corruption," he murmured as he flicked the pad of his thumb over the aching tip of my breast. "I'm merely helping you along. Of course—" he stopped flicking and looked into my eyes as he brought my hand and placed it on the bulge under his jeans "—as you can see, I'd like to come along for the ride."

His hardness excited me. The fact that I'd brought it on. The fact that the man I'd thought about so often for so long was touching me like this, the fact that I was touching him like *that...*

I stroked my hand against the hardness under his jeans. He groaned, then dragged me up against him and took my mouth again. We were still in the throes of the kiss when Moira threw open the door of the van and climbed back in.

"Well, I can see I wasn't missed," she announced.

I jerked back from Jack's arms and straightened my sweater. "What happened?"

"I think it's safe to say that Amy Westcott will no longer be spreading this particular rumor. In fact, Amy Westcott will be phoning all of her friends and would-be victims within the next few days and admitting that she's made a horrible mistake and the rumors about Lauren Campbell and a certain handyman are just that—rumors."

"That's going to just about drive her crazy," I said.

"As it should," Moira said emphatically. "Ah, don't you love the irony? Our Amy finally has some really hot gossip, illustrated, no less, and now she has to say it ain't so and keep it to herself for the rest of her life." Moira rubbed her hands together gleefully. "It's just too delicious. And, speaking of delicious, I'm going to let the two of you get back to what you were doing— only I'd suggest a different neighborhood. You leave this mess parked here too long and someone from the block watch is going to be nervously dialing 911."

Moira got out of the van, then turned and stuck her head back in. "Oh, and tell all your friends, there should be a going out of business sale at a little gift shop in the Cove soon." She wiggled her fingers. "Nitey-nite."

She slammed the door and Jack started the van, but I was laughing hard enough to be heard over the rumble.

"This has got to be one of the best nights of my life!" I crowed.

"Silencing a suburban gossip ranks right up there with the first time you had sex and childbirth?"

I slapped his shoulder playfully. "Okay, Gordy's birth was better."

"But, not, I take it, your first sexual encounter?"

"Ken Swartz—the summer I was eighteen. He was beyond horrible. Who was your first?"

"Gloria Ritchie. Under the bleachers. I was in ninth grade, she was a senior. She was far from horrible. I learned more from her than I ever did from science class."

As we drove through the dark streets of Milwaukee we talked about other things from the past. Worst hot lunch food. First beer. First time we thought we were in love. I sat next to him all the while, his arm around my shoulders, my palm on his knee, while we talked all the way back to Prospect Avenue.

He double-parked the van in front of the apartment building.

"I promised this guy I'd get his van back to him tonight," Jack said.

I was both relieved and disappointed.

"Well, thanks for helping us."

"No problem. Any time a suburban mom turns badass, I'm there."

"So now I'm a badass?"

He put his arm around my waist and pulled me to him. "You're just about everything a man could ask for," he said. "Except you keep saying no."

"But you're the kind of man who doesn't give up easily. Right?"

He threw back his head and laughed. "Right," he said when he was through. "I don't give up easily at all."

I was still buzzed by his flirting when I crawled into bed a half-hour later. When the phone rang, I prayed it was him and refused to look at the caller ID for fear I'd jinx it. It was Moira.

"Was that out of control tonight, or what?" she asked.

"I just hope it doesn't have any negative repercussions."

"If it does, you at least got special benefits. If Amy had more fortitude I have the feeling that that old van would have been rockin'."

I grinned. "Well, you did say that if it happened in a car, it doesn't count."

Moira laughed seductively. "Then I'm definitely sorry Amy didn't hold out longer."

"Don't be. I've got to get some things straightened out first—"

"—with Gordy," Moira finished for me. "Honey, that guy with the limp isn't getting any younger and neither are you. If I were you, I'd get busy working on the Gordy situation before 'ole blue eyes needs a splint on something more than his leg."

CHAPTER 16

I was at my workstation the next day, dealing with some last minute things to do with the fashion show, but I kept hearing Moira on the phone the night before. Maybe it was time again to push Gordy up to another level. I picked up my cell phone and called him.

To my surprise, he accepted my invitation to dinner at my apartment that night.

I made him meatloaf, garlic mashed potatoes and glazed carrots. All his favorites. The April night was warm enough to have the windows open, and the street sounds floated up and entered the room like energetic music.

Gordy showed up right on time.

"Come in, honey. I'd give you the grand tour but it would take about thirty seconds."

He looked so tall standing in my tiny galley kitchen. "Yeah, it's a little small."

"I gave you the biggest bedroom, though."

He raised his brows in surprise. "Me?"

"You know—in case you ever decided you wanted to live here—or even just spend the night sometimes."

He went to take a look at it. "You brought some of my stuff from the house over here."

"When I rented the place, I thought you'd be living with me—not your father."

He checked out my bedroom, then the living room. It was impossible for me to tell what he was thinking.

Finally, he noticed what I'd hung on the walls.

"Ma—these are all my paintings."

I grinned. "Don't you think I know that?"

"You know, I'm not some little kid that's going to get all excited about having my scribblings taped to the refrigerator door."

"They're hanging there because they're good. Even Moira agrees with me. She helped me choose the frames."

He stood there shaking his head as he studied each one. I guess you'd have to say that Gordy's style was of the impressionist school, but they were also modern and a little reckless. He had already started developing his own style by the age of fifteen.

Dinner was ready and we sat at the breakfast bar while I tried to entertain him with the tales of Bernice and me working together.

"If I'd known that all I had to do to get respect from her was to demand it, I would have done it years ago."

"How come it takes so long to learn stuff?" he asked as he stabbed a carrot.

My mommy antennae were quivering again. I concentrated on eating mashed potatoes while I waited and hoped.

The next words out of his mouth were nothing like I was expecting.

"Why are we such fuckups, Ma? I mean, Dad never makes dumb mistakes."

I sensed it wasn't time to ask him what he meant, so I told him what in my heart I believed.

"Maybe it's because we're more human than he is."

I could see he was thinking it over. "Maybe. It's for sure his girlfriends are robots. The latest one is a twenty-two-year-old flight attendant."

"What happened to Tiffany?"

He shrugged and hung his head. "Beats me. One day she was just gone."

He kept his head down for a long time. The changing light lit his hair and turned it the same white color it used to get every summer because he loved being outdoors so much. In those days, I worried about whether he remembered to put sunblock on at the beach. I had a feeling the mistakes he was thinking about right now were in a whole different class.

I put my fork down and leaned my elbows on the counter between us. "Would you look at me, please, Gordy?"

Slowly, he looked up.

"You know all about the mistakes I've made. I think it's time for you to tell me about the mistakes you've made."

He shoved his plate away and put his head down and started to cry. I was torn between taking him into my arms and rocking him while I told him it didn't matter, we'd simply begin again, and treating him like the adult he was trying to become.

I opted for a combination of the two and started to stroke his hair softly while I said, "Gordy, it's time. You know that. It's time for you to tell me why you got kicked out of school."

He jerked his head up to look at me. His face was red and wet with tears. "Cheating," he said, dashing angrily at his tears just like he'd done as a little boy. "Mom—I'm a cheater!"

"You—you mean you cheated on a test?"

"Everything, Mom. I cheated on everything. That's what I used Dad's hundred for. That's what I used the money for when I sold the electronics I charged on your account. I bought homework papers, term papers, advance copies of tests—anything I could get my hands on so I wouldn't flunk out."

Finally, I knew. It was bad. But not so bad that we couldn't handle it.

"Jesus, aren't you going to yell at me or something? Aren't you going to tell me how disappointed you are?"

"No—I'm going to hug you." I slid off my stool, skirted the breakfast bar, and pulled him off his. It felt good to hold him with the secret no longer between us. "You know what you've done is wrong. I don't have to tell you that. But don't think you're going to get off scot-free with this, though, cause you're not. First, you have to tell your father the truth."

"Hell," he said, his words muffled against my shoulder, "can't you just ground me for the rest of my life?"

I pulled back to look into his face. "Adults don't get grounded."

"Sometimes this adult shit sucks."

"Ha—tell me about it. And after you tell Roger, you're going to go out and get a job so you can pay us the money back."

"Ma—there's something else."

My heart seized up in my chest. "What?" I asked carefully.

"I don't think I want a life like Dad's. I mean, I thought that it was so cool he had so much money, but I can't see myself wearing a suit to an office. After these past eight months, I can't see myself fitting in that way. I don't even know if I want to go to college, anymore."

"What do you think you want to do?"

He looked at the framed painting hanging over the sofa. "I think I want to paint."

My heart relaxed, then swelled. Partly with tears because I knew what a hard road it would be and partly with pride to be the mother of a son who was willing to take that road.

"Then maybe that's what you should do," I said.

* * *

I tried to get him to spend the night, but he said he needed to go back to Roger's place and get about two days' sleep before he confronted his father.

"I could easily sleep a straight forty-eight there and nobody would come looking for me."

I hated the idea of him going back to that environment, but I wasn't about to push him to move in with me that night. We'd come so far in one evening, I didn't want to lose any of the ground we'd gained.

After Gordy left I grabbed a sweatshirt and waited for the elevator to come back up. I needed some fresh air. Needed to walk. Otherwise, I was going to throw myself on the sofa and spend the next couple of hours crying.

The elevator reached my floor, the doors creaking open. I jumped the six inches down into it and rode it to the lobby. I pushed the lobby doors open and walked out into the evening.

I finally knew the truth, I thought as I started to walk, but it hurt like hell. Hurt that Gordy hadn't felt he could come to me. Hurt to realize that I'd made so many mistakes when I thought I'd been doing everything right. And now I was going to have to go to work tomorrow, and act like nothing had happened, and make nice and smile plus work my butt off.

When had life become so complicated?

"Maybe when you started really living it," I muttered to myself.

"Muttering to yourself in this part of town is frowned upon," a voice behind me said. "You should head down Brady Street instead. It's a much more common occurrence there."

I turned around and smiled. It was Jack. "Maybe you should do a handbook for the demented."

"Not a bad idea," he said as I waited for him to catch up with me. "I could do a series on all the major cities. Areas where it's okay to act loony, areas where just crossing your eyes and sticking out your tongue will get you arrested."

"Now you've got it," I said.

"What has you walking the streets tonight?" he asked.

"Gordy, who else? He told me something today, something I wanted badly to know, and it's got me scared and confused and sad."

"Can you talk to me about it?"

I looked up at him. I wanted to tell him. And somehow it felt more natural to talk to Jack about it than to turn to Roger or Bernice—or even Moira. We turned onto Brady Street and walked on to the coffeehouse. We ordered coffee and I started to tell Jack the truth about my son.

"I can try to say all the right things here," he said when I'd finished. "All the platitudes, all the standard lines. But the truth is, people mess up. We all do. It's all part of the process of becoming who we really are. I mean, sometimes we end up where we never dreamed we would when we started. But sometimes, if we're lucky, that turns out to be exactly where we need to be."

We sat there for a while longer, talking about the different roads our lives had taken, roads we never even knew existed when we'd started out on life's journey.

Finally, I took my last sip of coffee and said, "I think we better get out of here or neither one of us is going to get any sleep tonight."

He reached for my hand across the table. "Do you think you'll sleep tonight?"

I nodded. "Oddly enough, yes. Knowing, no matter how bad it is, is always easier than not knowing."

We walked down Brady Street toward Prospect, holding hands in silence. At the elevator in our building, he gave me a hug that lingered, and while it felt good to be held like that, good to be comforted and cared about, there was nothing sexual in it. He'd known what I'd needed that night. And he'd given it to me.

* * *

The next day I took a drive over to Moira's after work to see if I could stuff a few more things into her attic. When I got there, there was a little boy sitting on the steps of my old house.

"Hi!" I called.

He waved shyly just as a woman came out of the house. She looked as young as I had been when Roger and I had moved in. I decided to take a walk over.

"Hi, there. I'm Lauren Campbell. I used to live here."

"Really? Well, we just love the place. It's exactly what we're looking for. My husband is talking over terms with the Realtor right now."

"Well, good luck. It's a great neighborhood to raise kids in."

"Thanks," the woman said. "If we get it, you'd be welcome to come over and see it again anytime."

"That's very nice of you," I told her. But I knew I would never take her up on her offer. The house was in the past. Right now, the future looked too wide open to look back.

I walked back to my car, opened the trunk and hauled out a box. When I reached Moira's front porch, she was waiting for me.

"I wasn't sure how you'd take seeing someone looking at the house."

I smiled. "They seem like nice people. I hope they get it. That house needs life in it again."

She grinned. "Okay, let's take a look at what kind of junk you want me to hang on to now."

I looked down at the box. It was full of Gordy's old books, the ones I'd read to him when he was a child. "On second thought," I said, "I think I'll hand this over to your new neighbor. I don't think Gordy will be wanting to read *Make Way for Ducklings* ever again."

* * *

To my surprise, when I got back to my apartment, Gordy was waiting for me on the stoop.

"I didn't know if I should call first or what," he said.

"Don't be silly. You don't have to call first. And I'm glad you waited. Come on up."

Once in the apartment, he sat on the sofa and stared quietly out the window.

"Gordy? What is it?"

He looked at me. "I told Dad the truth last night."

"You did?"

"Yeah, I suddenly wanted to just get it over with."

Slowly, I sank down onto the sofa next to him. "How did he take it?"

Gordy shrugged. "To tell you the truth, I think he was more upset when I told him I wanted to go to art school. He kind of freaked about that. Said he wasn't paying."

I put my arm around my son's shoulders and hugged him to my side. "I'm glad you decided to tell him right away. It was the right thing to do. And don't worry about art school. He has to pay. I wasn't completely stupid about the divorce agreement, you know."

"Seriously? He has to pay for it?"

I nodded. "He has to pay for any kind of education you want."

Gordy laughed. And it sounded almost like my old Gordy. "Dad's gonna freak about that."

"Let him. But while you're deciding what school you want to go to, you're getting a job."

"I know—so I can pay the money back."

"And I think maybe we should look into some counseling. What do you think?"

"What kind of counseling?" he asked warily.

"Oh, just someone to talk to. Someone who can help you to understand why you made the choices you did and help give you the tools to make better choices in the future."

"Is that what you wished you had done?"

"Sometimes. Who knows, maybe I'll follow my own advice and do it now."

"Can I think about it?"

"Of course. Meanwhile, the fashion show is Saturday. I know your grandmother would love to see you in the audience."

"Come on, Ma, that's unreasonable punishment to make a guy go to a fashion show."

"It's not a punishment, it's a request."

There was a knock on the door.

I got up to answer it. "Just think about it, okay?" I said over my shoulder.

I checked the peephole. It was Jack. Were they ready to meet each other? Was I ready for them to? What the hell, I thought, and opened the door.

"Package came for you earlier," he said as he handed over a box.

"Thanks. Come on in. My son's here. I'd like you to meet him."

"Ah, the artist," Jack said as he walked past me. "Pleased to meet you. I was admiring your work the other night. Pretty interesting stuff."

"Thanks," Gordy said.

Jack stopped in front of the sofa and held out his hand. "I'm Jack Neuhouse, by the way."

Gordy stood up and shook Jack's hand.

"Jack's a writer," I told Gordy. "Sci-fi."

Gordy's eyes lit up. "Are you the J. C. Neuhouse who wrote the We're Not Alone series?"

"Guilty."

"Wow—that's so cool. I heard you lived in Milwaukee. Is the series really over?"

Jack nodded. "'Fraid so. The last book comes out in a couple of months. Right now I'm playing super of this building for free rent while I try my hand at something different."

"No kidding. I never thought of doing something like that."

"Of course, tenants like your mother can drive you crazy, but otherwise it's a pretty decent gig."

"I'll have you know that there hasn't been a complaint lodged against me in days," I said primly.

Their laughter blended and I swear I could feel the sound of it in my heart.

"I just got the cover the other day for the last book. Want to come down and take a look at it?"

"Are you kidding? Sure."

Once again, Gordy took off without a backward glance. Only this time, it didn't bother me one bit.

Just after quitting time the next day, I poked my head into Dora's office to see if she needed anything before I left. I was surprised to find my mother there. Even more surprised to see her with her shoes off and her feet up on the corner of Dora's desk, drinking something from a plastic cup.

"Come on in here, kid," Dora said. "If anyone deserves to put her feet up about now, you do."

I looked at Bernice. "She's right," my mother said. "You've worked your tail off on this show."

I checked around. Nope. Didn't look like the Twilight Zone. Apparently, my mother had actually just given me a compliment in front of my boss. I was certainly willing to put my feet up to that.

I pulled another chair closer to Dora's desk, kicked off my shoes and stretched out my legs.

Dora bent and pulled a half-empty bottle of brandy and another cup from a desk drawer. She poured and handed me the cup.

"Here's to us," she said.

My mother raised her cup. "All these years and we're still here," she sang out merrily.

Dora laughed heartily. "Bernice and I were just reminiscing about the old days and all the people whose asses we had to kiss when we were starting out."

I nearly choked on my brandy. "Mother, you kissed ass?"

"Honey, everyone kisses ass sometime."

I grinned and with my feet up on Dora's desk, listened as two very extraordinary women gossiped and laughed about the good old days. I was thoroughly enjoying myself, perfectly happy to be a part of it, however small, when my mother turned to me.

"Lauren, I've been wanting to ask you about that white ensemble I'm wearing Saturday."

"What about it?"

"Well, I know I chose the picture hat to wear with it, but there's one in the window that I think might be even better."

"Oh, the little one with the veil and pearls?"

"Right. What do you think?"

My mother was asking my opinion on a hat. This would have been an extraordinary turn of events even without the buzz from the brandy.

"Well, I don't know, Mother. Why don't we go fetch it and see."

We put on our shoes and took the elevator to the main floor.

In one of the front display windows, I was tiptoeing gingerly through a garden of reflective stands of different heights that held shoes, jewelry and hats, when I heard a tapping on the glass.

It was Jack.

I gave him a little wave just as I reached the hat.

"Who are you waving at?" Bernice asked from behind me.

"Oh—just the super of my apartment building," I said as I climbed out of the window and handed my mother the hat.

Bernice craned her neck to get a look. "Wait a minute—I recognize that man. He's the one who called me an old bat—among other things. What's he doing out there? I'm going to go have a talk with him."

"No! Mother. Please don't."

"Why ever not?"

"Because he doesn't remember who I am, and I'd just as soon leave it that way."

"Don't tell me you're *dating* him? He's got all the suitability of a rhinoceros."

Jack might have something in common with a rhinoceros but it wasn't anything I planned to discuss with my mother. "We're friends," I said, "that's all." I handed the hat to Bernice. "Now get that scowl off your beautiful face and try the hat on."

There was a mirror to the side of the window. Bernice took her time putting on the hat, then tilted her head this way and that.

"What do you think?" she asked me.

"I think it's gorgeous. Definitely a better choice."

"Good. I think so, too."

"Would you mind adding it to the wardrobe list? I'd like to get going."

She put her hands on her hips. "I hope you're not rushing off to meet that aging ruffian, because—" She stopped. I liked to think it was because of the big grin on my face. "Oh, go ahead. I'll take care of the hat."

"Thanks, Mom," I said, giving her a kiss on the cheek before I hurried off.

"I hope you're waiting for me," I said when I joined Jack on the sidewalk.

"Nah, I was sort of hoping to see a naked mannequin but since you're here, I might as well walk you home."

"That's very sweet of you," I said.

"My pleasure. I seem to find you endlessly fascinating. Why else would I choose to walk three miles round trip on a bum leg?"

I winced. "Does it hurt?"

"Only when I move."

"Then let's get a taxi."

"No! It's too fine a day. Smell the lilacs. Do you know how lucky we are to be living in this part of the city? It's sheer beauty."

It was, indeed. We discussed architecture—from the winged Calatrava addition of the art museum to the wonderful fifties high-rises that had survived here and there. The trees were leafing out. The grass was greening. It was a splendid April day and I couldn't have been in better company.

"You were great with my son last night," I said.

"He's a pretty interesting kid. Which, considering his mother, doesn't really surprise me."

When we got to the apartment building I could see that Jack was in real pain.

"You never should have walked so far."

"I walk that far all the time. It's just that sometimes, my leg wants to stay home."

He leaned on me while we went up the two shallow steps to the lobby. I waited for him to unlock his door, then followed him in. His limp was noticeably worse and the lines in his face, the ones caused by pain, had deepened.

"Tell me what to do for you."

"There's some ointment—on the dresser—and a bottle of pills. If you could get them for me and a glass of water—"

I rushed around, gathering what he'd asked for. When I got back, he'd taken off his jeans and I could see how his one leg was twisted. He took a pill, then handed the water back to me and held his hand out for the ointment.

"Let me," I said.

To my surprise, he did. He stretched out on the bed and I propped his leg up on pillows and started to massage it. Little by little I could feel his muscles relax under my touch. His breathing quieted and when he gave a soft snore, I knew he had fallen asleep.

I didn't want to leave him in case he woke still in pain. I went into the living room, which was cluttered with books, magazines, manuscript pages that had been half wrinkled and tossed aside. His desk was layered with legal pads, notebooks, stacks of manuscript pages scribbled with notations.

I sat down at his desk and looked at the computer screen. He'd been playing solitaire—and losing. A legal pad fell to the floor when I nudged it with my elbow. Under it was what looked like the final draft of a manuscript. I took it with me when I tiptoed over to the bedroom door. Jack was still snoring lightly.

I sat in an old stuffed chair near the bedroom door where I could keep an eye on him and started to read.

The sky grew dark and I turned on a light. I read for what felt like hours. What felt like minutes. What felt like a lifetime.

"Women, you just can never trust them."

I jumped at the sound of his voice. "I didn't hear you wake up."

"Understandable." He yawned. "You were too busy snooping into my life."

"I was too busy reading an engrossing, wonderfully written novel."

"You couldn't have just cleaned out my refrigerator or something?"

I laughed. "I saw myself in the role of Elizabeth." I got up and started for the bedroom. "It's like you knew me—inside and out."

He smiled softly. "I do know you. Don't you know that it's every bad boy's dream to find the one good girl who would give it all up for him?"

I stopped a few feet from his bed and looked down at him. He was raised on one elbow, the sheet bunched around his hips, his face with it's usual scruffy five o'clock shadow, his eyes steady on mine. "Is that what I am to you," I asked, "a conquest?"

"A conquest. A joy. A necessity."

I stared into those eyes. "I think about you all the time," I said.

"Don't you think it's been the same for me?" He held out his hand. "Come over here."

I walked the final three feet to the bed and he pulled me down to him and took my mouth with his.

It was so ferocious it astounded me. This was no cool, slow lovemaking. This was being consumed. His mouth was everywhere as his hands pulled ineffectually at my clothes. We were still half-dressed when he rolled over onto his back so I was straddling him, pushed my pleated skirt up and my panties aside and thrust himself into me. I moved on him in sensual ways I'd thought my body had forgotten and all the while those blue, blue eyes watched me while his hands touched and teased until my body tensed and jerked while I came harder than I ever had in my life. And then he reversed our positions, throwing me onto my back and pumping himself into me until I was delirious and pulsing. I felt the liquid heat inside of me when he came and I heard it—heard it as he cried out. And then he rolled to his side, holding himself inside me, and we fell to sleep like that— attached and tangled.

I woke to find him grinning down at me like the devil.

"What?" I asked as I stretched languidly.

"I was just thinking that this disheveled-schoolgirl look is very fetching, but maybe you could wear your bonnet and braids next time we make love."

My mouth fell open. "You knew it was me all along?"

"Of course. I even admit I was a little jealous of that naked mannequin you were dancing with."

"You knew that was me, too!" I picked up a pillow and started to hit him with it. He dodged most of my blows, laughing and trying to grab the pillow from my grasp. Who knew, I wondered, that you could be playful with a man like this after sex?

I settled into his arms again and felt his chest rise and fall beneath my cheek.

"When I turned around that day," he said, "and saw you in my apartment, my heart almost stopped."

"You certainly hid it well. I was so relieved when I thought you didn't recognize me."

"I would have known you anywhere, anytime. You could have been wearing pitch-black in the rain at midnight during a power outage and I would have known it was you."

I brought myself up on my elbow so I could look down at him. "Why?" I asked in wonder.

He thrust his hand into my hair and held it back from my face. "Damned if I know. But it happened the first time I saw you. You're under my skin, Lauren. Under my skin, in my head and in my heart."

This time we took off our clothes before we made love.

"Are you my girl?" he murmured afterwards as he held me and stroked my hair.

A shot of anxiety disturbed my peacefulness. "Your girl? What does that entail, exactly?"

"You know, like going steady."

"And what does going steady mean when you're middle-aged?"

"Ouch."

"Well, I'm forty-one and you're—"

"Fifty, but don't gloat about it."

I grinned up at him. "I wouldn't dream of it."

"You know, some might argue that you've been taking the kind of liberties that might make a passerby think we're already a couple."

"Liberties? Me?"

"You've been feeding me—"

"One meal," I protested.

"And necking with me out in public…"

"It was the middle of the night and no one saw us."

"Letting me get to second base in a van…"

I started to laugh. "Moira claims if you do something in a car it doesn't count."

He rapped the headboard behind him. "Sounds more like a bed than a car. Therefore, it must have counted when we made love."

"Damn fine print again," I said. "But you still haven't answered my question. What does going steady mean for the middle-aged?"

"Well, despite my dashing appearance, I haven't had a lot of experience with it, but I think it works like this—we spend a lot of time getting to know each other and having fun. We always have someone to go to the movies with. We have increasingly awesome sex, of course. We spend holidays together."

The more he talked, the more nervous I got. "That's investing a lot."

"True."

"And don't forget—I have baggage."

He held up his bad leg. "You think I don't?"

"But this thing with Gordy, it's going to take time. And I still want him to have a room of his own at my place."

"So? We'll just have to have sex at mine all the time."

"Everything is happening so fast."

"Is that a no?"

"No. I mean, no, it's not a no. It's more of an 'I have to think about it,' okay? Things happened fast with Roger, too, and there were no happy endings."

"Did you feel this way with Roger in the beginning?"

"No," I said. I hadn't felt this way with anyone. Granted, I had small experience. But if there was anything better than what was between Jack and me I figured it had to be on another plane of existence. I'd never talked so much to a man, never listened so much, never laughed so much. And the sex. No— *passion*. Call it passion. Quint had been a practiced lover despite his *aw shucks* charm. But Jack just went for it. Body and soul.

"This is going to sound terrible, but I think with Roger, I fell in love because he was offering me the kind of life I always wanted. Now, I wonder if it was love at all."

"The life of a writer can be chaotic and uncertain. I get insane when I'm near a deadline. If this book doesn't make it, I might have to go back to sci-fi. It's a steady income, but I'll never get rich. And I'm never going to want a life in the burbs like your ex gave you."

"I don't want that kind of life anymore, either. I see now how a lot of it was just window dressing."

"What is it you do want now?"

I thought about it for a moment. "I love my job. I want to stay there and learn as much as I can. And when I can afford it, I want to take some classes."

"You should look into applying for some grants—"

The conversation went on like this for over an hour, then we shifted to favorite movies. It turned out we both loved *Casablanca*. Jack owned the DVD, so we watched it, cuddled together on Jack's leather sofa. *Casablanca*. I mean, it's practically a chick-flick. I was besotted. Absolutely entranced. A man who talked after sex and cuddled to *Casablanca*.

When the movie was over, Jack asked me to spend the night. I wasn't ready for that. Not yet.

So I walked to the elevator while he leaned in his doorway, watching me, his jeans unsnapped and slung a little low, no shirt. He was lean, the hair on his chest was gray and any six pack he might own was in the back of his refrigerator. But I liked what I saw.

Once I was safely inside the elevator with the doors shut, I thrust my arms into the air and did a silent cheer. I thought that maybe, for the first time, I was really in love.

When Saturday came, miraculously, the props were ready, the fresh flower arrangements had arrived, the rental company had sent enough gold organza covers for all the folding chairs and a very posh bakery downtown had set up a table of coffee, tea and pastries that were gorgeous enough to rival the best hat in the show. For weeks, Grant's had been advertising in the paper and there had been posters of my mother all over town. "The golden girl of the fifties is now a 24-karat woman," they read. I peeked out from behind the curtain. The chairs were filling up. The golden girl could still draw a crowd.

My cell phone rang. Thinking it was someone in Grant's with a last-minute request, I answered it without looking at the caller ID.

It was Roger.

"We need to talk. Today. Meet me for lunch at—"

"No, no, no, Roger—not possible. I'm swamped today. I can look at my calendar and give you a call tomorrow."

"Have you any idea," he said tightly, "what's going on with Gordon?"

"Yes," I was pleased to answer, "I do. He's made some mistakes, and he's going to pay for them."

"But he wants to go to art school! There's no way I'm paying for art school."

"Excuse me, Roger, but I think you better check with your lawyer because I believe you are paying for it. Gotta run," I said, then disconnected the call.

"What are you grinning about?" Stuart demanded. "One of the models just ripped the seam of her dress. I swear she must have been scarfing at buffets all week."

"I'll take it down to tailoring. They'll get working on it and we can just shift the numbers around in the show a little."

By the time I got back from the tailoring department, the harpist had begun to play and the rest of the guests had taken their seats. The room where I used to have tea with my mother looked as beautiful and elegant as it had all those years ago.

The announcer started and after that, everything was a blur. I helped with zippers, with making sure every model made it to the runway with the right shoes and accessories. I helped my mother into one of her ensembles and noticed that she didn't appear to be at all nervous. In fact, she was putting everyone else at ease with her calm charm.

When she walked out on the runway for the first time, I couldn't stop myself from peeking around the curtain. She still had it. The walk. The stature. The poise. The beauty. She was a natural. I think that maybe for the first time I was seeing what my mother had given up for me. Understood for the first time how she must have struggled to reconcile her needs with the needs of a child. And she'd had to do it all alone.

Just as she made it to the end of the catwalk, I saw her wink at someone. I followed her line of vision, and there was Gordy, sitting smack in the front row, looking both embarrassed and delighted.

When it was over, the models all walked out together, my mother in the center, and got a standing ovation while all of us behind the scenes sighed in relief that it was over for another year. Suddenly, there was the sound of a loud wolf whistle out front. I peeked around the curtain again. Sure enough, Jack Neuhouse was standing behind the back row, clapping louder than anyone else.

It took a while for Mom's dressing room to clear out. When we were finally alone, I said, "You were wonderful, Mom. Just wonderful. How on earth did someone like you end up with someone like me for a daughter?" I had to ask again.

She put the palm of her hand on my cheek and looked into my eyes. "Just lucky, I guess," she answered. "Now, if I'm not mistaken, I think you've got a man waiting out there for you," she said. "One who definitely knows how to whistle."

"What do you think, Mom? Should I go for it? Should I take a chance?"

Bernice looked more surprised than I'd ever seen her look in my life. "*You're* asking *me* for relationship advice?" she asked, her eyes glittering with humor.

I laughed. "Yeah—I guess I am."

"Well, he's a charming rogue. Which makes him too much like your father by far. But you're not me. You could probably make it work. And, hell, who am I kidding? There are still times that I wish I was down there in the Keys with him."

I hugged her. And she hugged back. No kiss on the forehead but a nice messy, hard hug. "Now get going. My grandson is escorting me out to dinner tonight—and you're not invited."

I ran off to find Jack, hoping he'd hung around. He was leaning against the building outside.

He lifted a brow. "Mad, I suppose?"

"I think I've made a decision about us," I said.

"Look, it was just one wolf whistle. I bet the old bat even liked it."

I started to laugh. "Actually, I think she did."

"Well, that should count in my favor."

"Do you want to hear my decision or do you want to make droll remarks all night?"

His blue, blue eyes looked right into mine. "I want to hear the decision."

"I've decided that I want to see where this goes from here. I want the journey—wherever it leads. Just as long as you're the one walking beside me."

"Are you my girl?" he asked me yet again.

"I'm your girl," I answered.

And then he kissed me, right there on Wisconsin Avenue. As good a place as any to start a journey.

* * * * *

Life.
It could happen to her!

Never Happened just about sums up
Alexis Jackson's life. Independent and
successful, Alexis has concentrated on
building her own business, leaving no
time for love. Now at forty, Alexis
discovers that she still has a few things
to learn about life—that the life unlived
is the one that "Never happened"
and it's her time to make a change....

Never Happened
by Debra Webb

Available July 2006
TheNextNovel.com

Just let it shine, it's payback time!

When a surprise inheritance brings
an unlikely pair together, the fortune
in sparkling jewelery could give
each woman what she desires most.
But the real treasure is the friendship
that forms when they discover that
all that glitters isn't gold.

Sparkle

by
Jennifer Greene

HN50

Available July 2006
TheNextNovel.com

Home improvement has never seen results like this!

When she receives a large inheritance,
Stacy Sommers decides she is finally going
to update her kitchen. Her busy husband has
never wanted to invest in a renovation, but now
has no choice. When the walls come down,
things start to change in ways that neither
of them ever expected.

Finding Home

by Marie Ferrarella

REQUEST YOUR FREE BOOKS!

2 FREE NOVELS TO INTRODUCE YOU TO OUR BRAND-NEW LINE!

There's the life you planned. And there's what comes next.

YES! Please send me 2 FREE Harlequin® NEXT™ novels and my FREE mystery gift. After receiving them, if I don't wish to receive any more books, I can return the shipping statement marked "cancel." If I don't cancel, I will receive 3 brand-new novels every month and be billed just $3.99 per book in the U.S., or $4.74 per book in Canada, plus 25¢ shipping and handling per book plus applicable taxes, if any*. That's a savings of over 20% off the cover price! I understand that accepting the 2 free books and gift places me under no obligation to buy any books. I can always return a shipment and cancel at any time. Even if I never buy another book from Harlequin, the two free books and gift are mine to keep forever.

156 HDN D74G   356 HDN D74S

Name	(PLEASE PRINT)

Address	Apt. #

City	State/Prov.	Zip/Postal Code

Signature (if under 18, a parent or guardian must sign)

Order online at www.TryNEXTNovels.com

Or mail to the Harlequin Reader Service®:

IN U.S.A.	**IN CANADA**
3010 Walden Ave.	P.O. Box 609
P.O. Box 1867	Fort Erie, Ontario
Buffalo, NY 14240-1867	L2A 5X3

Not valid to current Harlequin NEXT subscribers.

**Want to try two free books from another line?
Call 1-800-873-8635 or visit www.morefreebooks.com**

* Terms and prices subject to change without notice. NY residents add applicable sales tax. Canadian residents will be charged applicable provincial taxes and GST. This offer is limited to one order per household. All orders subject to approval. Credit or debit balances in a customer's account(s) may be offset by any other outstanding balance owed by or to the customer.

NEXT05

They were twin sisters with nothing in common...

Until they teamed up on a cross-country adventure to find their younger sibling. And ended up figuring out that, despite buried secrets and wrong turns, all roads lead back to family.

Sisters

by Nancy Robards Thompson

Sometimes you're up... sometimes you're down. Good friends always help each other deal with it.

Mood Swing

by Jane Graves

A story about three women who discover they have one thing in common—they've reached the breaking point.